To Sandy,
Dreams &
Blessings.

When the Lilacs Bloom

Linda Colwell 6/8/00

Linda Colwell

avid pressLLC   Brighton, Michigan USA

AVID PRESS, LLC
5470 Red Fox Drive
Brighton, MI 48114-9079
http://www.avidpress.com

Copyright 2000 by Linda Colwell

Cover illustration copyright 2000 by Chris Dodge.

Published by arrangement with the author
ISBN: 1-929613-09-1

All rights reserved, which includes the right to reproduce this book or portions thereof in any form whatsoever except as provided by U.S. Copyright Law.

For information contact Avid Press, LLC.

First Avid Press printing January 2000.

Printed in Canada.

"Enough, Mother! Elinor is my wife."

"We are going out west, Mother, with or without your blessing. It's as simple as that."

Harriet's dark gaze rested on Elinor. "This is your doing, isn't it? You have filled his head with all of this nonsense. Well, we will see—we will see!" Harriet Langford left the room, slamming the door behind her.

Elinor shuddered. Though she was happy Nicholas had finally stood up to his mother, there was something very chilling about Harriet's words and expression. The woman would stop at nothing to keep her son at Langford Manor.

"You're shaking, darling, are you cold?" Nicholas pulled the sheets up under her chin and held her close. "Don't worry about her. She can't stop us, Elinor."

"I'm not so certain," Elinor whispered as she cuddled against her husband.

"If you never were afraid of the dark, you will be after you read this gripping, powerful story of revenge. Linda Colwell crafts a story wrought in the paranormal and tempered with a heroine who leaves you cheering."

Sally Painter, author of **Shadows of Love**

To my family—my husband John, and sons, John, Mark and Dan, and my sister, Carol. Their constant love, support and belief in me have brought me to the realization of my dream.

I must also say thank you to fellow writers: Sally, Helga, Theresa, Holli and a very special thank you to Colleen and Kate.

Prologue

Langford Manor
July 4, 1900

Carrying a candle to dispel the shadows, Harriet Langford crept into the darkened bedroom. Clad from head to toe in her usual black taffeta, she resembled a large blackbird as she approached the bed of the sleeping woman.

Harriet sneered when she saw the way Elinor's sun-streaked hair cascaded over the pillow and picked up the candle's golden glow. She reached up and smoothed her own dark knot of hair that nested like a coiled snake on the top of her head.

She looked at Elinor's lovely blue dress, and had to admit that some might think her daughter-in-law a Sleeping Beauty. *The gown will make a pretty shroud*, Mother Langford thought; but, unlike the fairy princess, Elinor wouldn't be waking up in a hundred years.

Harriet pushed the happy thought from her mind and turned her attention to the half-empty wine glass. Had the girl drunk enough of it to put her into a deep sleep? Harriet swore under her breath. She must hurry up and get this done.

Emitting a low chuckle, she pulled a small jeweled box from her pocket and edged closer to the bed. Her ragged breath signaled her high level of excitement as she set the tiny box down on the pillow near the back of the young woman's ear. Carefully, she opened the jeweled lid and waited.

A small, black spider hurried to the rim of the box then stopped. Frustration grew on Harriet's malevolent face as she waited in the stuffy room for the creature to move again. Perspiration beaded on her forehead and ringed her mouth. When a large dollop slid down her nose, she swiped at it without looking away from the tiny spider.

Finally, her patience gone, Mother Langford took a tortoise shell comb from her hair and used it to tilt the box.

The shiny black spider flipped out onto its back, exposing a red hourglass marking on its underside. Magnified by the candle Harriet held close by, the spider's shadow loomed large.

Wanting to make sure the black widow did its work, Harriet Langford prodded it with her comb, pushing it toward the tender skin behind Elinor's ear just at the hairline. A bite there would never be found.

She watched and waited, clenching her fingers, but the spider just sat there. Again growing impatient, she poked the reluctant creature with the tooth of her comb. A crooked smile broke her narrow slit of a mouth when the spider bit into Elinor's flesh. Harriet goaded the spider again to make sure it pumped a lethal dose into the victim.

"Foolish girl!" she whispered, "did you really think I would allow you to take my son away from me?"

The task completed, Harriet used her comb to scoop the venomous creature back into the box, but it did not stay long enough for her to snap the lid shut. Instead, it darted toward her hand.

Again using the comb, she knocked the spider off the bed and stomped it when it landed on the floor. She scraped up the flattened remains and deposited them back inside the tiny jeweled container. After slipping the box into her pocket, she wiped the tortoise shell comb on the side of her dress and then stuck it back in her hair.

Smoothing her rustling skirts, Harriet walked over to the bedside table and picked up the wine glass. After dumping the remaining liquid onto the soil of a potted fern, she put the empty goblet back on the table.

When Elinor became deathly ill within a few hours, the true cause would not be discovered. The doctor would think she had a relapse of the stomach flu that she had suffered the week before. Or, he might conclude that she had eaten some tainted food at the morning's Fourth of July festivities. Yes, it was the perfect plan!

Harriet touched her own abdomen. Perhaps *she* would fake a stomach ailment. Everyone would think she had eaten the same bad food that Elinor had, or that she had caught the young woman's flu.

"Only I won't die from it," she chuckled under her breath.

Suddenly, the candle flame jerked. Harriet's hair stood on end as she felt a draft from the open door behind her. She whirled around but saw no one. Concluding that she must not have closed the door tightly and it had come open on its own, she headed toward it, anxious to be out of the stifling room.

Harriet gasped and the color drained from her face when she saw Nicholas standing there.

His dark gaze resting on her, he raised a questioning eyebrow.

"Mother," he said, suspicion in his voice, "What are you doing here?"

Chapter One

West Virginia
June, 2000

"Elinor, my Elinor, come to me." Nicholas reached for her. Melting against his firm body, her eager lips burned with the nectar of his kiss. The delicate aroma of lilacs delighted her nostrils as did Nicholas' scent of lye soap and sandalwood.

Suddenly, a dark mist crept from the corners of the room, bringing with it the beating of a thousand wings. As the shadows enveloped Nicholas he reached out and touched her face. "Elinor, my love, come home to me."

Emily Foster bolted upright, pushing herself from the cushiony embrace of the sofa and its many toss pillows. She touched her cheek, feeling for any warmth that might have been left by him. How could it have been a dream? Her cheek still tingled from his caress.

Sniffing the air, she picked up the sweet scent of lilacs coming through the open window behind the sofa. There was something else—an unusual scent—sandalwood, perhaps?

Again, she felt a touch on her cheek. Gasping, she turned to find that the sheer window curtain had blown against her face. So, that's what happened. She had dreamed it. How could she have thought otherwise?

For one thing, she was Emily Foster, not Elinor Foster

Langford. Elinor had died a hundred years ago, as had her beloved husband, Nicholas. The gossips of the day called it a murder/suicide with Nicholas being the culprit. Emily's grandmother had never believed him guilty and neither did Emily.

Emily leaned back against the cushions. This wasn't the first time she'd had the dream. She'd experienced it several times when she was growing up. In those days, her grandmother's stories about Elinor, her nineteenth century relative, had fueled a young Emily's imagination. Now, coming home to the old Victorian house had likely created fertile ground for resurrecting long-forgotten childhood fantasies.

The sudden shrilling of the telephone startled Emily. Though still unsettled by the dream, she reached for the telephone receiver on the end table.

"Hello."

"Emily? This is Betty Hanson. I just got back in town and heard the sad news about your grandmother. I can't believe she's gone! Why I was just talking to her two weeks ago and she was fine."

"It was very sudden, Betty. I had no warning that things weren't right with Grams. If I had, I'd have been here sooner. I didn't even get to say good-bye." Emily's throat tightened.

"I'm sorry I missed the funeral. If someone had called me, I would have cut my trip short and come home in time for the services," Betty said.

Emily swallowed hard, trying to hide her emotions. "Grams wouldn't have wanted you to do that. She knew how you looked forward to your yearly visit with Bill and the grandkids."

"Yes, I suppose you're right. Twila was always thinking of others. How are you doing, dear? Your grandmother loved you so and I know how much she meant to you. Look at the way she took you in after your parents were killed in that horrible accident. You were only seven or eight at the time, weren't you?" Betty droned on without waiting for an answer.

"Why you almost died yourself, didn't you? Twila certainly put the bloom back in your cheeks. She was a good woman, she was."

Tears welled up in Emily's eyes. "Betty, I really can't talk now." She choked out the words. "Thanks for calling."

"I didn't mean to upset—"

Emily hung up the phone before Betty finished speaking. Grabbing one of the toss pillows, she hugged it to her as tears trickled down her cheeks.

"Grams, how can I do without you?" she whispered. "I thought you'd always be here for me to come home to."

She sat, hugging the pillow, and crying for Grams, for herself and even for those long-ago lovers, Nicholas and Elinor, who had died so tragically in the fire that destroyed Langford Manor.

When there were no tears left, Emily got up from the sofa. She stepped into the foyer just as the grandfather clock struck one. Its comforting chime connected her with the family history that had become especially important to her after her parents were gone.

The old clock had stood in the entryway for over a hundred years, counting out the hours and days of several generations of Fosters.

Emily caught a glimpse of herself in the ornate hallway mirror. Running slender fingers through her long, silken hair, she studied her reflection. She was tall with good cheekbones and large, expressive eyes that were now red and swollen. Grams had always said she was a Foster, through and through.

Going to the bathroom off the main hallway, Emily splashed cold water on her face. After wetting a washcloth, she wrung it out and dabbed her eyelids and cheeks. Then, she held it to the back of her neck for a moment before discarding it.

Deciding to get a breath of fresh air, she headed out the front entrance of the house. Exiting the shady porch with its hanging baskets of ivy, she followed the cobblestone sidewalk to the recently-added wooden deck in back of the house.

As she had done so many times while growing up, she stood at the top of the sloping embankment and gazed across the jade waters of the Kanawha River.

Expecting to see the familiar blackened stone ruins of Langford Manor, she was surprised to find a new house standing in its place.

When did this happen? she wondered. Why hadn't Grams told her that the old mansion had been razed?

The stately house of gray stone with black shutters at the windows and white columns gracing the veranda looked like a lone outpost surrounded by a sea of greenery. Tall mountains rose in sharp angles behind the small patch of civilization.

Then, Emily noticed them and a shiver rippled up her back. A man and a woman stood on the lawn facing the river. Though she couldn't make out much detail, she noticed the woman was wearing a long skirt. The man appeared to be clad in an old-fashioned suit, although it was impossible to be sure at such a distance.

"Nicholas and Elinor," the words popped out as her thoughts raced back to the dream. It couldn't be them of course. Still, it was uncanny the way the man and woman stood there like statues.

Though she had never seen an actual picture of Nicholas, she knew exactly how the man in her dreams looked— graced with black, wind-tossed hair, pronounced sideburns, and dark gypsy eyes that could look straight into her heart. She even knew about the strawberry birthmark of the Langford males. Nicholas' was just beneath his chin and was only visible when he tilted his head.

Emily smiled at the remembering. Then she shuddered. There was no escaping the dark side of the dream or the fact that Nicholas and Elinor had died before their time.

The scent of lilacs wafting on the breeze chased away the disturbing thoughts. Lilacs! How she'd missed the sweet country air while living in the city.

She took a deep breath. Grams had said that lilacs were in bloom when Nicholas and Elinor fell in love in the spring of 1899.

Emily looked across the river again. The two people hadn't moved. Concentrating on the man, she was struck by how much he reminded her of the Nicholas of her dreams. She wished she could see his face clearly.

"Maybe I can," she said. "Grandpa's binoculars!" She turned and raced for the house. Rushing through the back entrance, she allowed the screen door to slam behind her. Her shoes clicked on the hardwood floors of the long hallway as she hurried to the foyer.

Stopping in front of the entryway closet, she opened the door. She bent down and pulled out a footstool and stepped up on it. Thrusting her hand to the back of the top shelf, she fumbled until her fingers finally grasped the familiar object.

She pulled out the dusty carrying case and stared at it for a moment, a flood of memories washing over her. Caught up in her thoughts, she paid little attention to the crawling sensation on her arm, thinking it was only the strap of the carrying case brushing against her.

Suddenly, she saw a small, dark spider creeping toward her shoulder. Stumbling off the stool, Emily screamed and with a flailing motion, knocked the spider away.

She watched as the fleeing creature disappeared beneath the grandfather clock. Afraid to move, she remained there for a moment as her heart pumped madly. She'd always had a 'thing' about spiders.

"Oh no!" she groaned when she finally looked down and saw the binoculars on the floor. In her panic she had dropped them. She picked up the case and unsnapped the lid. Relief washed over her when she found the binoculars intact.

Then she remembered the people across the river. Though still weak-kneed, she dusted off the carrying case with a cloth kept in the closet and slipped the leather strap over her head. Determined to get a better look at the strange-looking couple, she headed for the front door.

Her spirits sank when she saw a patch of fog hovering over the river, blocking her view of the man and woman. Odd to see fog on a balmy, sunny afternoon, she thought. Even stranger, the thick mist was limited to the section of river that bordered the Langford property.

Removing the binocular strap from around her neck, Emily set the case on the patio table. Hoping the smog would soon lift, she sat down in a lawn chair. She glanced at her grandmother's rose bushes and flower beds and made a mental note to see about hiring someone to come in and tend them.

She looked at the weeping willow remembering how those thin limbs had created sheltering walls for her childhood playhouse. Its branches nearly touching the ground now, it seemed a bit sadder.

The swing, its rusted chains still attached to a sturdy branch of the maple tree, stirred slightly in the breeze. As a young girl, Emily had spent hours in that swing, flying out over the embankment. Soaring and dipping like a bird, she had been at peace.

Getting up, Emily walked over to the swing and gave the chains a hard pull. Satisfied they were safe, she sat down on the weathered seat and grabbed hold of the chains. She pushed backward with her feet and then lifted them up, allowing the swing to carry her. She pushed again and the swing went higher.

Suddenly, she was a child again, gliding in the dappled sunlight, breathing deeply of the sweetly-scented air. Her long sun-streaked hair touched the ground as she tilted her head back and gazed up into the branches of the aged tree.

For the first time in days, Emily's mood lightened and she smiled. Raising her head up, she again pushed with her feet, sending the swing out over the embankment. As she had done so many times during her childhood, she gazed at the river.

As she watched, the low hanging mist thinned. Slipping away in eerie tentacles, it peeled back the curtain of darkness exposing the sunbathed stones of the new mansion.

The woman and man were still there.

Slamming her feet to the ground to stop the swing, Emily leaped off and reached for the binoculars. Removing them from the case, she slipped the strap around her neck and held the field glasses to her eyes.

At first she saw only green foliage and steep mountains. She scanned the area slowly. Suddenly the house loomed before her.

Turning the adjustment in the center of the binoculars, Emily brought the scene into sharper focus. Where were the people? She moved the glasses slightly to the left, and there was the man—staring back at her.

Startled, she let go of the binoculars and hardly felt their weight when the safety strap chafed against her neck. The man was Nicholas!

"That's impossible," she said, again lifting the binoculars to her eyes. Her scalp prickled as she focused on him. Tall, he wore an old-fashioned cutaway suit complete with stiff collar and bow tie. His black wavy hair curled at the edges and wide sideburns framed a strong jaw line. His face spoke of aristocracy, but it was his dark smoldering eyes that captivated Emily.

Then, he tilted his head and Emily saw the strawberry birthmark. Had there been any doubt about his identity, it was now erased. She was looking at Nicholas Langford.

He stared at her, a smile playing at the corners of his mouth. He knew she was watching him. In turn, he was looking at her. She sensed that he could even read her thoughts.

Hot blood coursed through Emily's veins as his dark gaze bore into her soul. His mouth moved and he gestured to her. Though she could not read his lips, she heard his voice as it beat in her heart.

"Elinor, my Elinor, come to me!"

Chapter Two

Suddenly, the dark mist returned. Emily watched as it wrapped Nicholas in its wispy arms. Frozen to the spot, she stared at the thick fog that again blocked her view of the manor house and the people. Hoping the smog would soon dissipate or float down river, she waited. She wasn't sure how long she stood there.

When the vaporous fingers finally parted, her blood turned to ice. The new mansion was gone. In its place, rising starkly like an accusing skeletal fist, were the blackened stone ruins of the former Langford Manor.

"This can't be," Emily whispered, "there was a new house there."

She thought about the man she'd recognized as Nicholas Langford. Had she imagined it all?

Checking her watch, she was surprised to find that she had been outside for over an hour. She had almost forgotten that Becky was coming to dinner. Taking a last glance at the old house, she shivered again. "It seemed so real," she said before turning and heading inside.

After putting the binoculars back in their proper place, Emily went into the large, country kitchen with its numerous oak cupboards and blue ceramic countertops. Opening the refrigerator, she removed a plump roasting chicken, fresh broccoli and the makings of a tossed salad. Although Emily usually followed a healthy diet, she would have opted for the junk food she and Becky had voraciously consumed when they were teenagers had her friend not insisted otherwise.

"Now, Em," the plumpish Becky had said, "I've lost five pounds and I don't want to gain it all back in one evening!"

While preparing the rice side dish and putting together a fresh fruit salad for dessert, Emily thought about her friend. Becky had always wanted to be a history teacher. Who'd have thought she would end up teaching at Benson High School, their old alma mater? Those hallowed halls had to be much more lively now that Becky had joined the faculty.

Later, as Emily removed the chicken from the oven, a knock sounded at the screen door.

"Yoo hoo, anybody home?"

"Come in, Beck. You're just in time."

Becky Hall stepped into the kitchen, bringing a ray of sunshine with her. Her red hair carried a touch of fire and the freckles on her face constantly changed patterns to accommodate her broad and frequent smiles. Though several inches shorter than Emily, what Becky lacked in height she more than made up for in determination.

She gave Emily a hug. "Gosh, it's good to have you back! You're the talk of Benson. It's not everyday a famous New York actress returns to our sleepy little burg."

"If you call understudy and minor parts on Broadway 'famous', I suppose I fit the description."

"Come now, Em, we know it will only be a matter of time before you hit it big, and with top billing too!"

"Is it okay if we eat in the kitchen? It's cozier, don't you think?" Emily changed the subject.

"The kitchen's fine. Here, let me give you a hand."

After dinner, the two young women cleared the table and set about the task of washing and drying the dishes.

"What is it, Em? You seemed distracted all through dinner. If you want to talk about Grams, you know I'm a good listener. I know I breezed in here with my silly jokes, but I was only trying to cheer you up." Becky's voice softened. "I loved her too. She was like the grandmother I never had and I know she would want us to celebrate her life rather than mourn her death."

"I miss her terribly, Beck, but I agree with you. She wouldn't want us to sit around with long faces."

"There's something more, isn't there?" Becky didn't wait for an answer. "Are you concerned about your career? I noticed how quickly you changed the subject when I mentioned it."

"I never could keep anything from you, could I?" Emily smiled as she rinsed a plate and placed it on the drainboard. "I've lost the drive I once had—the fire isn't there anymore. I'm beginning to think it was all a mistake. I should never have left Grams. If I had stayed here, we'd have had more time together."

"Now stop right there, Em. Do you realize how proud Grams was of you? She would have hated it if you had given up your dreams to stay by her side."

"Thanks, Beck, I needed to hear that." Emily smiled at her red-headed friend. "Still, I doubt that I will go back to it. Everything has been turned upside-down in my life. I need time to get a fresh perspective. The money left me by my parents was invested wisely and there is also Grams' estate, so I don't have to be immediately concerned with earning a living. For the time being, I intend to remain right where I am. I may even decide to stay here permanently."

Becky flashed a green-eyed smile. "I was hoping you'd say that. But, I want it to be for the right reasons. This town hasn't been the same without you, kid." She wiggled her darkish eyebrows and did her Groucho Marx impersonation.

Emily giggled. She'd missed her friend's zany antics.

Becky wiped a plate and put it in the cupboard. Then she turned to Emily, a serious expression on her face. "I suppose your break-up with Jeff has something to do with your reluctance to return to New York?"

The mention of Jeff's name no longer caused Emily the stab of pain it once did. "Not as much as you'd think. Even though our break-up was fairly recent, I can honestly say I have put Jeff behind me."

Emily lifted her hand from the sudsy water and looked

at the thin faded line where her engagement ring had been. "I'm glad I found out about his cheating before I married him. Grams warned me. When I brought him home to meet her, she saw right through him. You weren't exactly taken with him either, were you?"

"To be completely honest, I had him pegged for a phony from day one."

"Why couldn't I see what others saw so clearly? I had to catch him in bed with another woman before I got the message."

"The important thing is that you did wise up before it was too late. Besides, we all know that love is blind." Becky patted Emily's arm.

Emily stopped and looked at her friend. "Beck, do you remember the old Langford place across the river and the stories Grams used to tell us about the family that lived there at the turn of the century?"

"I sure do. Who wouldn't remember Tobias and Harriet Langford? Their wealth couldn't buy them respectability. I also remember the crush you had on the long-dead and very psychotic Nicholas." Becky flashed an impish grin.

"Nicholas was not psychotic, Beck!" Emily's blue eyes clouded.

"I know he was your hero when we were kids, Em, but it hardly matters what people are saying now."

"Just what are they saying?" Emily asked.

"It's the same old story that's been around for years. The high school kids say that Nicholas Langford set the fire that killed his parents, Elinor and himself. They say he became insanely jealous when he saw another man looking at Elinor at the Fourth of July Festival. When she went home to rest before the evening Ball, he set fire to the manor house." Becky lowered her voice. "Some say the ghosts of Nicholas and Elinor roam the Langford property. The guys love to take their dates there. Naturally, the girls scream in fear and the boys protect them from the Langford ghosts."

"That's terrible! Nicholas never murdered anyone. Grams said he and Elinor were deeply in love and that, if the fire was deliberately set, it wasn't Nicholas who did it."

Becky sighed. "Come on, Em, you're taking this too much to heart. It's been a hundred years! So who cares if he did it or not?"

"I care. I always have." Emily whispered.

"I know, I know." Becky patted Emily's arm again. "Just look at it this way, Em. The kids have Nicholas to pick on, we had Crazy Charlie. Remember him? He haunted the cemetery off Route Sixty. Nobody ever really saw him, though several claimed that he chased them with an ax—the same ax, no doubt, that he used to murder his wife. It was just our way of having fun."

Emily smiled in spite of her serious mood. "How could I ever forget Crazy Charlie?"

"Remember the time we went to the old cemetery with Mitch Ames and Bruce Hobson?"

"It was fun, I'll admit it. That's when we heard about the girl who was locked in the mausoleum overnight. They said she was found dead the next morning and her hair had turned white from fright. Do you remember that story?"

"Remember it?" Becky's freckles danced, "I'm the one who made it up!"

"Beck! I was your best friend and you never told me!"

"I didn't want to spoil your fun," she giggled. "Don't you see? We had Crazy Charlie to pick on. Today, the kids have Nicholas Langford."

Emily sighed. "I do understand their need to have fun but I wish they would pick on Crazy Charlie and leave my Nicholas alone."

Becky touched her friend's arm. "*Your* Nicholas? Nicholas Langford lived a hundred years ago."

"It's just a figure of speech. You know how we used to play when we were kids, Beck. I suppose I became rather possessive of Nicholas, but I know he's not my Nicholas. He is Elinor's."

"Is?" Becky raised her eyebrows.

"All right, *was* Elinor's."

Now that the dishes were finished, Emily pulled out a

chair and sat down at the round, oak table. "Did you say the kids claim to have seen ghosts at the Langford place?"

"Well, yeah, that's the current fad. I'm sure they've seen ghosts the same way we saw Crazy Charlie. Youthful imagination is wonderful!' Becky wiped the last bowl and, putting it in the cupboard, joined Emily at the table.

"I'm not so sure it's imagination, Beck. I saw something when I looked across the river."

"I gotta hear this." Becky leaned closer to Emily. "Don't tell me you saw Crazy Charlie brandishing an ax?"

Emily looked her in the eye. "This is serious, Beck."

Her freckles drooped and a contrite expression splashed across Becky's face. "I'm sorry, Em. You know me and my big mouth. Please, tell me what you saw."

"This afternoon when I went into the backyard, I looked across the river and instead of the old ruins I saw a new house with people in the yard."

"Do you want to run that one by me again?"

Emily hesitated, realizing how strange she must sound. Then she told Becky everything that had happened.

"Whew! That's quite a story. If it was anybody else telling me, I just flat wouldn't believe it."

Emily searched her friend's face. "Then you do believe me?"

"I know you wouldn't lie about it and I am sure you think you saw something. There has to be a logical explanation, though. I'm skeptical when it comes to ghosts and haunted houses."

"Beck, I never said anything about ghosts and haunted houses. What I saw wasn't some transparent specter. He was flesh and blood and the house was solid stone."

"Are you sure you didn't just dream this? Dreams can seem so real and you said you had taken a short nap. Maybe you only thought you had awakened and were, in fact, still dreaming."

"Really, Beck, I think I'd know the difference."

"Look, Em, you're living in the same house where Elinor resided a hundred years ago before she married Nicholas.

They met on the very riverbank that you and I have strolled a hundred times. Grams made those stories come alive for us. I can understand how you might get confused, especially at a time like this when you are under so much stress. That and a lack of sleep can cause the lines between dreams and reality to blur."

Emily stared at Becky. "Do you really think that's it?"

"Think about it, Em. What else could it be?"

"You're right. It's the only reasonable explanation."

Relief flooded Becky's face and Emily was glad she had gone along with the theory, though in truth, she still wasn't convinced.

Leaving the kitchen, they went to the living room where they took out Grams' photo album. Pictures of Emily with Jeff were still inside. As Emily looked at them, she saw how large a part he had played in her life.

Becky must have reached the same conclusion. "It's good that you're home where you're appreciated. You know, Em, there are several local bachelors who would kill for a chance to go out with you."

"I don't think they would 'kill,' Becky, and anyway, I don't want to be involved with anyone right now." Emily changed the subject, "How are you getting along with that professor you mentioned in your last letter?"

"Fred is falling madly in love with me. He just doesn't know it yet." Becky explained how Fred Johnson, professor of Archeology at Kanawha State University, was so engrossed with the digs at the Indian burial mound that she had to wear a name tag so he wouldn't forget who she was.

"Oh, Beck," Emily laughed, "I'm sure you're exaggerating."

"Well yeah, I guess he isn't that bad. It's just that he is so focused. I don't have to worry about another woman, at least not a live one!"

"Don't underestimate the value of that, Beck. It could be worse."

Following the good-natured bantering, Emily made coffee and Becky suggested they have it on the patio. Though she didn't want to admit it, Emily was reluctant to go outside after the experience she had that afternoon.

"It might be a little chilly out of doors. Why don't we stay inside?" She should have known she couldn't fool her lifelong friend.

"Now, Em, what better time to confront your dream or whatever it was? I'm here with you. We stood up to rattlesnakes when we were kids. I think we can handle this."

Becky was right. Emily needed to face this illusion. Having her friend beside her made it easier.

The crickets and frogs had begun their evening choruses as the two young women stepped outside with steaming cups of coffee in hand. The evening shadows had already crept over the patio, swallowing it up, as the setting sun dipped behind the mountains on the other side of the river.

Emily's gaze automatically traveled to the Langford Manor property. The dull blackened stones gave off no light so she could barely see them against the dark backdrop of the steep hills.

"See," Becky said, "same old house we've always looked at. It's a wonder no one has torn it down. The land still belongs to the descendants of Nicholas' sister, Geneva Langford. She's the only family member who survived the fire. You'd think they'd want to be rid of the old eyesore."

Sipping her coffee, Emily continued to stare at the remains of the manor house. "I think it's charming. I would hate to see it torn down."

A balmy June breeze kissed Emily's cheek, carrying with it the sweet fragrance of lilac. She was struck by a wistful longing. "I had forgotten how wonderful it was here, away from the glaring city lights and pollution. You were right, Beck," she added as an afterthought, "I must have dreamed about the new house and Nicholas and Elinor. At least, I think the woman was Elinor. I never got a close look at her. Even if I had, I wouldn't necessarily recognize her. It was always Nicholas who dominated the dreams." She hesitated for a moment. "It sounds so ridiculous when I put it into words."

"There you see? I told you we would get this thing figured out." Becky took a final sip of coffee. "I'd never think you were ridiculous, Em. As I said before, you've been under a great deal of stress."

Emily sniffed the air. "Beck, do you smell that?"

"Smell what?"

"The lilacs. I didn't realize they bloomed this late. I guess I'm really out of touch with nature." Emily took a slow, deep breath and closed her eyes. "Ah, isn't that wonderful? It's always been my favorite scent."

"If you say so, Em. I guess my sinuses must be acting up because I can't smell a thing. Besides, the lilacs have already bloomed. You must be smelling the roses."

Emily opened her eyes and sniffed again. "No, I'm sure it's lilacs."

"You're probably right. I suppose there are several varieties. Maybe some of them are late bloomers—just like us." Becky laughed. "I've got a stack of papers to grade, so I've got to go. If I'd known you were going to be home, I would never have signed up to teach summer school."

Emily got up and walked Becky to her car. "How are your parents? Are they enjoying their new home in Florida?"

Becky said they were and that she enjoyed having the West Virginia homeplace to herself. "Are you going to be all right, Em?"

"I'm going to be fine. Thanks for your help."

"Hey, what are best friends for? I'll call you in a day or so. Maybe we can take in dinner and a movie."

Emily watched Becky's car pull out of the driveway and head down the street. Remembering that the coffee cups had been left on the patio table, she followed the path into the ebony shadows at the back of the house to retrieve them. Here, away from the city lights, the darkness was so pronounced she had to walk carefully to avoid stumbling.

The minute she approached the wooden deck, she noticed the difference. Electricity filled the air, causing her hair to stand on end. She willed herself to turn around and leave, but a dream-like paralysis gripped her and her limbs would not respond. All of her senses were finely tuned, particularly her sense of smell. The scent of lilacs was now so overpowering, Emily swayed. Reaching out, she grabbed the wooden railing to steady herself.

Out of the velvety shadows a cool breeze slithered across her arm. Suppressing a cry, she let out her breath slowly, as though the sound of it rushing out would break the fragile thread on which her emotions were suspended.

"Who are you?" She heard herself say.

Then he was in front of her, close enough to touch. His dark, wavy hair framed a face that was surprisingly visible even in the darkness. But it was the black, gypsy eyes that held her gaze captive. They spoke of longing. His full, sensual lips bade her to come to him.

"Who are you?" she asked again. She needed to hear the sweet melody of his name echoing from the ages.

"Elinor, it is I, Nicholas." He reached for her. "It is time, dearest—please, come with me."

"Yes, Nicholas, yes," Emily heard herself say, though the words were not her own.

Then, a great white light enveloped her and the power of a thousand exploding stars coursed through her body. The last thing she remembered was the overpowering scent of lilacs.

Chapter Three

West Virginia
April, 1899

Elinor Foster sat on the large stone, her feet dangling in the river. She wiggled her toes in the cool water and delighted in the wafting breeze that kissed her nose and ruffled the strands of her long, golden hair. Leaning back, she closed her eyes and tilted her face upward to soak up the sun's warmth.

Basking in the peacefulness of a perfect spring day, she gave no thought to her unladylike appearance. A smile curled her lips as she exalted in the sweet, heady scent of lilacs, her favorite flower.

Suddenly, a shadow came between her and the sun, blocking out the warmth. Opening her eyes, she gasped when she looked up into the face of a stranger.

Attempting to scramble from her seat on the rock, she slipped and would have ended up in the river had the man not caught her in his strong arms and pulled her to safety.

She rested against her rescuer's firm chest for a brief moment before pushing herself away.

"Are you all right?" the deep, male voice asked.

She could see the man clearly now. Tall, and trim with black wavy hair, he appeared to be in his early thirties. The fact that the trousers of his cutaway suit were wet from the knees down did noting to detract from his gentlemanly bearing. Smiling, he tilted his chin, revealing a strawberry birthmark.

Elinor remembered someone saying that Nicholas Langford and his father, Tobias, had unusual strawberry birthmarks, a trait common to the male members of their family. The Langfords lived in the isolated stone mansion across the river and, in spite of their money, were not well accepted by the people of Charleston and surrounding areas. Obviously, Nicholas had decided to row across and make his own introductions.

Her cheeks flamed. Had he watched her remove her shoes and hairpins and interpreted it as a sign that she was a woman of loose morals? She knew she should turn and run up the embankment. Since they had never been formally introduced, remaining and speaking with him would only enhance any negative impression he might already have of her.

The look of genuine concern in his eyes, however, kept her from leaving. She could not turn away; though by staying, she was implying that she welcomed his bold behavior.

"You look a little pale—perhaps you should sit down," he said.

"I am fine. You needn't concern yourself further about me, Mr...?"

She was not going to let this man know she recognized him. Elinor smoothed her hair back and with her other hand, attempted to refasten the top buttons of her bodice.

"My name is Nicholas Langford." He smiled and bowed.

Elinor watched as his hand slipped inside his breast pocket. When he withdrew it, he was clutching a bouquet of lilacs which he offered to her. "For you, Elinor Foster. Would that they were roses. But then, even a rose cannot equal the sweetness of the lilac. The lilac grows wild and free and roses are so pampered and cultivated. That makes roses rather boring, don't you think?" He regarded her with a faint amusement. "There is something special in the air today. Do you feel it? That's how I knew it was time we met."

Elinor did not reach for the flowers, though a part of her wanted to. "How is it that we've never been introduced?" she asked.

"I assure you, Elinor, if we had, our lives would have been forever changed."

"What an odd thing to say, Mr. Foster. You keep calling me by my name as though you know me." She tried to sound calm, but in truth, she hadn't felt so alive in months. She chastised herself for finding this brash man so exciting.

"Our souls have known one another for a very long time. I have also made inquiries. There is no need for pretense between us."

"Mr. Langford, I am not in the habit—"

"I know you are a proper lady and I assure you, my intentions are honorable. You have no idea how long I have wanted to row across and tell you that I would very much like to call on you. I will ask your father if I may do so."

Elinor was breathless. Her entire upbringing was being challenged. But, hadn't she been waiting for something special, different to happen? She reached for the lilacs and clasped them to her bosom. The intoxicating fragrance delighted her.

"We're alike, the two of us," he said, apparently encouraged by her acceptance of the flowers. "I can't explain how I know that, but I do. I have sensed your longing and dissatisfaction because I have felt exactly the same way. Convention can be so confining. I want to be free to live without being weighted down by family obligations and expectations."

"Really, Mr. Langford, you assume a great deal. Please don't allow my bedraggled appearance to mislead you. I did not expect to see anyone. This is private property."

"Ah, but the fragrance of spring flowers and the whisper of anticipation on the breeze tempt you—as well they should. You are a free spirit, Elinor Foster. You're not like those stuffy, narrow-minded women who are already old before their time. When I look into your lovely blue eyes, I find the ocean that I someday hope to see. I'd love you to see it with me."

Uncertainty shook Elinor. "How can you say these things to me when we aren't even acquainted?"

"Dear Elinor, as I said before, our souls know one another. They have reached across the river and touched. I know you feel it too."

Staring at him in disbelief, Elinor asked herself if this was really happening. "This is insane, Mr. Langford. Not only have we not been formally introduced, but there is also the matter of Sophie Gilmore. What about her?"

"Miss Gilmore is the young lady my parents would have me marry. I refuse to marry someone I don't love. I have known since I first saw you that someday we would be together."

Elinor's heart pounded with fear and exhilaration. Good sense dictated that she should send him away, but when she looked into his dark, gypsy eyes, she could not.

"My father will be home tomorrow evening," she said, though she could hardly believe her own voice, "if you wish, you may call on him at seven o'clock."

A broad smile broke across Nicholas' handsome face. "I will be there."

"You had better go now. There would be a scandal if someone should see us before you have asked my father's permission to call." She broke a sprig of lilac from the bouquet. "Here, put this in your bible as a remembrance of our meeting."

Their fingers touched when she handed it to him. The brief contact set off a jolt that traveled to the center of Elinor's being. She felt weak-kneed, wary—yet at the same time drawn to this man she had only just met.

Stepping closer, Nicholas teased her lips with the lilac blossom. "I shall keep it forever," he said, "but there is something else I mean to take with me."

Folding her in his arms, he touched his lips to hers, gently, sweetly, as he pulled her closer, and she melted against the firm body that seemed to have been made just for her. Holding her so tightly she could scarcely breathe, he buried his face in her windblown hair. "My beautiful angel," he whispered before releasing her. "Someday you will be mine, Elinor. Until tomorrow, then."

Shaken by the powerful emotions his kiss—indeed his very presence had created—she watched him as he got into his boat and rowed toward the opposite shore. She watched as the setting sun settled over him, outlining his form with an aura of burnished gold. Once he reached the other side, he raised his hand in farewell, then headed toward the hulking stone house. Soon, he was lost in its shadow.

She stood there for a moment asking herself if it had all been a dream. She touched the lips that still burned from his kiss. No, he was not a phantom. That kiss was real. She smiled, not minding that her cheeks must be flaming. If this was the behavior of a wanton woman, then so be it. She'd been stifled long enough. Today, it was as though she had been reborn.

A chill slithered up her back as the spring evening turned suddenly cool. Nicholas had taken the warmth with him. Gazing at Langford Manor, as Nicholas' home was called, she noted the contrast of a fiery sunset and the dark stones of the manor house resting in ominous shadows. It sent another chill down her back as she again reminded herself that everyone said the Langfords were a strange lot. That seemed to be especially true of the mother, Harriet.

Elinor sensed that if she intended to turn back, now was the time to do it. A voice inside told her to play it safe, to refuse Nicholas' intentions. She shivered again. She couldn't shake the sense of danger that seemed to accompany him. Was that why she found him so attractive?

She'd seen sadness and longing in his dark eyes. It was just as he had said. Their souls did, somehow, know one another.

What would she do if her father refused to allow Nicholas to court her? The Langfords' questionable reputations made that a possibility. She told herself she mustn't think about it. Her father had never been one to refuse Elinor anything, but he was also very protective of her. Now, in a matter of minutes, her life had changed dramatically. She had an important decision to make. One that would shape the rest of her life.

The ocean. Like Nicholas, she, too, had yearned to see the blue swells of endless water, to smell the salty tang of sea air and watch the gulls glide overhead.

Suddenly, the flapping, beating sound of rustling wings shook Elinor from her musings. She looked up almost expecting to see a flock of her imagined gulls. Instead, a large crow circled overhead. It was unlike any she had ever seen.

Dipping and diving in weird patterns, it swooped down and just missed the top of her head. Its loud shrieking drowned out her own screams.

Flailing her arms in an attempt to keep the vicious bird away, Elinor scrambled toward the embankment and began climbing upward.

"Caw! caw!" the winged creature shrilled as its menacing form continued circling overhead.

When Elinor reached the top of the incline, she glanced over her shoulder. The crow made one more pass and then turned and headed toward the river. Its shrieks grew fainter as it soared across the water and disappeared into the black shadows that now enveloped Langford Manor.

Chapter Four

The following evening, as she brushed her long, golden hair, Elinor studied her reflection in the mirror. The lamplight accented her high cheek bones and added brilliance to her large, blue eyes. She kept glancing out her bedroom window. It was almost seven o'clock. Would Nicholas change his mind?

She thought again of his dark probing eyes and the feel of his warm, eager lips upon her own. New and powerful feelings had been awakened in her. Consumed by these exciting emotions, she knew she wanted more—so much more. She could not turn back. Elinor felt the warmth spread over her face at the mere admission, even to herself. Respectable young ladies weren't supposed to think or talk about such intimacies.

She steered her thoughts back to Nicholas' visit. Her parents would certainly be surprised. Judging from her mother's curious glances at Elinor, she seemed to know something was afoot. Even though Mary Foster had a knack for reading her daughter's mind, she would never guess that Nicholas Langford was the reason for Elinor's preoccupation.

"They must accept him!" Elinor whispered.

Hopefully, her parents' anxiety about her lack of a serious suitor would outweigh any prejudice they might have against a member of the Langford family. She knew they had heard the stories about the ruthless Tobias Langford who, it was said, had won his first coal mine in a poker game. There had also been whispers about Harriet Langford, Nicholas' mother. One of the kinder descriptions labeled her as odd. Others called her a witch. One thing was certain: she craved a social acceptance she had not yet achieved.

Elinor jumped to her feet at the sound of carriage wheels. Standing in front of the lace-curtained window, she watched Nicholas alight from an elegant brougham complete with coachman and a team of sleek, black horses. Her heart raced when Nicholas looked up at her. A smile creased his handsome face and he waved.

Running to her bedroom door, Elinor opened it and stood poised, listening. The sound of the front door opening and closing was followed by muffled conversation. Then Jacob Foster said, "Step into the library, Mr. Langford."

Elinor heard her mother's soft, quick footsteps padding up the stairs. Mary Foster stepped onto the upper landing and approached her daughter. Her blue eyes, so like Elinor's, clouded and a worried look washed over her serene face.

"Elinor, dear," she began, "Nicholas Langford has come to speak to your father. Do you know what this is about?"

She already knows, Elinor thought. "He wants to call on me. Isn't that wonderful?" Elinor looked into her mother's eyes and saw the disappointment.

"Oh Elinor! A Langford? And what of Sophie Gilmore? I can't believe you would consider this man suitable."

"Mother, you taught me to turn a deaf ear to gossip. As far as Sophie Gilmore is concerned, she is his parents' choice, not his. He has not pledged himself to her."

"How is it you know all of this?"

"I know enough to have reached these conclusions but, after all, the reason he wants permission to call is so that we can get to know one another."

"You have been introduced, then?"

Elinor hesitated. "We ran into each other. There was no formal introduction. He asked permission to speak to Papa. I told him I would welcome his intentions." Elinor's cheeks flamed.

Mary Foster took her daughter's hand. "Look at me, dear." She returned her mother's gaze.

"You seem quite smitten." Mary's demeanor softened, "He is very handsome, I'll grant you that. But, dear, the Langfords live in that gloomy old house that's practically cut off from civilization. And that mother! No one speaks well of her. Yet they say Nicholas is a devoted son. Are you prepared to deal with that?"

"I don't care. I just want the chance to get to know him, Mother. I find him..." Elinor hesitated, searching for the right word, "interesting."

'Exciting' would have been a more correct term, but she thought it unwise to use it. "Please, Mother, just give him a chance. You've been so concerned that I haven't shown an interest in anyone. I had hoped you would be happy for me."

Then, Elinor threw caution to the wind and gave her restless spirit full rein. "I sense in him the one that I have been waiting for. He is the man I will someday marry."

Her mother paled. "Elinor! Such talk is foolish. Even you admit that you really don't know him."

Elinor tilted her chin. "When you met Papa, you told me you knew right away that he was the one for you."

"Yes, I knew. Jacob was the handsomest, kindest man I had ever met." A wistful look passed over Mary's gentle features. "But, dear, he came from a family of good standing."

"Would it have mattered if he hadn't? You didn't fall in love with his family, did you?"

Mary Foster ignored the defiance in her daughter's voice. "Now we're talking of love, are we?" She tilted her head and returned Elinor's gaze. As far as family's concerned, when you marry a man, you marry his family, too. You're young and inexperienced and don't know that yet. If you don't fit into the family you will have a hard row to hoe."

"Then, so be it."

Tears brimmed in Mary's eyes and Elinor's heart broke for putting them there, but she would not give up Nicholas even if her parents demanded it. The realization shook her.

Mary Foster pulled a handkerchief from her apron pocket and dabbed at her eyes. "You're headstrong, my dear, but I don't suppose you get it from a stranger." She put her arm around Elinor. "I see myself in you. When I was young, I was also restless and yearned for adventure. I was lucky I met a good man like your father. He has made me very happy."

"Mother, how can you be so sure Nicholas isn't a good man, too? It doesn't seem fair to prejudge him based on what his parents may or may not have done."

Mary smiled at Elinor and patted her on the shoulder. "Well, let's see what your father says. Come on downstairs, I made a pitcher of lemonade. I believe we could use some."

A few minutes later, while sitting at the round oak table finishing the cool drink, Elinor heard the library door open.

When her father called her, she sprang to her feet.

"Yes, Papa," she answered as she reached out and clasped her mother's hand.

"Would you and your mother come into the library?"

The two women left the kitchen and stepped into the hallway.

Jacob Foster and Nicholas stood at the far end, next to the library. Both wore somber expressions.

"Elinor," Jacob began, "Mr. Nicholas Langford has asked permission to call on you. I told him I did not believe a daughter of mine would be interested in a man who is promised to another. He insists that he is not the intended husband of Sophie Gilmore. He also tells me he believes you would welcome his intentions. Is that true?"

"Yes, Papa, it's true." Elinor felt her cheeks turn crimson as she met her father's blue-eyed gaze. A lump formed in her throat when she saw the disappointment there. She looked at his thin, graying hair and the stoop of his shoulders, evidence of years of hard work. Hurting him was the last thing she wanted to do.

"I have never denied you anything within reason, my girl. But I cannot in good conscience give my blessings." Jacob Foster started to turn away.

"Papa, don't do this. Don't make me choose."

Startled by her words, he turned back. "Has it come to that, then? You would give up your family for this man?"

"If I have to." Elinor's heart was breaking. She wanted to run to her father's arms and ask forgiveness for the words that she knew were like a knife through his heart.

Then, she looked into Nicholas' eyes and saw love, pride and compassion. She went to stand beside him. "If I must, I will go with him."

"No daughter of mine will be turned out!" Jacob's voice boomed. "Very well, I will give my consent under one condition. You will not see one another for a month. If you still feel the same four weeks from today, then I will withdraw my objections. Mr. Langford may come calling at that time."

Her heart bursting with relief, Elinor went to her father. "Thank you, Papa!" she cried as he folded her in his huge embrace. Speaking in soft, hushing tones, he soothed away the hurt as he had done when she was a child and had fallen and scraped her knee.

A moment later when she looked up and saw Nicholas smiling, she knew he would accept the conditions.

"A month seems like a lifetime, Papa, but it that's what it takes to have your consent, I will gladly abide by it."

"I, too, accept your terms, Mr. Foster."

"Then I have your word as a gentleman on that, Mr. Langford?" Jacob asked.

"You have my word, sir. In fact, I will use the time to clear up the misconception regarding Miss Gilmore and myself."

In the coming days, Nicholas kept his word. When Elinor took Sunday afternoon walks by the river, she often saw him doing the same, but he made no attempt to communicate with her. A part of her was disappointed. She wondered if a month might bring about a change of heart. She knew it wouldn't in her. She had set upon a path and there was no turning back.

Nicholas was no longer seen with Sophie Gilmore but that had not stopped the tongues from wagging.

Elinor's best friend, Celia Morgan couldn't believe her

ears when Elinor told her about Nicholas. "Ellie! Do you realize what you're doing?" she'd exclaimed.

At last the month was up. Elinor was anxious for seven o'clock to come. That was the hour decided upon. What if Nicholas forgot? Even worse, what if he changed his mind and didn't show up at all?

Her skin tingled with anticipation when, at precisely seven o'clock, she heard the sound of a carriage. Nicholas! He had come for her.

A short time later, Elinor's parents waved good-bye as she and Nicholas left in his brougham for an evening ride.

A chill of anticipation swept over Elinor as they drove down the winding drive past the weeping willow trees. The scent of lilacs permeating the twilight and the rhythmic sway of the carriage as the horses clopped along lulled Elinor's finely tuned senses into a state of pure happiness.

When Nicholas slipped his hand in hers, she did not pull away. There would be no pretense between them. A delicious shiver swept over her when she turned and looked into his eyes.

Smiling and pointing to the front of the coach where the driver sat, Nicholas put his finger to his lips indicating the coachman might be listening to their conversation.

Elinor doubted that he could hear through the walls, especially with the steady clip-clop of the horses but she played along anyway.

"It is a lovely evening, isn't it, Miss Foster?" Nicholas said, mocking the way the ramrod straight coachman was likely sitting.

"Indeed, Mr. Langford," Elinor replied, suppressing a giggle. She loved the way his lips curled into a mischievous grin as his dark-eyed gaze locked with hers.

"I thought we would stop at the recently-opened Mountain Inn for a dish of ice cream and a glass of soda."

"That sounds wonderful, Mr. Langford. I haven't been

there and I hear it's quite the place." Seeing a lock of hair slip down his forehead, Elinor reached over and smoothed it back.

Nicholas caught her wrist as she withdrew her hand, and gazing into her eyes, kissed it, right where the button hole exposed a small patch of skin.

A tingling sensation coursed through her body and it was all she could do not to gasp.

A playful smile again broke across his handsome face. He held her hand for a moment before releasing it. "You look especially lovely tonight in that beautiful blue dress."

"Thank you. Blue is my favorite color."

"You will be the loveliest woman at the inn, tonight. I understand they have a piano player, violinists and a dance floor. Do you dance, Miss Foster?"

"I wouldn't have graduated from Miss Springwell's Academy for Young Ladies if I hadn't learned the fine art of terpsichore. How about you?"

"Yes, my mother insisted on it. I hated it at the time, but now I see the merit in it."

Elinor felt a chill go up her arm when Nicholas mentioned his mother, but she ignored it. Now that she and Nicholas were together, noting was going to interfere with their happiness.

Twenty minutes later, the carriage pulled in front of the Mountain Inn. A rambling building in the new Victorian style, it boasted hotel rooms in the upper stories and a vast dining area and ballroom on the main floor.

Nicholas helped Elinor from the brougham and, with a protective arm around her, guided her to the entryway. Stepping into a huge lobby where colorfully-clad people milled about, they heard the strains of violin and piano music. Following the sound, they entered the large dining room.

The tables were covered with lace cloths and each had a candle that flickered in a red glass chamber. The delicious aromas of baking bread and roasting beef drifted through the dimly lit room. In the far corner, the musicians began playing *Fantasie Impromptu*. Several couples arose from their seats and went to the dance floor.

"It's one of my favorite melodies," Elinor remarked as a waiter led them to a table near a window. After they were seated, Nicholas asked if she would like something more substantial to eat, a late supper, perhaps?

Elinor declined, saying the ice cream and soda would be fine.

After placing the order, Nicholas asked Elinor if she would like to dance. "I'd love to," she replied.

Nicholas put his arms around Elinor in the appropriate fashion which kept them at a greater distance than Elinor would have liked. When she gazed into his eyes, she knew he felt the same way.

Being in Nicholas' arms and swaying to the beautiful melody gave Elinor goose bumps. She wanted to *be* with him completely. She was glad the dim lighting obscured the color in her cheeks. She had never felt this way before. She inched closer so that their bodies touched. When her breasts brushed against his chest, she felt fire, even through the layers of clothing.

Seeing in his dark eyes the same desire that gripped her, she yearned for the feel of his lips against her.

He tilted his head forward to quench her burning thirst.

"Elinor, Elinor—"

Hearing her name being called, Elinor pulled back, the spell broken.

Celia Morgan approached with her fiancé, Jonathan Wilkes, in tow. "Why didn't you tell me you were going to be here?"

Celia's blonde ringlets bounced and her dimples creased as she smiled and hugged Elinor. Eyeing Nicholas, she waited for an introduction.

"Oh, Celia! Isn't he wonderful?" Elinor asked later, when the two young women went to the powder room.

"I'll admit, he is quite dashing—even if he is a Langford." Celia flashed a saucy grin.

"I love him, Celia. I don't care what his name is. When I marry him, my name will be Langford, too."

Celia gasped. "Marry him? Has it really gone that far? Oh, Ellie, I hope you won't jump into anything. Don't forget that mother of his. I would hate to go up against her. They say Harriet Langford is very possessive of her son. There is also gossip about her unusual habits."

Elinor smiled as she applied a little rice powder to her shiny nose. "I don't care about any of it, Celia. I love Nicholas. That's all that matters."

"I am assuming that Nicholas feels the same way about you?" Celia rearranged a blonde ringlet that had slipped loose from her upswept do.

"Yes, Celia, he does. As I said, there is an unspoken bond between us."

"Then, I am happy for you," Celia put her arm around Elinor and gave her a hug. "It's just like when I met Jonathan. We both knew then. Now you know how it feels to be in love."

The haunting strains of *Moonlight Sonata* filled the room as Celia and Elinor joined their escorts at the table. Elinor caught the wistful look in Nicholas' eyes. Without asking, she knew that he, too, loved this piece of music.

Celia chattered on and Jonathan smiled and nodded. But Elinor, lost in Nicholas' gaze, was oblivious to what was being said.

Later, after saying good-bye to the other couple, Nicholas helped Elinor into the waiting brougham. Her skin tingled where he touched her. The heady scent of lilacs floated on the night air as Nicholas climbed into the coach. It was all she could do to keep from going into his arms. Instead, she looked away.

"Elinor," he reached for her hand, "What is it?"

She shuddered at the sweetness of his touch.

Then, he pulled her to him and his lips brushed hers. But her hunger would not be satisfied with a mere feathery touch.

Her eager hands sought the planes of his face and the

luxurious thickness of his dark, wavy hair. She pulled him closer, not caring that such boldness was unbecoming to a lady.

His lips took possession of hers, until the smoldering fire between them fully ignited and he pulled her so close she could hardly breathe. She had no desire to stop now. Her head spinning, she melted against him. She felt herself slipping backwards against the leather carriage seat as Nicholas' hand stroked her back and slipped forward to the softness beneath her bodice.

Suddenly, the brougham lurched forward. The action brought Elinor to her senses. She sat up, smoothing the front of her dress with one hand and catching the loose wisps of her hair with the other.

"Nicholas, I—"

"Don't say anything, dearest. We are alike, you and I. Our feelings run deep and they have been too long denied. I love you and want you to be my wife."

"And I want to be your wife, Nicholas. I am as sure of that as I am of my own name. But I am equally sure that our families will not approve of a quick marriage. Convention dictates waiting awhile and then becoming engaged. After that, we should wait another year before getting married."

Nicholas took Elinor's hand. "I detest convention! But, you are right. I wouldn't want to compromise your reputation. And, our parents' wishes can't be ignored."

"I think we must do things properly, Nicholas. Our families will expect it. Once we are married, we will have the rest of our lives to enjoy one another."

Nicholas bent forward and brushed her lips with the sweetness of his own. "Then, we will do as you say." He fell silent for a moment, an odd expression flashing across his handsome features. "I must arrange for you to meet my parents. I'm sure Mother will want to invite you to dinner. I'll discuss it with her and an invitation will be forthcoming."

A chill swept over Elinor when Nicholas mentioned his mother. Suddenly, she felt very uneasy about meeting the formidable Harriet Langford.

Chapter Five

On a warm Saturday afternoon two weeks later, Nicholas helped Elinor into a buckboard and they set out for Langford Manor. Going across the river in a boat would have been faster, but the carriage seemed more appropriate for the occasion and the ferry was only four miles away.

Besides, Elinor wasn't in a hurry to get there. She couldn't shake a growing fear that gnawed in the pit of her stomach. She tried to conceal her nervousness, but Nicholas wasn't fooled. He assured her his family would give her a warm welcome.

"How could they not love you?" He patted her hand and smiled.

"They wanted you to marry Sophie Gilmore and I have interfered with those plans. It will be very easy for them to dislike me, Nicholas."

"Sophie Gilmore is no longer an issue. I have made my feelings clear in that regard. My parents assured me that they are only interested in my happiness. Naturally, I want their approval. They understand I am determined to make you my wife. I don't anticipate any problems."

Elinor hoped his optimism was based on fact and not wishful thinking. Her parents now accepted Nicholas. If the Langfords disliked her, she would just work very hard to win them over.

"Besides," Nicholas said, giving her hand a squeeze, "one day, you and I will go out West. My father wants me to remain in the family business, but I have something different in mind. Soon, I will have saved enough of my own money to make a fresh start in a place where the Langford name is not known."

"Nicholas—"

"I know what people say about us, Elinor. In some instances, I can't say that I blame them. I want to get away from it and be my own man. I want you to be by my side as my wife when I do."

Elinor looked into his eyes and saw the love that was always there. She would go to the ends of the earth with him if that was what he wanted.

"I thought we could announce our engagement at the Fourth of July Ball. Some people, of course, will be shocked since our courtship has only recently begun. We will marry in the spring, when the lilacs first bloom. Does that meet with your approval?"

"Yes, darling. Only—"

"I know. A year engagement is considered appropriate. I think spring is close enough, though. Don't you? We will have known one another for a year. That will just have to do." He slipped his arm around Elinor.

When he held her close and dazzled her with his smile, any objections she might have had disappeared.

"I think an April wedding will be wonderful," she said. "Lillies, lilacs, tulips and apple blossoms will be blooming. It's a perfect time." She hesitated for a moment as an uneasy feeling swept over her. "I think it would be wise for us to say nothing about this until we have announced our engagement."

Nicholas gave her a companionable squeeze and, reaching over, kissed her on the cheek. Then, meeting her gaze with a twinkle in his eye, he said, "I can keep quiet, but does this mean that you're not going to tell Celia?"

"Celia's different, Nicholas. She will keep our secret."

He laughed, "Then by all means feel free to tell her."

Elinor thought again about her future in-laws. She suspected they wouldn't be too happy if they knew about the plans she and Nicholas had just made.

She had been sitting with Nicholas' arm around her. She pulled away when they approached the ferry at Malden. Once the horses and carriage were on the large, flat barge, they began the journey across the green waters.

A chill slithered up Elinor's back as they neared the lush wilderness on the far shore. She had been on this side of the river before but not this far downstream. She wondered again why the Langfords had built their home so far away from the nearest neighbor. The question was on the tip of her tongue, but knowing Nicholas was sensitive about his odd family, Elinor didn't ask him.

"It won't be too long now," Nicholas said, as the coachman guided the team off the ferry and onto a road that looked like a tunnel of greenery. As the team of horses plunged deeper into the wilderness, Elinor's apprehension grew. The dank smell of fresh earth and vegetation was suddenly oppressive. Her skin was clammy. She felt she was being swallowed up by a great bird of prey.

After a mile and a half, the tunneling trees thinned and Elinor relaxed a little. Seeing the blue sky now, she didn't feel so enclosed. Instead, the bright, relentless sunlight bore down on them.

"Are you all right, darling? You look a bit pale." Nicholas studied her, concern creasing his brow. I should have brought a covered carriage."

"I'm fine. I like being out in the open. It just seemed a little close for a moment there. It is a very humid day."

Nicholas looked up at the sky. "We'd better hurry. It looks like rain."

Apprehension took hold of Elinor as she watched dark, menacing clouds creep across the horizon. They provided an ominous backdrop for her first glimpse of Langford Manor from this side of the river. She swallowed hard, trying to dispel the growing fear that knotted in her stomach. She loved Nicholas, but his world seemed suddenly very foreign to her.

The manor house rose up out of the small clearing of

foliage like an accusing skeletal fist pointing upward to heaven. The house was bathed in shadows, its weathered stones like hungry entities, swallowing up the light.

Elinor couldn't shake the feeling of dread. All of her senses told he that she was heading to an evil place, a place where heaven's protection was suspended and anyone who entered would be left to the mercy of the forces of darkness.

I must stop this foolishness, she told herself. She looked at Nicholas and found reassurance in his easy smile and loving gaze. She told herself that with him at her side, she would be safe. Langford Manor was only a house! She had to pull in on the reins of her overactive imagination. She mustn't allow anything to spoil her first meeting with Nicholas' parents.

Another long, winding tunnel of greenery greeted Elinor on the last mile of road to Langford Manor. This one was even more oppressive than the first. The road was rutted and narrow, and vines and branches scraped the sides of the carriage. Elinor took a deep breath and tried to ignore the goose bumps that rose on her skin—goose bumps that had nothing to do with cold. In fact, the heat was even worse than before and was accompanied by man-eating mosquitoes, delighted to have fresh victims. She waved her hand to ward them off, wishing mightily that they had rowed across the river from her house instead of coming this way.

Another thought occurred to her that only added to her uneasiness. Where would she and Nicholas live when they married? Langford Manor was Nicholas' home and, as the only son, it would someday pass on to him.

Since she and Nicholas were planning to go out West, it made no sense to purchase a residence that they would have to sell again. Marrying Nicholas was becoming more and more complicated.

Finally, the buckboard broke free of the green tunnel and pulled into an open area surrounding Langford Manor. The main entrance was opposite the river and fronted by a circular drive.

Suddenly, the clouds that had been hovering overhead darkened the sky like an eerie hand pulling a cloak of yellow-green over the landscape. A lightening flash, immediately followed by an ear-splitting clap of thunder, shook Elinor from her seat, causing her to cry out.

Nicholas put a protective arm around her as a torrent of summer rain pelted them. Stopping in front of the carriage house, and turning the reins over to a stable boy, Nicholas helped Elinor from the carriage.

"Let's get inside," he shouted over the sound of the wind buffeting the trees. Buckets of rain, splashed the parched earth.

Shielding Elinor with his body as best he could, he pulled her along as he dashed for the front entrance of Langford Manor. The driving rain splashed against them, showing no mercy to Elinor's new dress and shoes.

When they reached the door, Nicholas put his shoulder to it and shoved it open. He pushed Elinor in ahead of him and following closely behind her, he closed the massive oak door to shut out the fury of the thunderstorm.

Three people stood in the drab, dimly lit foyer. Their stiff, ramrod postures and sober demeanors melted the last shred of any optimism Elinor might have had.

Feeling self-conscious, she reached up and smoothed the wet tendrils of hair away from her face. She knew she must look like a drowned rat as she stood there, dripping on the well-worn rug. This was not the way she had wanted the first meeting with the Langfords to go.

The dripping was not lost on Nicholas' mother. Harriet Langford stared at the puddle on the floor, and then turned around and called for the housekeeper to bring some rags and mop up the mess. Uncomfortable under his mother's critical stare, Elinor wished Nicholas had postponed this trip.

Dressed in black taffeta from her neck to her toes, Harriet Langford's slightest movement elicited a rustling sound. A harbinger of evil, Elinor thought, then immediately chastised herself for being too fanciful. Still, she couldn't shake the feeling. She thought of a great black vulture-like bird, flapping its wings, ready to swoop down on its unsuspecting prey.

Harriet folded her claw-like hands together and tilted her chin. Her dark, beady eyes were shrewd and alert. She may have had a handsome face at one time, Elinor thought, but the coldness in Mrs. Langford's gaze would not allow any softness to mellow her sharp facial features. Her black hair was pulled severely on top of her head and twisted into a knot.

A tortoise shell comb was the only ornamentation the spartan Harriet Langford allowed herself.

Nicholas' sister, Geneva, a younger, perhaps less forceful, version of the older woman, stood two steps behind her mother. Geneva's receding chin gave her a permanent pout. Her brittle-eyed gaze mocked Elinor. She wasn't even attempting to hide her glee at Elinor's discomfort. Clad in the brown gabardine that suited her status as a spinster, Geneva looked like a lackluster sparrow.

Nicholas' father stood next to his wife, a bored smirk on his face. Elinor could see that in his younger days, Tobias Langford must have resembled Nicholas. But there was a striking difference. While Nicholas had an easy smile, Tobias' full lips rested in a cruel twist and his intent gaze was mocking and arrogant.

Tobias had the strawberry birthmark. Unlike Nicholas' whose small birthmark was just beneath his chin, his father's mark was much more prominent. It resembled a large, red dollop of jam that had dribbled onto

his chin and remained there.

After barking her orders to the housekeeper, Harriet returned her attention to Nicholas and Elinor. Her thin slash of a mouth tried to form a smile, but the seemingly permanent scowl won out.

"Well, Nicholas, don't just stand there—introduce us to your little friend who obviously forgot her parasol. Tsk,

tsk." She shook her head. "She is soaking wet and so are you!"

Harriet turned around once more. "Millie!" she yelled, "where are those rags? This rug is going to be ruined."

"Mother!" Nicholas' voice was tinged with anger, "Let's not spoil your first meeting with Elinor. The rug is old. If need be, I will replace it."

Harriet Langford flushed. "Very well, Nicholas. As you say, it is an old rug. Still, in my day, a young lady would not be caught without her parasol. Geneva," she said, turning to her daughter, "once Nicholas has introduced us to his guest, please take her upstairs and see if you can find something dry for her to put on."

Elinor was stung by the rudeness of Nicholas' mother. After the brief introductions in which Elinor felt like a piece of meat being looked over before the purchase, Geneva motioned for her to follow her up the stairway.

Nicholas nodded. "Geneva will help you," he said, "I don't want you to catch your death. I'm going up to change too." As Geneva led the way, Nicholas took Elinor's hand and they mounted the massive staircase.

Elinor hoped that once she was alone with Geneva, the woman would adopt a friendlier attitude. This was not to be, in spite of Elinor's repeated efforts at conversation once they were inside of Geneva's room.

"Here, you can wear this." Geneva thrust a gray gabardine dress at Elinor. "You're awfully tall," she said, wrinkling her pointy nose, "it might be a little short, but it should serve the purpose. I'll step outside while you're changing. Just leave the wet clothes on the window seat, I'll have Millie hang them by the kitchen stove to dry." Then, without looking back, Geneva left the room.

Elinor peeled off her sodden, pink frock and looked at herself in the full length mirror. She was five feet seven inches, a little taller than most of her friends, but not tall enough to have warranted Geneva's remark. Noting that her corset and pantaloons were also wet, Elinor had no choice but to remove them.

Quickly, she put on the drab, ill-fitting dress and fastened the buttons. She was at a disadvantage without undergarments but she would rather go without than ask Geneva to provide them.

Elinor untied the limp, pink ribbon from her hair and shook the wet strands. Using Geneva's hairbrush, she pulled the stiff bristles through her mass of blonde tangles. She would have preferred to just leave her hair free so it would dry faster, but instead, once she finished brushing it, she tied it at the nape of her neck with the wet ribbon. From what she'd seen of the Langford women so far, she knew that unbound hair would be frowned upon in this house. While she had no desire to knuckle under, she wasn't going to be so foolish as to totally alienate Harriet and Geneva on her first visit.

Elinor took a last look at herself in the mirror. She appeared drab, but suitable. Her cheeks pinked when she thought of Nicholas. He loved her. That was all that mattered.

Nicholas was waiting for her when she left Geneva's sparse, stuffy room. He smiled and, bending forward, whispered into her ear. "You do a lot more for that dress than Geneva ever could."

The twinkle in his dark, loving eyes brought a smile to Elinor's face. When Nicholas slipped his arm around her and guided her toward the staircase, the uncertainty faded. She would brave anything the Langfords threw at her as long as Nicholas stood by her side.

Chapter Six

A dank, musty smell permeated the dining room, mingling with the charred aroma of an overcooked leg of mutton. The windows were closed and the draperies shut in the stifling room.

Elinor listened. The thunderstorm had passed. The air would be fresh now. She loved to throw open the windows after a storm and breath the clean, sweet scent. In fact, she often left windows open during the rain, allowing the cleansing waters to pelt against her face and body. The feel of it against her skin was exquisite, rejuvenating. Clearly, such a ritual would not be tolerated at Langford Manor.

Though Nicholas tried to make up for his family's chilly reception, Elinor still thought dinner would never end. More than once, she felt Harriet Langford's cold gaze resting on her.

She wished she had not come. Either Nicholas had misread his parents' reaction or he had lied to Elinor when he told her that the Langfords had accepted his choosing her over Sophie Gilmore.

That became clear when Mrs. Langford set her fork down and stated, "I saw Thelma and Sophie Gilmore yesterday. They couldn't have been more charming and Sophie looked so radiant! She inquired after you, Nicholas. She has been waiting for you to ask her to the Fourth of July Ball. I told her I was sure an invitation would be forthcoming."

Elinor couldn't believe her ears. She looked at Nicholas and saw the color drain from his face and the muscle in his jaw tighten. He folded his napkin and placed it on the table.

"Perhaps I have not made myself clear, Mother. I am keeping company with Miss Elinor Foster and no other lady. I will not be calling on Sophie Gilmore in the future. I told her as much. I'm surprised she would be expecting an invitation from me."

He looked down at his plate for a moment, collecting his thoughts, before speaking again. "Sophie Gilmore means nothing to me. She never did. Elinor, on the other hand, means everything. At the Fourth of July Ball, Elinor and I will announce our engagement."

Harriet Langford's mouth dropped open and she looked to her husband, Tobias, for support, but he remained aloof, concentrating instead on cutting a tough piece of meat.

Without looking away from the task at hand, he said, "Well Harriet, the fat's in the fire now. It seems the boy isn't interested in that stick of a girl, Sophie Gilmore. Can't say that I blame him either."

Tobias looked up and stared at Elinor. "This one's an improvement as far as looks go." He eyed Elinor. "What does your father, Mr.—uh, what did you say your surname was?"

"It's Foster, her name is Foster. Her father is Jacob Foster." Nicholas answered for Elinor, his voice tinged with irritation.

Forking a piece of the meat he had finally succeeded in cutting, Tobias champed down on the tough mutton and addressed Nicholas while he chewed it. "What does this Jacob Foster do for a living?"

"He owns the blacksmith shop and livery on the Kanawha Road three miles outside of Charleston."

"Of course—Foster's Livery. I've passed it many times but can't say I've stopped there. A real self-made man, upstanding businessman, no doubt."

The ridicule in his tone was not lost on Elinor. She felt the heat rise in her cheeks. She was about to get into the conversation and defend her father when Tobias Langford wheezed and made choking sounds.

Harriet Langford jumped to her feet and pounded him on the back until the offending piece of mutton popped out.

By the time Tobias was settled in again, the moment had passed and nothing more was said about Elinor or her family. Several times, during the meal, Elinor caught Mrs. Langford glaring at her, but if Nicholas happened to look up his mother's expression softened and she smiled. Once she even looked at Elinor and said, "She really is lovely, Nicholas."

Tobias had coughed when he heard that and for a moment Elinor thought he was choking again. However, he quickly recovered, sparing himself another pounding on the back from his dutiful wife.

By the time dinner was over, Elinor felt as though it was she, not the leg of mutton, that had been served up on a platter. While Nicholas had defended her, she noticed a certain hesitation in standing up to his parents. She couldn't fault him. It was a natural response, and they were a formidable pair. Now, more than ever, she realized the importance of getting along with Nicholas' family. She wouldn't want to put him in the position of having to choose between her and them.

The sun was setting when Elinor, in her dry, but soiled dress, climbed up on the buckboard for the homeward journey. The rain had passed and a cool breeze would make the return trip pleasant.

Harriet Langford had followed Nicholas and Elinor to the stable. She pulled a stern face when he announced that he might be saying in town for the night.

"Nicholas! That would be most unseemly."

"Not at all, Mother. I can take a room at the Mountain Inn, or for that matter, Jonathan Wilkes has issued me an invitation to stay with his family whenever I'm in town."

Mrs. Langford's face brightened. "*The* Wilkes of Charleston society?" She reached a claw-like hand to the tortoise shell comb in the knot of hair on top of her head. Yanking it out, she combed into order a wisp of hair that had slipped loose. The task completed, she put the comb back in its place. "How is it you know the Wilkes? I don't believe we've actually met them."

Nicholas grinned and glanced at Elinor. "Jonathan Wilkes is engaged to Elinor's best friend, Celia Morgan. Elinor introduced us."

If Harriet was grudgingly impressed, she didn't show it. "Well, son, perhaps you could arrange an introduction between Mrs. Wilkes and myself?"

"We'll see, Mother. I'll be home tomorrow." Waving goodbye, he urged the horses out of the barn.

A fiery sunset gave a red glow to the sky, but it was soon swallowed up by the steep mountains that hovered nearby. The jungle-like thicket was now even more foreboding in the gathering shadows of darkness.

"I could have rowed you across, Elinor, but I wanted to have more time alone with you. Please forgive me for revealing our marriage plans. Here I was teasing you about not being able to keep it from Celia. I did it to make my family understand the seriousness of my intentions toward you. I can't believe their rudeness! Dearest, can you forgive them—Mother in particular? She will come around eventually, she just needs more time. You'll see. Mother has some high and mighty ideas about what I should do with my life. But now that she sees my determination, she will have to accept my decision. In time, she will grow to love you as I do."

Elinor wasn't nearly as sure as he but she didn't want to spoil Nicholas' hopes by voicing her doubts. He seemed a bit naive when it came to his mother, but he obviously knew her better than Elinor. Things had gotten off on the wrong foot. She renewed her resolve to do everything in her power to win the Langfords' respect.

The moon and a sprinkling of stars were visible in the night sky when Nicholas drove the buckboard out of the first thicket of trees. She was grateful the mosquitoes weren't as ferocious on the return trip. The night air, cool now, washed over

Elinor's exposed skin, leaving it tingling. When they entered the next thicket she edged closer to Nicholas. She felt the muscle twitch in his arm when their shoulders touched.

"It's so dark and the road is narrow. What would happen if another carriage came in the opposite direction?" Elinor asked, recalling that they had not passed anyone on their trip to Langford Manor.

"This is a private road my father built. It leads directly to Langford Manor and nowhere else, and we really don't get may visitors. So, it's highly unlikely we would ever meet another wagon."

Elinor shivered. It made Langford Manor seem more isolated than ever.

"Dearest, you're cold." Nicholas pulled on the reins and commanded the horses to stop.

Dappled shafts of moonlight filtered through the trees so that Elinor could see Nicholas' face.

He pulled a blanket from the bed of the buckboard and placed it around her shoulders. His touch lingered, sending a thousand sprinkles of starlight over her entire body.

Then, his arms encircled her. When his lips found hers it was not in the gentle manner as before.

His insistent, burning kisses fueled a fire that smoldered within her. Her eager lips pressed against his and she clung to him, wishing that her body could touch his without the cumbersome clothing between them.

Trailing kisses of flame down her neck and to the top of her bodice, Nicholas whispered her name, over and over.

Elinor's head was spinning in a delicious vertigo when she felt his fingers fumbling with the numerous hooks of her bodice. She pulled back long enough to help him undo them. All of her pent-up emotions and caution were tossed aside into the darkness of the balmy summer night.

Elinor cried out when his lips burned the soft rises of her breast, touching, licking until she thought she would go mad with desire. The sweet scent of lilacs and the velvety darkness created a dreamlike atmosphere in which nothing was to be denied.

"Nicholas," she gasped, as the full realization of what was about to happen intruded upon her thoughts, "we mustn't."

Suddenly, he lifted his head and kissed her on the cheek. "You're right, my love." Then he buried his face against the softness of her bare shoulder. "We will wait." He sighed and continued to hold her for a moment.

Though Elinor knew they had done the right thing by stopping, her body still yearned for his. The fire within was not so easily squelched. A part of her wanted him to ignore her words. She wanted him to tell her that it was all right for them to make love here and now—that nothing or no one else mattered.

Nicholas must have read her thoughts. "Dearest," he said, cradling her in his arms, "I want you, ache for you. But, you are right. We mustn't compromise our love."

Sighing, he released Elinor, leaving her to re-fasten her bodice. He whistled to the horses and they lurched forward through the tunneling trees.

By the time they reached the ferry, Elinor had regained her composure. *Darling Nicholas*, she thought, glancing at his profile, *we will have the rest of our lives together*. But, next April seemed such a long time to wait before this recently awakened desire could be satisfied.

Attempting to move her thoughts in another direction, she thought again of Langford Manor and the chilly reception she had received. It was all the more reason not to give in to the desire of the moment. Nicholas' mother already had a low opinion of her. If she ever learned that they had gone even a far as they had, Harriet Langford would paint Elinor as a fallen woman.

Elinor shivered as she remembered the disgusted look on Harriet's face when they were introduced. Being her daughter-in-law was not going to be easy, but Elinor was willing to brave that and more to be Nicholas Langford's wife.

Chapter Seven

The sun was peeking over the rim of the mountains on the far side of the valley when Elinor awoke. Stretching and smiling, she rose from her bed. It was the Fourth of July—a day of great celebration in the Charleston area.

Today's festivities took on an added importance since this was the day she and Nicholas would become officially engaged. She looked at the ring finger of her left hand. Before the evening was over, a diamond solitaire in a white gold setting would rest there. She and Nicholas had chosen the ring together.

Elinor put on her blue gingham dress, combed back her hair and tied it with a silky, blue ribbon. She pulled the yellow and blue patchwork quilt over her bed. After smoothing out its wrinkles, she left the room.

As Elinor descended the stairs, the delicious smell of frying bacon and freshly brewed coffee drifted up from the kitchen. The familiar aroma had greeted Elinor most of the mornings of her life. Would it be the same at Langford Manor? She shivered at the thought.

It had been decided. She and Nicholas would live with his parents for the first year or so. After that, they should have saved enough money to give them a good start out West, probably California.

Elinor was less than enthusiastic about living with her in-laws, but if she and Nicholas were not moving into their own residence, living with the Langfords was considered proper. Elinor would have preferred leasing a house, but if they did, it would take them longer to save the money they needed to start out on their own.

While the Langfords favored having the newlyweds share their home, Elinor sensed they were still not happy with Nicholas' choice of a bride. Elinor had noticed the way Harriet Langford looked at Sophie Gilmore the day of the riverboat races in Charleston. Sophie had found another beau and seemed none the worse for wear from Nicholas' perceived rebuff.

Harriet had eyed Sophie the way a cat does a mouse. She nearly salivated, Elinor thought. Sophie Gilmore, the trophy mouse, had almost been within Harriet's clutches and Elinor had stepped in and ruined everything. Harriet's goal of being linked to the esteemed Gilmores had slipped through her fingers.

Elinor hoped the Langfords would accept her as Nicholas' wife. She again resolved to do everything in her power to get along with her future mother-in-law. Nicholas loved his mother, so Harriet Langford couldn't be all bad.

Having settled that, Elinor breezed into the kitchen. Mary and Jacob Foster were already sitting at the round, oak table. As Elinor greeted each of them with a kiss on the cheek, a lump formed in her throat and she blinked back a tear. This would be the last Fourth of July she would have breakfast with them in this manner.

"Good morning, dear," her mother said, "the biscuits are hot from the oven, just the way you like them."

"Umm, they look delicious." Elinor was too excited to be hungry but she wanted to remember this breakfast. So, she helped herself to the bacon, scrambled eggs and a hot biscuit with butter and honey and joined her parents at the table.

An hour later the three of them set out in the buckboard for Charleston. There, they would join her two older brothers' families at the fair grounds. Nicholas and the Langfords would arrive a little later.

Each year the county residents turned out in great numbers to participate in the various events and offerings of

Independence Day. Artists displayed their wares, food of every kind was available and numerous tents and exhibits featured such things as a two-headed cow and the world's tiniest man. There were games of chance and quilting booths, horse and boat races. A band played patriotic music and other popular tunes at the town square, the center of the festivities.

In the afternoon, while the men occupied themselves with sharpshooting and endurance contests, the women would go home and rest. In the evening, the gentlemen would escort their ladies to the dance. The nighttime festivities always began with a gigantic fireworks display. After that, the small children were sent home and the formal dance commenced.

Elinor and Nicholas intended to announce their engagement during the ball. Since their romance had become quite the topic of conversation, it was not likely anyone would be too surprised.

Even as a child, Elinor had been fascinated by the sights, sounds and tastes of the Fourth of July. The aromas of pork roasting on the spit and corn and potatoes baking in the coals, mingled with the smell of ripe, sliced watermelon and freshly baked cakes and pies. In spite of her mother's repeated warnings, as a child Elinor had always stuffed herself with the delicious food and topped it off with ice cream and sodas. She smiled as she thought of the warm, loving upbringing her parents had given her.

"Thank you, Mother," Elinor said, giving her a hug after they stepped down form the buckboard.

"What was that for?" Mary Foster smiled and patted her daughter's arm.

"I've been so lucky to have you and Papa. I'll take so many wonderful memories with me when I marry and leave home. The Fourth of July celebrations have always been special—second only to Christmas."

"Why, you sound as though you were going a million miles away. Dear, you're only going to be across the river. We will see one another often." Mary Foster's smile suddenly faded. "Elinor, are you having second thoughts? Dear, you don't have to go through with this if you don't want to."

"Oh Mother, I love Nicholas so. I have no second thoughts about him. It's just that I will miss living at home. Things will be different. I'll be a married woman." Elinor and Nicholas had told no one of their plans to settle out West. Since it wouldn't take place for at least a year after they married, and knowing that both of their mothers would be upset, the young couple had decided not to mention the move until their plans were finalized.

Mary touched Elinor's cheek. "Yes, and you will be very happy as Nicholas' wife. It's plain that he adores you and I can see how deeply you love him. But why be in such a rush? Most people are engaged for a year or two. Maybe you should give yourself more time."

"I couldn't bear that, Mother. As it is, spring seems so far away. I yearn to be Nicholas' wife."

"And you shall, dear. It's just that there is no need to hurry." Mary touched her daughter's face.

But there is, Elinor thought. She felt her cheeks grow warm as she recalled the time she and Nicholas had stopped in the grove of trees on their way from Langford Manor. They had carefully avoided such situations since then. But Elinor doubted that either of them could hold out for a long engagement.

"There you are!" Elinor heard her brother William's voice as he and his wife, Kate, with their two children in tow, walked over to join his parents and sister. Following closely behind was Elinor's other brother, David, and his wife of one year, Melanie. Melanie's condition was beginning to show and she glowed with the anticipation of motherhood.

Elinor's brothers had met Nicholas at a family dinner. The three of them had taken to one another immediately and before the evening was over, Nicholas, William and David had planned a hunting expedition.

Elinor had loved her brothers even more that day. They had always been her knights in shining armor. When she was growing up, they protected her from the school bullies and any other threats that came her way.

Her brothers had not judged Nicholas by the gossip circulating about his family. They accepted him as an individual and had given their whole-hearted blessings to a marriage between Nicholas and their kid sister.

Tall, blonde David, who was closest to Elinor's age, slipped his arm around her. "How are you, Sis?" he whispered. "Not having second thoughts, are you?"

"Now why would you say that? You know how much I love Nicholas." David had always been able to pick up on Elinor's thoughts. His marrying and moving away from home hadn't changed that.

"And Nicholas loves you. That's not the point. You seem distracted and I have to wonder if you're feeling pressured because of the announcement you'll be making tonight. If you have any misgivings, just postpone it. It's that simple."

"Oh I couldn't, David. I wouldn't want to. I love him so. You have Melanie, so I know you understand. I want to be with Nicholas. The wait already seems unbearable. I don't want any additional delays."

Elinor's brother smiled and his face flushed, "I do understand, but, I still think there's something you're not telling me." He gave her arm a squeeze.

"Oh, I'm just feeling sentimental, David. I have been reminiscing about past Independence Days. This time next year I will no longer be a young woman, riding into town with Mother and Papa. I will be Mrs. Nicholas Langford."

"And a credit to their name, Ellie. Now, are you going to stop worrying and enjoy the fair?"

"Yes," Elinor smiled at her brother. "I intend to enjoy myself to the fullest. Let's start with something sweet!"

Nicholas arrived just as the Foster family got in line for ice cream. Elinor felt him looking at her before she turned around to meet his gaze. When she did, her heart leaped. She wanted to run and throw herself into his arms but she knew it wouldn't be seemly.

His smile told her that he had read her thoughts. He

quickened his pace until he stood beside her next to the ice cream tent. His parents and Geneva followed behind.

In spite of the warm July weather, Harriet Langford was clad in her usual black taffeta. She rustled her way to the tent, indicating to Tobias that she would like a dish of ice cream. Then she turned her frosty gaze on the Fosters.

"Mrs. Langford," Mary Foster smiled at the tight-lipped Harriet, "I would like to invite your family to our home for dinner. It seems we should get to know one another better since we are going to be related by marriage."

A look of amusement slithered across Harriet Langford's face. "Really? I will, of course, have to check our social calendar. I'm not sure when we'll be able to fit you in." Harriet's gaze slid up and down Mary, inspecting her and obviously finding her wanting.

"Do that, Mrs. Langford. Let me know when you are free and I will do my best to fit you in." Elinor's usually gentle, soft spoken mother, apparently couldn't resist the jab, but she said it in such a polite way, Harriet seemed unsure as to how to take it.

Caught off guard, she stammered, "Yes, well, of course, we shall have to see." she turned away quickly, dismissing the Fosters. "I don't think I care for ice cream just yet, Tobias. Let's go to the White Elephant Sale."

Elinor flashed her mother a congratulatory smile as Nicholas purchased the ice cream. After eating it, the young couple strolled down by the river and, sitting on a wooden bench, watched the colorful boats gather for the race.

Although the morning had been pleasant, the sun was high overhead now and the day had turned hot and humid. Eating ice cream had made Elinor thirsty. When Nicholas asked her if she'd like a cold drink, she accepted gratefully.

"Stay here by the river where it's cooler, Elinor, I'll go get us one." Nicholas gave her a quick peck on the cheek.

Elinor flushed and glanced around to see if anyone had noticed. She loved Nicholas. The imprint of his kiss on her cheek still teased her flesh, leaving her wanting much more.

She leaned back on the bench and closed her eyes, giving

herself over to the feel of the sun on her skin and the peaceful sound of the river's green waters lapping against the rocky shore.

Suddenly, a screeching noise startled her. Elinor opened her eyes and looked up into the blinding sunlight believing the sound had come from overhead. Shielding her eyes, she didn't see anything at first, but she heard a "Caw! Caw!"

Then a large, black shadow winged across the sky. A crow! She thought about the one she had seen the evening she and Nicholas met. Like that crow, this one dipped lower and lower, as though aiming at her.

As quickly as the black bird appeared, it vanished. Elinor scanned the area to see where it had flown, but it was nowhere in sight. In spite of the heat of the day, a shiver slithered down her back.

Distracted by the unsettling event, she failed to notice an unusual sound coming from beneath her bench.

"Elinor, don't move!" Nicholas shouted from behind her. Then she heard the rattling. Glancing to her side and down, Elinor saw a large rattlesnake coiled next to her foot.

She froze, knowing that any movement on her part might set the snake off. Out of the corner of her eye, she saw Nicholas running toward her with a large stick.

Suddenly, the fanged creature lunged and a hot jabbing pain pierced Elinor's ankle. She heard herself screaming as blackness edged her field of vision, blotting out the light. No, she told herself, I can't faint. I must stay alert.

Then, she felt Nicholas beside her, angrily cursing the snake, and beating at it as the poisonous reptile slithered away, disappearing among the rocks.

Nicholas called to the townsmen who had gathered when they heard the commotion. "Find that snake and kill it before it bites someone else."

He then dropped to his knees and with frantic fingers, undid the numerous buttons on Elinor's shoe. "Don't fret, dearest, I'll take care of you. You'll be all right."

Elinor was stunned, though the encroaching blackness had receded. She sat, her muscles rigid, not knowing what to do. The hot pain was spreading up from her ankle, encircling her leg. She watched with a morbid fascination as Nicholas pulled the shoe from her foot.

Not caring what other people might think, Nicholas slipped his hands under her skirt and found the garter that held up her stocking. He quickly unfastened it and yanked the stocking down and off of Elinor's foot. Twisting the silken strip of fabric into a tourniquet, he tied it just below Elinor's knee.

"It could have been worse," she heard Nicholas say, "the shoe leather kept the fangs from going in deep. Still, the skin is broken."

Fighting waves of blackness that threatened to envelop her, Elinor looked at the tiny red markings just as Nicholas bent down and covered the area with his mouth. Elinor gasped, not immediately understanding what he was doing. Her thinking became fuzzy and a new wave of darkness again distorted her vision. The last thing she remembered was the feeling of Nicholas' warm lips against her ankle, sucking, drawing the poison away from her and into his mouth.

Chapter Eight

Elinor felt herself being lifted by strong, familiar arms—Nicholas'. She clung to him as he carried her away. She wanted to open her eyes, but she was too weak.

"You're going to be all right, Elinor." Nicholas whispered. "Your father has gone to get the doctor. Then we're going to get you home."

"Put her in here," she heard her mother's voice. "I've made a pallet in the back of the wagon."

Elinor recognized the feel of the quilt that she was placed on. Its familiar softness and lye soap smell told her that she was in good hands. In spite of the reassurance, the pain in her ankle felt like a searing poker prodding mercilessly at flesh and bone.

Again, she tired to open her eyes and this time, she succeeded. Looking up, she at first saw tree branches and sky. Then she saw Nicholas standing next to her by the side of the wagon. Her mother stood beside him, her blue eyes clouded with concern.

The conveyance, resting under a shade tree, offered some degree of relief from the heat.

"Nicholas, my leg hurts so bad. Am I going to die?"

"No, Elinor," he said, tugging at a strand of her hair and smiling. "The wound is not deep and the fact that you can feel the pain is a good sign. It's the numb ones that are the most serious. The doctor will be here any minute, my love. Don't fret." Taking her hand in his and kissing the tips of her fingers, he looked into her eyes and added, "Besides, I wouldn't allow even death to take you away from me. My love will keep you by my side."

It was as though time stopped for an instant. Elinor knew he meant it and she believed him.

Mary Foster climbed in beside Elinor and took her daughter's other hand. She managed a reassuring smile, "Nicholas' quick thinking saved you. He risked his own life to do it." Mary looked at Nicholas. "I will be proud to have you as my son-in-law."

"Thank you, Mrs. Foster. I appreciate that." He looked down at Elinor. "She is my life. Besides, there was no harm done to me. What about you, Elinor? How are you feeling?

"Very thirsty and a little sick to my stomach," Elinor answered through lips that felt twice their normal size. Suddenly, she remembered the snake and cried out. "Did they find that snake?"

"The men are still looking. Don't worry about it." Nicholas squeezed her fingers. "They'll find it and kill it."

A chill swept over Elinor and a dark shadow passed by, making her think she was blacking out again. But she soon learned otherwise.

"What has happened here?" The high-pitched voice of Harriet Langford, accompanied by the sound of her rustling taffeta skirts, provided the answer. "Someone said Elinor was bitten by a rattlesnake!"

She stood at the foot of the wagon to get a closer look. "Poor girl," she said, shaking her head. "Nicholas! How could you allow this to happen?" She glared at her son.

"I only left her for a minute to get us something to drink."

Elinor saw him flinch at his mother's accusing words. "Nicholas," she said, though her voice was weak, "it wasn't your fault. You saved my life! That's all that matters."

"You're absolutely right, dear." Mary Foster said. "Would you like a drink of water?" She removed the lid from a jug and poured the liquid into a tin cup. "Here Elinor, don't drink it down too fast, just sip it."

Nicholas put his arm behind Elinor's head and lifted her

forward so she could drink more easily.

Harriet Langford stepped away from the wagon.

A throng of people had gathered by the time Doc Landers arrived, accompanied by Elinor's father and Tobias Langford. Climbing up into the wagon, the short, white-haired doctor examined the puncture marks.

Peering through the small round spectacles perched on the end of his nose, he checked the pupils of Elinor's eyes. He asked if she had vomited or experienced numbness, paralysis or had difficulty breathing.

She answered 'no' to all the questions but told him that her leg throbbed and that she was nauseated.

"I'd say you're a lucky young woman," he said. "If it hadn't been for the shoe leather between you and that snake and for Nicholas' quick thinking, you might be feeling a lot worse. I'll give you something for pain. You go home and rest. You should be feeling better within a couple of days." The elderly doctor smiled and patted Elinor's arm. He left after administering a dose of laudanum.

Elinor noticed Nicholas talking to Silas Hemmings. The ruddy-faced farmer pulled off his hat and wiped the sweat from his face with his shirt sleeve. He shrugged, a puzzled look on his face.

Though the drug was making her drowsy, Elinor managed to overhear part of the conversation.

"Can't none of us find that snake, Mr. Langford. It's like it done disappeared from the face of the earth."

"How could a big rattler like that disappear?"

"Don't know, Sir, but twenty of us men turned over every rock and limb in that area and ain't none of us could find it."

Elinor turned away and closed her eyes. As the blessed numbness from the laudanum swept over her, the memory of the events by the river came flooding back. The incessant beating of wings and the terrible cawing of the circling crow. And then the snake, rattling, hissing, striking, filling her leg with pain. A moment later, the full effects of the laudanum began and the vile memories faded as she drifted off.

Chapter Nine

Elinor studied the diamond solitaire Nicholas had placed on her finger last Fourth of July. After her run-in with the snake, she had received the ring later that evening at her home.

Now, that unfortunate incident was all but forgotten and Christmas was only two days away. Elinor looked out her window at the snow drifts and wondered if Nicholas would come to see her. It had been terribly cold for days, with temperatures dropping below zero for two nights in a row.

That old familiar longing stirred within her. She hadn't seen Nicholas for a week. Now it was Saturday and if she knew her husband to be, he wouldn't allow a snowstorm and freezing temperatures to keep him away. She smiled, recalling the way her heart always leaped when she first caught sight of him.

Last week he had arrived during a snow squall, his hair tossed and windblown, and fringed with ice and snow. Calling him Jack Frost, she had kissed his cold lips to pass her warmth to him.

They had spent the day in the parlor by the crackling fire, roasting chestnuts and popping corn. Elinor's life had been good before, but she'd never imagined it could be this wonderful.

Occasionally, when they were alone, Nicholas would steal a chaste kiss. Elinor reveled in the knowledge that in a few months, there would be so much more.

Suddenly, a knock sounded downstairs followed by the sound of boots stomping, to clear off the snow.

Nicholas! Elinor did a quick check in the mirror. She straightened the plaid bow that fastened her hair and smoothed the skirt of her green woolen dress.

Leaving her room, she paused at the top of the stairway to look down at her beloved. His smile washed over her, leaving her aching for his touch.

It was all she could do to keep from running down the stairs. Instead, she descended in a lady-like fashion. Cold air from the outside had entered the foyer when the door was opened. The cool draft swept over her now as she joined Nicholas in the entryway that had been decorated for the holidays. She went to him, finding a delicious warmth in his arms, even though his greatcoat was dusted with snow. Along with his usual lye soap and sandalwood, he smelled of pine, wind and ice.

Her lips pressed against his cold ones, sending warmth to them.

"Darling, I was afraid you wouldn't come," she said, nuzzling the hollow of his neck. There, his skin was warm because of the woolen scarf he had just removed.

"There's a blizzard out there!" she said. "Though I would have missed you terribly, I would have understood if you chose not to come in this weather."

"Do you think I would let a little ice and snow keep me from you? Besides," he grinned and tweaked her nose, "It was one of the easiest trips I've ever made."

"How can that be? The drifts must be two feet high?"

"Not so on the river, my little snowflake. It's frozen solid. I rode across on the sleigh, and just like Saint Nicholas, I brought presents." His lips twisted into a mischievous grin.

"My very own Saint Nick—" a delighted Elinor exclaimed. Then her face sobered. "But darling, wasn't that dangerous? What if the ice had broken?"

"During a normal winter, yes. But this is one of the coldest winters we've ever had. That river is as solid as the road itself and a lot easier to cross." His dark eyes sparkled. "Anyway, I couldn't stay away from my girl." He bent down and kissed the tip of her nose.

Elinor blushed as she helped Nicholas out of his great coat. "Let's go in by the fire, and then when you've warmed up, maybe you'll take me for a sleigh ride. I've been feeling cooped-up lately. The fresh air would be a welcome change."

"That's a great idea! We can go across and surprise my parents. Mother was complaining that you haven't visited lately." Nicholas took Elinor's hand. "She's beginning to grow very fond of you, Elinor. I told you she would come around."

He bent down and kissed Elinor on the cheek and then on the lips. When they heard the sound of footsteps from the back of the house they quickly pulled apart.

Mary Foster came down the hallway with a tray containing a pot of hot chocolate, two cups and saucers, and a plate of warm cookies. Clinging to Mary were the pleasant smells of chocolate, cinnamon and ginger.

"I'll put this in the parlor," she said, disappearing through the doorway to her right.

Later, after Nicholas placed the presents he'd brought under the huge balsam tree that stood by the bay window, they sat down near the fire that crackled in the hearth. Warmed by the red and yellow flames and smoldering logs, they sipped their warm cocoa and ate ginger cookies.

"Mother will be so surprised to see you." Nicholas said. He hesitated when Elinor didn't respond. "You do want to go, don't you?"

"Of course, I want to go, darling. It's been a while since I've been there. It'll give me a chance to see Langford Manor in its holiday decor. I hope there is some strategically placed mistletoe."

Nicholas' face reddened. "I don't need mistletoe to kiss my girl." He leaned over and kissed her on the cheek and then fell silent for a moment. "I should warn you, though, Christmas decorations at our house are rather sparse. Mother is against bringing a tree into the house. She doesn't like pine roping, either. She says they both make her sneeze." Sighing, he glanced into the fireplace. "Of course, we have a nice dinner on Christmas Day and we usually exchange presents."

Elinor swallowed hard. *Usually?* She looked around the parlor at the sprigs of holly and mistletoe, the festive tree with popcorn and cranberry roping and ornaments that had been handed down for three generations. On Christmas Eve, bayberry scented candles, tied to the pine branches, would be lighted. It was one of Elinor's favorite sights and smells. How sad that Nicholas had not grown up with such festivities. She made a silent vow that when she and Nicholas had their own home, there would be a Christmas tree and mistletoe.

Shaking the serious mood, an impish grin flashed across Nicholas' face. He put his hand inside his jacket and pulled out a small package wrapped in red paper with a frilly white bow on top.

"Why don't you open this one now?"

"Oh Nicholas!" she squealed, "May I? You must open one of yours, too." She went over to the tree and selected a package from beneath it.

After giving Nicholas his present, Elinor carefully opened the brightly colored package he had given her. She gasped with delight when she saw the beautiful jade earrings inside. Realizing they matched her dress, she put them on.

Nicholas, in turn, was thrilled with the tan sweater Elinor had spent weeks knitting for him. He slipped it on, deciding to wear it under his suit jacket and great coat. "This will keep me warm on our trip across the river."

An hour later, they were making their way down the river bank. Steps had been formed in the ice and a rope was tied to a tree at the top to help guide them down the steep slope.

"We could take a toboggan down but it would slide so far, we'd probably end up halfway across the river before it came to a stop," Nicholas said as he held onto Elinor to guide her down the embankment.

The wind had died down and the air was crisp and clean.

Still, the cold nipped away at their exposed skin. Elinor felt like a turtle as she pulled her neck further down into the thick muffler that wound around her neck and covered her mouth and nose. Points of cold air still found their way up her sleeve and beneath her voluminous skirts and petticoats.

The snow fell in big, swirling flakes. Elinor couldn't resist pulling the muffler away from her mouth long enough to stick her tongue out and taste a mouthful of the lacy-patterned ice crystals.

Somewhere high above, patches of blue sky peeked through the dancing white flecks. In the distance, the mountains, cloaked in their mantles of snow and ice, were barely visible.

The horses and sleigh had been secured in a stand of trees near the river. The animals huddled together under the sheltering branches.

Nicholas reached in the pocket of his great coat and pulled out two lumps of sugar. The horses scooped up the treat and nuzzled against him as he patted and spoke softly to them.

Once in the sleigh, Nicholas covered Elinor with a bear skin blanket that reached to her chin. "We'll be there in no time."

The wind picked up as they started out onto the ice. There, the snow wasn't deep, apparently having been blown away by the brisk arctic blasts. Suddenly, the sound of cracking ice startled Elinor.

Nicholas smiled and reassured her that it was only settling. "Dearest, I'd never bring you out here if there was any danger."

Trusting Nicholas completely, Elinor snuggled against him, determined to enjoy the bracing glide over the hard, frozen surface.

When they arrived, Harriet Langford had a startled look on her face when she saw that Nicholas had brought Elinor with him. She recovered quickly. "What a nice surprise," she cooed.

Elinor decided that Harriet Langford's smile was about as warm as the snow that blanketed the landscape.

Elinor couldn't help contrasting the barren look of Langford Manor with the brightly decorated Foster house. Save for a green ribbon placed at the base of the sconce in the foyer, nothing at Langford Manor indicated that Christmas was near.

"You two must be frozen. Come into the library and I'll have Cook prepare some coffee. You'd like that, wouldn't you?" Harriet asked.

Elinor nodded, "That would be nice." Acknowledging that Harriet Langford was trying to be pleasant, Elinor decided to try harder to build a good relationship with her future mother-in-law.

At first the afternoon went by pleasantly. Geneva smiled more than once and kept up her end of the conversation. At one point, Tobias joined them in the library and went into a little too much detail about his coal mining empire.

The moment of awkwardness came when Harriet noticed Elinor's earrings. "Nicholas gave them to me for Christmas," Elinor explained.

Harriet Langford paled and her lips drew into a tight line. "They're very much like a pair he gave me two years ago." She glared at Nicholas, then turned away and stared at the fire.

Elinor glanced at Nicholas. Surely these were different earrings. Elinor couldn't imagine Nicholas giving away something that wasn't his to give.

"I'm not surprised they're similar." Nicholas explained. "They were designed by the same jeweler. I requested that they be of similar design. After all, they are for my two best girls."

Harriet looked up, a bright smile on her face. "Well, son, since you put it that way, I forgive you."

Forgive him? Elinor thought. Elinor saw Nicholas return his mother's smile and she felt disheartened by the syrupy exchange. This was a side of Nicholas she had only glimpsed before. She'd been warned about his closeness to his mother. Now she'd seen first hand how easily Harriet manipulated him.

Then Elinor reminded herself of how he had stood up to his parents about choosing Elinor over Sophie Gilmore and she felt ashamed at her reaction. He'd proven himself time and again. He'd even saved her life.

His mother was probably feeling a little jealous and left out. It was the holiday season. Elinor could afford to be generous. She was engaged to a kind, sensitive man who cared about other people's feelings. It was only natural that he would be indulgent where his mother was concerned.

Harriet excused herself and went into the kitchen. A short time later, she returned with slices of walnut cake. Her face was flushed and she fidgeted, betraying what appeared to be a case of nerves—something Elinor had never expected form the older woman.

Was it possible that she actually wanted to impress Elinor? Maybe Harriet realized after the conversation concerning the earrings that Nicholas loved them both and that it was very important to him that they get along,. This just might work out, after all, Elinor thought. She had been dreading the prospect of living at Langford Manor once she was married. Now, the thought didn't seem quite as depressing.

When it was time to go, Harriet Langford pushed a package into Elinor's hand and gave her a hug. Elinor was surprised and touched by the gesture. "I should have brought your presents with me," she said. "I'll send them back with Nicholas. I had planned to wait until Christmas, but with the weather the way it is, I'd better send them now."

"My dear, you really didn't have to do that." Harriet flushed and turned away.

The wind was howling as Nicholas bundled Elinor into the sleigh. The afternoon shadows were lengthening, creating shades of mauve and purple on the horizon. As Nicholas lifted his foot to climb into the sleigh, his mother called to him.

"Come back for a minute, Nicholas. I forgot to give you the Fosters' presents." They could barely hear her voice over the sound of the moaning wind.

Frowning, Nicholas stepped down. "I guess I'd better get them or I'll never hear the last of it." He handed Elinor the reins. Here, hold on to these. I'll be right back."

Elinor watched him disappear into the swirling mist as he headed back towards the house. Suddenly, an ominous sound ripped through the air and a dark shadow appeared overhead. "Caw! Caw!"

Shrieking, Elinor dropped the reins causing the horses to bolt upright and lurch forward onto the frozen river. The menacing crow made a pass at them striking the head of one of the animals. The poor horse reared up, causing the other one to slip and skid.

Then, both horses raised up on their hind legs, pawing and whinnying at the darkening sky. The low flying crow cut through the curtain of blinding snow and dipped past Elinor.

The sleigh jerked, and skidded sideways, before tipping over. Elinor was thrown onto the ice, perilously close to the stomping hooves of the horses.

Elinor got on all fours and half-crawled, half-slid in an attempt to avoid the trampling hooves of the terrified horses. "Nicholas, help, help!" She cried out, hoping he could hear her over the wailing wind.

Suddenly, there was a cracking sound as the ice gave way under the weight of the terrified animals.

Elinor felt the numbing wetness seeping from the gaping hole that had opened in the ice. She scooted back from the dark abyss that pulled at her and the helpless horses whose front feet had slipped into the frigid water.

The creatures shrieked in distress as they struggled to keep their heads from becoming submerged. Frantically, Elinor pushed herself further away from the hole in the ice. But her best efforts were in vain as she slid closer toward the yawning hole.

"Oh God, don't let me die. I don't want to die. I have so much to live for," she cried as her feet and legs slipped into the water.

Then she heard Nicholas calling her name—or was it the sound of the howling wind or the shrieking horses? She listened. It was Nicholas!

"Give me your hand, Elinor." His voice was strong.

She heard Tobias and another man shouting back and forth as the shocking strength of the icy water threatened to pull her completely under.

In another minute, Elinor felt Nicholas grab her hand and pull her up against his chest. A rope was tied around his waist. When Elinor was secure in Nicholas' arms, his father and the stableman pulled on the rope, getting Nicholas and Elinor to shore.

Carrying Elinor back to the Manor, Nicholas turned her over to his mother. "I have to help with the horses, Elinor. Mother will take care of you."

Elinor was too cold and stiff with the accompanying pain to protest when Harriet and Geneva stripped off her wet clothing, there in the parlor. Soon, they had her in a long flannel night gown, wrapped in a quilt, and sitting before the fire. Her teeth chattering, she stretched out her feet and hands trying to get extra warmth to them.

"Thank you, Mrs. Langford, Geneva."

"There, there now, you'll be fine." Harriet said, her mouth drawn into a sullen line. "I'll get some extra quilts for you. I expect the men will need them too." She shook her head. "I don't know what possessed you to try to drive that team by yourself. Why, you could have been killed!"

"I didn't!" Elinor protested. "A large crow appeared overhead and spooked the horses."

Harriet glared at her. "That's the most ridiculous thing I've ever heard. I don't think I would be repeating such an outlandish story if I were you."

It was dark by the time the men came back inside. Though cold and exhausted, they had managed to save both horses.

It was then Elinor was told, much to her dismay, that she would have to spend the night at Langford Manor. Nicholas assured her they would set out for her home the first thing in the morning. He would have the stableman build a bonfire by the river to serve as a signal to the Fosters for the time being. After the stableman had warmed up, he would take a fresh horse and ride across at another point of the river to let Elinor's parents know that she was all right.

Later that night, as Elinor huddled in the guest room bed, tears that she had been holding back for hours trickled down her cheeks. Fear gripped her when she thought about how close she had again come to losing her life. Both times a crow had circled overhead. She couldn't help thinking the crow was a harbinger of death that would sooner or later return to claim her and destroy her happiness with Nicholas.

Chapter Ten

Elinor gazed at her reflection in the mirror. Was she really this golden-haired woman in the ivory, satin dress? The happiest day of her life had finally arrived! April 5, 1900—her wedding day. Her cheeks flamed when she thought of Nicholas. After today, she could give herself to him completely.

She looked at the diamond engagement ring on her finger. All the shadows were gone now. She had put her brushes with death behind her, refusing to dwell on them or the crow.

She and Nicholas were going to be so happy! Even the prospect of living at Langford Manor couldn't dampen her spirits this day.

A few minutes later, Elinor descended the staircase on her father's arm. The foyer was bursting with the lilacs and apple blossoms that had been brought inside for the occasion.

When Elinor saw Nicholas waiting, her heart leaped. She was oblivious to family and guests who filled the parlor. Overflowing with happiness, she approached her handsome husband-to-be.

The ceremony was brief but beautiful. She would always remember the moment when Nicholas lifted her apple blossom encircled veil and kissed her in front of all the guests.

As each person congratulated them, pressing kisses on Elinor's cheek and shaking Nicholas' hand, Harriet and Tobias played their part of parents of the groom to the fullest.

"Welcome to the Langford family, daughter," Harriet hugged Elinor and went on to compliment Mary Foster on the sumptuous wedding supper Elinor's mother had prepared with help from her daughters-in-law. Even Geneva got into the spirit of things. "You look lovely, Elinor. I suppose you and I are going to be sisters now," she said. Coming from Geneva, it was a high compliment.

However, when Elinor tossed the wedding bouquet from the top of the staircase and Celia Morgan caught it, Geneva glared at Elinor and then reverted back to her usual sullen self.

Nicholas and Elinor cut the wedding cake together and drank a toast with their guests. Then it was time to have their wedding photographs taken. Elinor posed for one by herself, another with Nicholas and a family photograph with their parents. By two o'clock, it was time for them to leave. Elinor's pulse quickened. Their honeymoon destination was three hours away. A remote cabin on the top of a mountain would be their home for the next week. The cabin had been built by Elinor's grandfather and had passed on to her parents when Grandpa died. Though too remote for everyday living, it was the perfect setting for a honeymoon.

The cabin had been prepared ahead of time. Scrubbed windows and floors, a stocked larder and fresh linen on the feather bed awaited the newlyweds.

After saying their good-byes, Nicholas helped his bride onto the seat of the carriage and, after hopping aboard himself, he signaled the horses. In a shower of rice, Nicholas and Elinor started down the winding driveway of the Foster home. After one more wave to the well-wishers, they turned onto the main road, to begin their new life as husband and wife.

Soon after, the shouts of family and friends faded away. A short time later, they left the main road and started the ascent up the winding, narrow pathway that would take them to the top of the mountain and their waiting cottage.

Mother Nature had gone all out to set the scene. Rhododendron, lilacs, apple blossoms and dogwood fringed the roadway, releasing their intoxicating fragrances.

It's perfect, Elinor thought, as she reached over and slipped her hand through the crook of her husband's arm.

He looked at her and she saw the longing in Nicholas' eyes—a longing that matched her own. The sweet scents that permeated the air added to the desire that became more insistent with each passing mile.

"We'll be there soon, beloved," Nicholas said.

The sun was low in the sky when they pulled into the small, open meadow that surrounded the log cabin.

"Oh Nicholas! Isn't it wonderful?" Elinor clapped her hands together.

Nicholas brought the horses to a halt and slipped his arms around her. "Yes, dearest, it is."

A steady breeze ruffled through a large lilac bush near the cabin, spreading the sweet aroma of the purple blossoms.

"This has to be the closest thing to heaven on earth," Nicholas said.

"It is paradise." Elinor's kissed her husband's cheek. "Are you hungry?"

"Not for food." He smiled and looked into her eyes. "Let me see to the horses, then we'll go inside."

A short time later, as a brilliant sunset crested on the far mountain peaks, Nicholas lifted Elinor and carried her over the threshold into the one room cabin. Once inside, he gently set her down. His dark-eyed gaze spoke of love, passion and a hunger too long denied as he stood for a long moment looking into her eyes.

Shafts of fiery, golden light filtered through the westward facing window, bathing the newlyweds in an ethereal glow.

Elinor touched Nicholas' face with the tips of her fingers, tracing the planes and lines as though mapping out the territory that was now completely hers to explore. In burnished light, he was a god—a god who loved and desired her. His dark hair, edged with the sun; his perfect form, tall and lean, belonged to her. She could explore, taste, love and grow old with this extraordinary man.

Nicholas leaned down, brushing her lips with his own,

sending a trail of liquid heat coursing through her alert being. Straightening and taking a step back, he removed his jacket and unbuttoned his shirt.

"No, let me," Elinor said, in a tremulous vice. Her need for him becoming more insistent, she reached a shaking hand and one by one she undid the buttons, kissing the warm, newly exposed skin beneath each one.

Once the shirt was off, Elinor gazed at the manly chest with its dark swirls of hair meeting in the center, and pointing downward. Her eager hands smoothed the curves of his chest, running her fingers through the soft, curly thatch, brushing ever so lightly against his small, hard nipples.

Feeling him shudder, she reveled in the powerful love that gave her this boldness. Her hands found the belt buckle and she quickly unfastened it. Pressing on, she slipped her hands against the burning skin beneath his trousers, cupping, slipping easing his trousers over his trim hips and down. Finally all of his clothing lay in a heap on the floor.

Looking at him in his beautiful nakedness, Elinor said, "Now it's your turn."

She saw his smile in the fading light. "At last, beloved, I will do now what I have imagined a thousand times."

He pulled her to him and sought her lips, pressing, burning, nearly taking her breath away—kissing her in a strange, deep, new way. Tasting his sweetness and wanting more, she melted against him.

Leaving her lips, his kisses trailed downward, nuzzling against her neck, burning her skin at his mere touch. His hands found the hooks on the back of her dress and expertly unfastened them. One by one, they came undone as his fingers traced a pathway down her spine.

She felt the satin gown slip down, exposing the soft swells of her breasts, concealed beneath her corset. Soon, the dress and petticoats were at her feet. She stood in her corset with garters and stockings attached.

Nicholas' large, warm hands touched and smoothed the tender skin peeking over the top of her laced-up garment. Then, he kissed and coaxed her breasts out of the confines of her corset. Lingering there, he pushed the corset farther down until his mouth found her erect, aching nipples. His tongue teased and darted against them until Elinor gasped with pleasure.

She ran her fingers through his thick, wavy hair, and massaged his neck and the tops of his shoulders. Her body pressed harder against him, seeking its firmness.

Then Nicholas fell to his knees, and his hands slipped down to Elinor's thighs. His fingers stroked and smoothed the soft skin beneath the garters as he slowly unfastened them. Placing his hands around her right thigh, he took hold of the top of her stocking and eased it down, trailing kisses as he did so.

Groaning and weak with the pleasurable sensations, Elinor dug her fingers into his shoulders as he helped her out of her white leather slippers.

He slowly removed her left stocking, all the while planting sweet, lingering kisses on her thighs, knees and ankles.

By now her legs were shaking and she leaned back against the wall to steady herself. Her entire body burned, aching for the union that had been so long denied. Her heart pounded and her breath came out in short bursts as she unlaced the ties of her corset. Anxious to free herself of the cumbersome thing, she tore at it and Nicholas pulled it away from her, dropping in on the floor. He clasped his hands around her waist, and pulled her to him until his face rested against the softness of her abdomen.

Shuddering at the feel of his warm breath against her sensitive skin, she cried out and fell to her knees. Slipping her arms around his neck, her lips sought his with a hungry fury. Elinor allowed herself to be guided to the floor, where she lay beside her husband, on top of her wedding dress.

The last rays of the sun dipped in a fiery exit, infusing her with its heat as Nicholas slipped above her. "Elinor, my Elinor," he said over and over as he kissed her forehead and eyelids before tasting her lips in a long, deep kiss. His tongue explored the inside of her mouth, darting, flicking.

Groaning, she arched her back, thrusting hard against him, begging to feel the beauty and power of him inside her.

The scent of lilacs, mingling with the sandalwood, lye-soap scent of him delighted her nostrils as she clasped her hands around his lean backside. She guided him down until at last, in one quick motion, he plunged into the depths of her softness.

Feeling the hot, shocking pain, she cried out. But very soon the cry turned to a pleasurable groan as the smooth gliding, rocking motion lulled her into a dizzying world of sensual joy. As Nicholas steadied himself above her, she was consumed, lifted to heaven, and satiated with a driving force that felt like waves of warm, golden honey flowing from a well deep within her. The sweet waves spread over her body, enveloping it in a soft cocoon of pleasure.

In one final shudder, Nicholas called her name and she repeated his. Their fingers intertwined, and with their lips only inches apart, they both cried out. His breath came in gasps, matching her own, as he slipped from above her, and falling next to her, nestled his face against her neck. They remained there, wrapped in one another's arms, until the sunset faded and the room glittered with silvery moonlight.

A short time later, Elinor awoke to Nicholas' touch. His hands explored her breasts, brushing her nipples with his skillful fingertips until she was consumed with a need to feel him inside of her. He continued teasing, as his hand slipped down her belly to the newly discovered place of her being. Slowly, his touched lingered there, further heating the warmth between her legs and sending a new wave of molten honey to pour over her.

"Let's use the bed this time," he whispered, his voice thick with desire. He stood up and helped Elinor to her feet. Her knees shook as she watched him pull back the quilt. He took her in his arms, and her body melted against his.

She flushed at the sheer joy of his naked skin next to hers. We're made for each other, she thought, as her hardened nipples nested in his chest hair. His hand slipped down to her hips and backside as he guided her into the bed.

Once there, he pulled Elinor on top of him. Then, wrapping his arms around her, he brought her lips down to meet his. Burning, teasing, taunting, his mouth probed hers before seeking the soft flesh of her throat and breasts. At the same time, his hands moved to align her at the appropriate spot astride him. Then he pulled her against his rigidity, and she slid into his waiting member, releasing shock waves of delight.

This time there was no pain, only starbursts of white heat as they moved in a rhythmic ecstasy so all encompassing that no part of her would ever be hidden or unfulfilled again.

The next morning, Elinor rose early and had bacon frying and biscuits baking by the time Nicholas awoke.

Elinor couldn't keep from looking at his splendid body as he slipped from the bed. Tempted to tear away her loose wrap and go to him, she smiled to herself and chose instead to serve him breakfast.

It seemed he had other plans. "How would you like to join me for a dip in the creek at the back of the cabin?" He smiled and arched an eyebrow.

"I'd love to." She gave him a saucy, knowing smile. "Shall we do that first and have breakfast afterwards?"

"Yes, if breakfast will keep. I'll be hungry as a bear after our swim."

"It'll keep. Just let me take the bread out of the oven first." Opening the door of the wood-burning stove, she pulled out a pan of nicely-browned biscuits and set them on top of the oven to keep them warm.

"It's hot in here," Elinor ran the back of her hand across her face, leaving a smudge of flour on her nose. "The cool water will feel good."

Nicholas approached her with an impish grin. Cupping his hands around the soft curves of her hips, he pulled her to him and kissed the flour streaks from her face.

Soon, Elinor's silk wrap lay in a heap on the floor and she and Nicholas were back in bed. This time, the lovemaking was slower, more deliberate. She lay trembling as he explored, kissed, stroked, every part of her. When the fire within her could stand it no longer, she pulled him to her. The sweet scent of lilacs surrounded her as he entered her, the powerful thrusts creating pleasurable waves that set her nerve endings to singing. She held on, climbing the heights of rapture with Nicholas until their bodies forged one perfect entity before relaxing in spent exultation.

Spent, they lay there for several minutes wrapped in one another's arms. Finally, Nicholas stirred, and kissing Elinor lightly on the lips said,

"How about that dip in the creek?"

Isolated on the remote mountain peak, neither of them felt the need for clothing. Hand in hand, they headed for the bubbling stream with only their towels and soap. The warm morning sun and a gentle breeze teased Elinor's skin, kissing and smoothing it. She was a woman now, alive, awake to her new needs. She looked at Nicholas, allowing her gaze to linger up and down his beautiful body. *Oh yes, we really were made for each other*, she told herself again, still marveling at how perfectly their bodies fit together.

After planting a kiss on her nose, Nicholas grabbed her hand. "Let's go!" he said, as he rushed toward the creek, pulling her along beside him.

She shrieked as the cold water enveloped her when she fell forward into its icy embrace. She laughed and splashed Nicholas who pretended that the water wasn't cold at all.

Surrounded by blue sky and distant mountains, they were in their own Garden of Eden. All around them the intoxicating scent of lilacs seemed to celebrate Nicholas and Elinor's new life together.

Later that evening, after a candlelight dinner, they lay in the soft, dewy grass and made love as the fiery sun dipped behind the distant peaks.

If only it could last forever, she thought.

Chapter Eleven

The honeymoon week went by all too quickly and soon it was time for Nicholas and Elinor to leave the idyllic cabin and return to Langford Manor.

Elinor had pushed aside any negative thoughts during her week at the cottage. Now, as she and Nicholas turned to have a last look, she found herself aching to stay.

"We'll come back again sometime," Nicholas said.

"May we?" she asked, her voice hopeful. As a shiver darted down her back, she fought a premonition that she would never gaze upon the place again. Why was she thinking such thoughts? She had just spent the happiest week of her life.

It was Langford Manor and her new mother-in-law that she dreaded!

She might as well admit it. Elinor was determined to make the best of the living arrangements and get along with Nicholas' family. She took comfort in the fact that in a year or so, she and Nicholas would be leaving the manor house for a home of their own out West. An uneasy feeling swept over her when she thought about it. Nicholas hadn't wanted to discuss the subject earlier that morning. Surely he hadn't changed his mind. When she'd asked him if that were the case, he'd said, "Of course not," but she wasn't entirely convinced.

Realizing it would do no good to press the issue at this time, she pushed the doubts from her mind and decided to enjoy what was left of their special week together.

As they descended the mountain, Elinor closed her eyes and breathed the sweet scents, taking them inside of her, cherishing the sights, smells, of their idyllic honeymoon paradise. It had all been so perfect, she didn't want to forget any of it. Even the weather had been unusually warm for early April.

All too soon, their special mountain was behind them and they were on the last leg of their journey to Langford Manor. The birds that had chirped along the way suddenly stopped their choruses once the house was in sight.

The closer they got to Langford Manor, the more apprehensive Elinor became. Nicholas must have sensed it.

"Dearest, you've grown quiet. Before you know it, you will feel quite at home at Langford Manor. My parents are happy for us. I'm sure they will do all they can to see that your are content. You'll see. There's nothing to be afraid of."

"I'm not afraid, Nicholas. It's just that I'm sorry we had to leave our cottage. Now we're going to be just like every other married couple."

"I think not. No one else could be as happy or as in love as we are," he answered, a teasing smile on his face.

She smiled and snuggled against him. "You're absolutely right. I guess I just have the jitters. Going to live at Langford Manor is a big change for me. But I will adjust."

"Of course you will, dearest. We will fill the house with love."

Silently, Elinor prayed that he was right, but she still had misgivings. She knew Nicholas had a blind spot where his mother was concerned.

When they arrived at Langford Manor, Elinor was surprised that no one greeted them at the door. She told herself the family probably hadn't heard or seen them approach.

Inside the shadowy foyer, Elinor's eyes needed a moment to adjust. It didn't take long, however, for her to see the tall dark form on the stairway. Startled, she stifled a cry when she thought at first she was looking at a giant blackbird.

"Well, well, look who's here." Harriet Langford's shrill

voice sounded from the top of the stairs. "Welcome home."

Elinor's hope that things would go smoothly was dashed when Mother Langford, as Harriet instructed Elinor to call her, told Nicholas he could retain his old room and that she had prepared a separate bedroom for Elinor.

"That was a waste of time, Mother. Elinor and I will be sleeping in the same room and in the same bed."

Harriet sucked her breath in sharply. "Son, a lady prefers to have her own room. You know that I have occupied the master suite alone. Your father is as happy in his own quarters as you will be. Besides, I've already had Elinor's things placed in her room."

"Mother Langford," Elinor said, figuring it was time to speak for herself, "this is one lady who prefers to share a room with her husband. You needn't fret about my things. Nicholas and I can move them into his room."

Harriet Langford descended the stairs and came to stop in front of the couple. Even in the dim light, it was plain to see that the color had drained from her face. "Well, if you want to behave in such a common way...."

"We do, Mother," Nicholas put his arm around his mother, attempting to cajole her into coming around to their point of view. "As Elinor said, we'll take care of everything—so stop fretting." He tweaked his mother's chin and kissed her on the cheek.

That night, Elinor lay in her husband's arms, fully awake, long after he had drifted off. Clearly, she had gotten off on the wrong foot with her mother-in-law. She would have to work hard to get along with the woman. But, she would make the effort for Nicholas' sake.

Chapter Twelve

The coming days and weeks were a mixture of bliss and misery for Elinor. Her happy times came when she was with Nicholas. When he was away at the office in Charleston, she missed him terribly. Aware of Elinor's bouts of homesickness, he frequently rowed her across the river to visit her parents.

One evening, two months after their marriage, Elinor and Nicholas made one of their trips. As they were descending the river bank after saying their good-byes, Elinor became light-headed and her temple ached. When she swayed against Nicholas, he picked her up and placed her on plush velvet cushions in the small gondola-like boat.

"Dearest, are you all right?" He bent over her, concern on his face.

The sweet scent of lilacs permeated the dewy night. Lulled into a dream-like state, she leaned back against the pillows as the deep, dark waters slapped and swished against the side of the boat. The stars were out but there was only a crescent moon to light their path.

"I'm fine darling, you mustn't worry so." Her lips felt thick and strange when she said the words. What was happening to her?

She could see Nicholas clearly as he skillfully guided the boat through the black waters to the distant shore. As he oared silently, his gaze never left her and she in turn could look at nothing else. The farther they got from land, the more confused she became until time itself evaporated into a mystical fog.

At first she could not recall her name. There was only the dark night, the lapping waves and this man, Nicholas. Then she saw the lights of lanterns on the dock just ahead and she remembered that she and her husband, Nicholas, often took these night excursions. Mother Langford constantly warned of the danger. Nicholas always smiled and tried to reassure her.

"Elinor?" Nicholas' deep voice broke the silence.

"Yes, my darling?" she responded.

"Now that we have had our boat ride, I think it is time to retire."

The invitation in his words was not lost on her. She could not get enough of her husband, her wild and wonderful lover. They had been together only a short time and already she could not understand how she had ever lived without him.

Remembering that Nicholas preferred to see her hair flowing freely, Elinor reached back and pulled out the pins that secured it. Shaking her golden mane, she was rewarded by Nicholas' sensual smile. Thrilled to the very center of her being, she knew that even greater delights awaited her. She yearned to be alone with him in their bedroom, an oasis in the midst of the barren place called Langford Manor.

After docking the boat, he reached out and pulled her to her feet. She raised her long skirts as he lifted her out of the skiff onto dry land.

"My beautiful wife," he whispered, pulling her to him. His lips found hers and took possession of them quickly, sending a thousand pins and needles through her body. Burying his face in her hair, he murmured, "Elinor, my Elinor, I could not live without you."

Hand in hand, they climbed the slate steps to the house. Elinor felt a chill as she looked at its impressive stone walls. She did not feel welcome here. Certainly Nicholas wanted her by his side, but the others did not accept her presence at Langford Manor. As she approached the house tonight, it seemed especially foreboding. An odd sensation that she was seeing it for the first time swept over her.

Nicholas led her to the back entrance an they slipped inside the darkened kitchen. "Hungry?" he asked, as he lit a lantern. "There are chicken and roasted potatoes left from dinner."

"Potatoes? I thought we had rice."

Nicholas raised a questioning eyebrow. "Rice? Why no, darling, we had potatoes."

Why had she said rice? It didn't make sense. But then she couldn't remember even having dinner on this particular evening. In fact, she didn't recall anything about the day prior to the boat ride. What was happening to her?

"You ate very little, that may be why it wasn't particularly memorable. Perhaps it's connected with that lightheadedness you felt back there. Why don't you eat something now?"

She wouldn't worry him by belaboring her lapse of memory. Though food was the last thing she had on her mind, she reached for a chicken leg to humor Nicholas. She didn't want him to worry about her.

"I wasn't so much faint, Nicholas. I just have a slight headache. It will pass."

"I have just the thing," he smiled, producing a bottle of wine from the cupboard. "There is no elixir equal to Mother's elderberry wine. Have some with the chicken."

Nicholas poured a glass of wine for each of them. The dark liquid looked like blood. Elinor rubbed her temple. Where were these thoughts coming from? After eating a few bites of the chicken, she lifted the glass to her lips and took a sip of the sweet drink. As she did so, she met Nicholas' passionate gaze and a fire exploded in her veins. Under his bold sensual stare, the faint ache in her head disappeared.

Nicholas took the glass from her hand, "Come, it's time to go to bed."

Elinor slipped her hand into his, her excitement mounting as they left the kitchen. How long had it been since they had been together as husband and wife? Strange that she could not remember. She sensed that it had been a very long time, but she couldn't understand why that would be.

Perhaps the headache blocked her memory. Yet, if that were the case, then her memory should have returned when the pain in her head subsided. It was all very confusing.

The single sconce that usually burned after dark was unlit this evening and there was no moonlight to guide them. They groped along the paneled walls of the long hallway. Elinor disliked total darkness. Even with Nicholas at her side, she imagined velvety hands reaching for her and she felt the presence of hideous creatures lying in wait in the dark shadows, ready to pounce.

"Why was the sconce not lit this evening?" Elinor asked.

"The servants are becoming remiss in their duties. I shall speak to Mother about it tomorrow."

This is Mother Langford's doing, Elinor thought, not the servants. Harriet Langford resented Elinor and was jealous of the time the young couple spent together. She knew they would be coming home in the dark after their boat excursion. She enjoyed making things difficult for Elinor, who had made the mistake of admitting her fear of the dark to her mother-in-law.

Once they found their way to the massive staircase their eyes had adjusted to the darkness and they could better see where they were going. Elinor clung to Nicholas' hand as they tip-toed up the stairs.

A thin stream of faint light shone beneath the door of the master suite. No doubt Harriet had waited up for their return. Motherly devotion was one thing, but she carried it to extremes.

At the opposite end of the hall was the bedroom Elinor and Nicholas shared. Desire coursed through Elinor's veins, but she was suddenly afraid of what lay ahead on the other side. She looked at Nicholas in the dimly lit upper hallway and for a brief moment he was a stranger to her. He must have sensed her withdrawal. He stopped and swept her up in his arms.

"You suddenly seem shy and bewildered, dearest." He kissed her on the lips, then the forehead. "I believe I have a remedy for that."

He carried her inside and set her gently down after closing the door. the room became enveloped in a soft glow when he lit the candle on the vanity.

Elinor looked at the familiar four poster bed and the mirror, which seemed to draw her. She approached it in the flickering candlelight, almost forgetting Nicholas' presence, and stared at herself. Her large, expressive eyes showed confusion, perhaps fear. Her soft blonde hair, its highlighted sun streaks picking up the glow of the candlelight, was in an exotic disarray. It was her face, eyes and hair but something had changed. She was somehow different.

Nicholas stepped behind her and touched his lips lightly to her neck.

He brought his hands around and deftly undid the buttons of her bodice.

She forgot the mirror, the strangeness, as her hot blood ignited. Turning around, she boldly helped him slip from his jacket. They stepped back, releasing one another only long enough to free themselves from the unwelcome clothing. Endowed with a tall, thin figure, Elinor frequently went without the customary corset. Her husband preferred it that way and she was only too glad to oblige, though her female in-laws thought it scandalous. She had ignored their advice, a perhaps unwise reaction. Now she was glad not to be so fettered as she went to her husband's waiting arms, reveling in the feel of his skin against hers.

Again, he lifted Elinor and carried her to the four poster bed. The coverlet having already been turned back, Nicholas placed Elinor on the fresh linen sheets that felt cool against her skin.

She breathed deeply of the lilac-scented air and her skin tingled in anticipation as she luxuriated in the large four poster bed.

Nicholas slid in beside her, further fueling the smoldering fire that coursed through her body. Leaning on one elbow, he hovered over her and with his free hand, traced her profile with a bloom from the vase of lilacs on the bedside table. He paused at her lips so that she might taste its sweetness. The feathery tracings of the cool, dewy flower set Elinor to shuddering as he brushed it down her neck, against her breasts and beyond.

Nicholas' long wavy hair fell forward as he discarded the lilac and bent to kiss the hollow of her neck.

"Dearest, we were destined to be together. Nothing will ever come between us." His dark eyes sought hers and as their gazes met, she was branded by him for all eternity. She touched his face, his lips, lingering just beneath his chin at the small strawberry birthmark that was common to the Langford men.

"My love," she said as he slid above her. His kisses burned a trail of fire upon her face, lips neck and down her breasts. She wound her fingers in his long, dark hair and held on tightly as though she were about to be swept away. She ached for him and reveled in the joining of their bodies and souls. Her spirit soared, and her body arched, then relaxed, spent and sated.

Later, after Nicholas had fallen asleep, Elinor went to the water pitcher and poured a small amount into the wash bowl. She splashed the water on her face and shuddered as it trailed down between her breasts. It was a warm muggy night and Elinor needed fresh air. She walked to the long windows that overlooked the river and unfastened one of the locks so she could raise it.

As she did so, she scraped her finger on something sharp. A dark spot of blood oozed from the wound. It stung mightily for such a small cut. She plunged her hand into the washbowl, swished it in the water, then held it still for a moment. Needing something to stem the persistent bleeding, she took a handkerchief from her vanity and wound it around the cut.

Feeling suddenly naked, she took a long, white nightgown from her armoire and slipped it on. Going back to the window she had opened, she stood in front of it and allowed the warm balmy breeze to blow against her. She looked across the quiet, dark river, to the other side where she saw a light coming from her childhood home. It seemed brighter than the other lights that dotted the shore, almost as though it were signaling her. Though she did not understand why, she felt unsettled.

A sudden breeze blew the sheer curtain against her face causing her hair to stand on end. Something strange was happening to her. She couldn't remember anything that had gone on earlier in the day and now, the pain in her head threatened to return as she turned away from the window and extinguished the candle.

As she joined her sleeping husband in bed, she took a moment to study his profile. He was so masculine and yet at this moment he seemed vulnerable, almost childlike. What was this love that consumed her to the depths of her soul?

Curling up against him and resting her hand against the soft thatch of hair on his chest, her breathing synchronized with his and she fell asleep surrounded by the sweet scent of lilacs.

It was not to be a restful sleep. She dreamed that she was standing in a fog, a green swirling vapor that slowly turned into smoke. A strange sound, like the beating of many wings could be heard in the distance. Choking in the acrid mist, Elinor coughed. Far away, she saw a red and yellow glow. Indistinct at first, it soon became clear that flames were advancing in her direction.

Then, the crying started, a faint whimper that grew louder. Elinor peered into the swirling smoke and saw the dim outline of a child, a young girl of eight or nine.

The vision came toward Elinor with outstretched arms. Her sobs changed to, "Help me, Elinor, help me." The girl hid her face in her hands and cried as though her heart were breaking. Then, she removed her hands from her face and looked directly at Elinor. Her large blue eyes filled with tears, she said, "Elinor, come home. I need you."

Elinor couldn't move. She could only wait for the little girl to come to her. When she got close enough, Elinor reached out and taking hold of the child, she pulled the small, thin girl to her bosom.

"Don't worry, Emily," she heard herself say, "I'm coming to help you."

Chapter Thirteen

West Virginia
June, 2000

Emily yawned and with an arm extended across her face, shielded her eyes from the full force of the morning sun that streamed through the window. She turned her head and looked at the clock radio. Nine o'clock. Stretching and yawning one last time, she reluctantly got out of bed. After a night filled with jumbled dreams, she was exhausted.

Her muscles seemed unusually stiff when she stepped into the shower a few minutes later. She was glad for the warmth of the water as it soothed away the sore spots and rejuvenated her spirits. Reaching her hands upward toward the stream of water, she pulled one hand back as a hot, stinging pain pierced her fingertip.

"Ouch!" she yelped, as she looked at the small, deep cut. "Now when did I do that?" She could not remember. "Those were some crazy dreams," she mumbled. Ignoring, the raw ache in her fingertip, she lathered the shampoo into her long, silky hair.

That hair really was a bother. She had threatened many times to cut it short, but Jeff had always talked her out of it. What a fool she had been to allow him to dictate anything to her.

After dressing in jeans and a blue t-shirt, Emily brushed

her hair and tied it back with a blue scarf. Later, while making the bed, she found a faded linen handkerchief with a smudge of blood on it. "I must have wrapped it around my finger when I cut it," she whispered, puzzled. But how could that be? She didn't even remember cutting her finger. As she unfolded the handkerchief, she noticed that it was beautifully monogrammed. In yellowed white scrolls were the letters 'EF.'

Those were Emily's initials, but the handkerchief wasn't hers. Grams' name was Twila, so it wasn't hers, either. From the looks of it, the handkerchief was very old. It might have come from the attic or could have been among Grams' linens. Wherever it came from, Emily couldn't remember picking it up.

"Wait a minute! I'll bet this was Elinor's!" A chill raced up her back as she closed her eyes and tried to remember when and where she had gotten it.

When Emily first lost her parents she had gone through a period of sleep disturbances. Grams had sometimes found her walking in her sleep. Because of her recent losses, could the pattern be repeating itself?

A familiar ache in her right temple distracted her from her thoughts.

Placing her handkerchief on the dressing table, she massaged the side of her head. She seemed to be getting far too many headaches lately.

She went into the kitchen and after preparing and plugging in the coffee pot, she poured a glass of orange juice and helped herself to some aspirin. She had no appetite, but knew she shouldn't take aspirin on an empty stomach so she popped two pieces of bread into the toaster and took the butter and blackberry jam from the refrigerator.

It was Grams' homemade jam. The name written on the paper label affixed to the jar was in her grandmother's wide scrawl. Emily pushed back the brimming tears and thought instead of the many days she and Becky had spent exploring the riverbank picking berries for Grams to turn into jams, jellies and cobblers. Grams always warned them to watch out for snakes, but Emily would have faced a dozen rattlesnakes for a piece of one of Grams' blackberry cobblers.

A moment later, as she was buttering her toast, Emily thought about how easy it was to toast bread. A hundred years ago there would have been no toasters, percolators, or refrigerators available to the general public. Even when electricity was more widely attainable, it had been slow in reaching the remote mountain regions.

"What brought all of that on?" she mumbled under her breath. She took a bite of toast that had been generously spread with the blackberry jam. After finishing her meal and draining the last sip of coffee from her cup, she carried her dishes to the sink. A sudden breeze blew through the window above the sink, causing the sheer curtain to billow out and touch Emily's face. A hint of lilac wafted on the breeze, causing her to shiver.

She remembered the eerie feeling she had yesterday when the curtain in the living room had blown against her face. Looking out at the river glistening in the sunlight, she suddenly imagined it in darkness with nothing but starlight to mark a pathway across its shimmering surface.

Shaking off the odd image, she parted the curtains to get a better view of the river. She wished the weeping willow tree did not block her view of Langford Manor.

It was then she noticed the coffee cups sitting on the patio table. Hadn't she brought them in last night? She remembered going back to get them, but she didn't remember bringing them in. In fact, she didn't remember anything about the remainder of the night.

Another shiver slithered down her back as thoughts of yesterday afternoon came rushing back. Obviously, a house couldn't change back and forth from old to new. She must have been dreaming, drawing on memories from Grams' stories and her own dreams. Her thoughts wandered again to the man—Nicholas—with the dark, gypsy eyes. Those eyes had locked with hers in an unmistakable sensual message that caused her to blush even now.

A warm glow swept over her as she thought of him. It was ridiculous, of course. He couldn't have seen her eyes as she looked at him through the binoculars. Suddenly a new picture flashed in her mind. He was holding her close and she could feel the pressure of his hungry lips as they pressed against her own. She could scarcely breathe as he pulled her even closer, probing for a deeper union.

"Good Lord, Emily," she said under her breath, "You had better get hold of yourself—you're losing it."

Remembering the handkerchief, she returned to her bedroom and retrieved it. Carrying it back to the kitchen, she squirted a little dishwashing liquid on it and running it under the cold water, washed and rinsed until the stain was gone. Feeling pleased that she had not ruined the lovely old keepsake, she hung it over the towel rack to dry.

As she studied the delicate lacy pattern of the handkerchief, she heard a knock at the kitchen door. Before she had time to answer, the knock sounded again, accompanied by a woman's voice.

"Are you in there, Miss Emily? It's me, Mattie Devers."

Hearing the familiar name and voice, Emily went to the door and opened it. "Come in, Mattie."

The older woman stepped inside the kitchen. Her wrinkled, sun-worn face crinkled into a smile. "It's good to see you again, Miss Emily, only not under the present circumstances, I'm sure. Your grandmother was a saint, she was." Mattie took a handkerchief from her pocket and dabbed at a tear that had slipped down her cheek. "I didn't know if you would still want me to come here and clean for you the way I did for Twila. She had me in once a week."

A spark of hope rose in Mattie's eyes as she watched Emily. "So I says to myself, just go over there and ask Miss Emily whether or not she needs you. Yes, your grandmother was a saint, she was. She was clean as a pin, too. Truth was, she knew I needed the work and she paid me very well. Yes, she did."

The small, bent woman who was also a nearby neighbor, eyed Emily hopefully.

Emily had known Mattie Devers since Emily was a child. Mattie was shunned by many of the village folk. Some of the more superstitious ones said she had the evil eye. Grams always said it was because Mattie had one green eye and one brown one. Mrs. Devers accepted the label and even capitalized on it to the extent that she could. She claimed to have gypsy blood in her and had made a few dollars doing astrological charts and card and palm readings.

Most of the villagers treated her with disdain until they felt a need for her services. Then, they would approach her on the sly. Grams had been a notable exception. Though Twila Foster had never availed herself of Mattie's fortune telling services, she felt sorry for the scorned woman and always treated her with respect.

As Grams grew older, she benefited from the help Mattie gave her as a part-time cleaning lady and Mattie, in turn, earned a little extra money.

Emily was aware of the mutually beneficial arrangement her grandmother had worked out with Mattie. "Mrs. Devers, I would very much like you to continue working here. I'm sure I can use your help. Grams didn't like to admit it but this big house was getting to be too much for her. I don't know what she would have done without you."

"Bless your heart, it's mighty kind of you to say so. I'll get busy right away and go on about my business. I know my duties, but if there is anything you want to add or change just let me know."

"Just continue as you always have, Mrs. Devers."

"Lord, Miss Emily, why don't you just call me Mattie?"

"Very well, and you can call me Emily, the way you did when I was a little girl." Emily smiled. "Meanwhile, I have some errands to do, so I'll be out this morning."

Not wanting to be underfoot, Emily decided to take a drive and she knew exactly where she wanted to go. She picked up her purse and went out the kitchen door. Immediately her gaze traveled across the river to the blackened stone ruins of Langford Manor. Even as she tried once more to convince herself that it had all been a dream, her heart could not forget the man with the dark, gypsy eyes.

"Nicholas," she whispered, "could it have been Nicholas?" Just saying his name caused her lips to burn for his phantom kiss and her body to long for his touch.

A short time later, Emily was on her way to the other side of the river. The decision gave her gooseflesh. She was apprehensive about going alone since it was a deserted area. She knew it would be wiser to wait and have Becky go with her. But she had seen the look of concern on her friend's face. Besides, she couldn't wait, she felt irresistibly drawn to the old burned stone ruins.

To get to the other side, Emily had to drive seven miles east to the Clawson bridge. She chose to avoid the interstate and opted for the local road, since she would have to go three miles out of her way in order to pick it up. It was a pleasant, scenic route, and she rolled down her window to enjoy it fully.

The pungent, pine-scented greenery delighted her senses. On the one side, the emerald slopes of steep, sheltering mountains paralleled the highway. On the opposite side of the road, a narrow ledge of land overlooked the calm, jade waters of the glistening river.

Rhododendron and mountain laurel burst forth in colorful profusion, the sweet, cloying scent mingling with the pine. God's country! Again, Emily realized how much she had missed it. The lure of the big city had promised much, but in the end had offered little. She was back where she belonged.

The Clawson bridge soon loomed before her, more rusted and smaller than she remembered. But, that was typical. Everything from her childhood seemed smaller now. Smaller and narrower, she thought, as she navigated the two lane span. She was glad there was little traffic and especially happy there were no oncoming trucks to pass.

Leaving the bridge on the other side of the river, she entered an even more rugged area than the one she had just left. Lush overgrowth greeted her and there were few signs of civilization. It was strange that no one had bothered building on this side of the river. But in truth, the narrow ledge of land running adjacent to the Kanawha River was too narrow or sandy in most places to support homes. To her left, a mountain climbed steeply, prohibiting the building of houses.

Emily knew that any people to be found on this side would be discovered along the creeks and hollows that dissected the formidable mountains.

Because of the few landmarks, she would have to watch carefully for her intended destination lest she go past it. She chided herself. Unless there was so much overgrowth along the road that her view was completely blocked, she would not pass it! Even now, she felt it drawing her. She took a deep breath and gooseflesh raised on her arms as she spied the blackened stone chimney protruding above the greenery just ahead.

Her instinct to turn and run was almost as strong as the one which urged her on. She nosed her car into a dark tunnel of overlapping trees. Feeling she was being swallowed by a great emerald bird, she bravely forged ahead into the depths of foliage, steeling herself for what lay ahead.

The moist dank smell of the damp earth and rotting vegetation left her feeling slightly nauseated. Small branches from the crowded, sapling trees reached through her open car window and slapped her face.

After what seemed like an eternity, she exited the thicket of trees and came into a clearing. Her breath caught in her throat as she stopped her car. The hot sun bore down and the bright sunlight nearly blinded her. Suddenly, a distorted vision wavered before her.

She saw a new stone house with shutters and a myriad of rose bushes surrounding it. She blinked her eyes and it was gone. It must have been a trick of the sunlight and her overactive imagination, she concluded, as her gaze settled on the blackened stone shell that had stood sentinel for as long as she could remember.

When the Lilacs Bloom

It seemed all the more foreboding up close, resembling a hovering bird of prey ready to swoop on an unsuspecting victim who happened by. She turned off the engine. After coming this far, she would not turn tail and run. She would do the exploring she had set out to do.

As Emily got out of the car, a breeze stirred, carrying with it a faint burnt odor. She doubted that the ruins would still harbor the smell of charred wood after a hundred years. In spite of the sun's warmth, she shivered when she thought about Nicholas and Elinor perishing here in a fire that must have been visible for miles up and down the river.

The clearing was dotted with a few soda pop and beer cans, evidence of the teenage thrill-seekers who came to do battle with the Langford ghosts.

Emily turned her attention to the stone ruins. Weeds and vines had claimed a good portion of the main floor. She followed the path toward the house, hoping she wouldn't trip over a snake sunning itself on the warm stones.

Her heart pounded as she came upon a crooked stone slab. It was the first step up to what was left of the wide verandah. A swishing in the grass caught Emily's attention and she shrieked as a blue-tailed lizard darted across her foot. Her heart pounding, she mustered the courage to stay put and not turn around and run back to her car and leave. She took a deep breath and proceeded.

Stepping onto the verandah, she gazed across the river. It seemed strange to be standing on this side, looking across at her property. The unique structure of her house made it easy to spot. For a fleeting moment, she had the odd sensation that she had stood on this spot and gazed across the river many times before.

The breeze stirred again, breaking the eerie silence that surrounded this forgotten place. It was like visiting a cemetery or a civil war battleground. Emily held her breath and listened.

After a moment, she looked at what was left of the Langford house. She stepped up on the stone porch and saw, upon closer inspection, that there was no flooring inside. Emily touched the smooth stones of the entryway, and closed her eyes trying to visualize how the house would have looked hundred years ago.

She imagined a wide staircase in the foyer and large bedrooms upstairs with long windows reaching almost to the floor. A woman with long sun-streaked hair, very much like Emily's, lived here with her husband, a man whose dark, soulful eyes were filled with love for his bride.

"Nicholas and Elinor," Emily whispered. The wind blew softly against Emily's cheek and her eyelids became suddenly heavy as the cloying scent of lilacs wafting on the breeze made her feel faint. She clung to the door post, steadying herself against the vertigo that swept over her like a tidal wave. The wind picked up in intensity and as it whirled and whipped about the empty shell of a house, its moans resembled a woman's voice.

In spite of the dizziness and eyelids that were so heavy she could not open them, her senses became very acute, alert to hear the name spoken on the wind.

Straining her hears as she clung to the post to keep her balance, Emily heard the low mournful tone whisper over and over again, "Elinor, Elinor...."

Chapter Fourteen

"Elinor, Elinor...."

Hearing her name being called, Elinor lifted her long skirts and stepped inside the foyer. "You called me, Mother Langford?"

The pinch-faced woman in her usual black taffeta dress tapped her foot impatiently. Her dark, gray-streaked hair was pulled severely back from her face and twisted securely in its usual knot on top of her head. The unflattering hairstyle accentuated the gaunt, sallow face and thin lips. She eyed Elinor suspiciously.

"What have you been up to, Missy? I've been looking all over for you. Janie Adkins is here to measure the hem for your ball gown. It is very inconsiderate of you to keep her waiting. I told you she would be here at ten o'clock sharp." The beady eyes were as keen and unrelenting as a hawk's.

Elinor flushed, attempting to maintain her composure. She did not want to be drawn into a confrontation with her mother-in-law. The woman detested her. It was becoming increasingly clear to Elinor that no matter what she did, Harriet Langford would never forgive her for committing the unpardonable sin of marrying her son.

"I'm sorry, Mother Langford, I took a walk and the time got away from me. I will apologize to Mrs. Adkins for any inconvenience I might have caused."

"You will do nothing of the kind! I will not have my son's wife apologizing to hired help. Really, Elinor, you must try to behave in a manner befitting a lady even if it is not what you are accustomed to. My son's position demands a woman of breeding and you must learn to act the part. I will not have him be the laughing stock of the county."

Elinor's face flushed and as hard as she tried to bite her tongue, she knew that this was one time she could not ignore her mother-in-law's rude remarks. "Mother Langford, I could never hope to be a better person than the woman who raised me. You may berate me, since you seem to find it so satisfying a pastime, but I will not allow you to vilify my mother."

Angry splotches rose on Harriet Langford's cheeks. "So the insipid girl has spirit. Don't think it will garner you any favor with me. At best it only makes you a more worthy opponent." She emitted a sarcastic chuckle. "Furthermore, young lady, I find it incredible that you would presume to dictate what I may or may not say in my own house."

"Is this not also the home of your son and his wife?"

Harriet Langford was not one to back down, but this time she must have realized that Elinor was not going to. "I would be happy to stand here and debate your dubious family tree, but as I reminded you, Mrs. Adkins is waiting. I think it best if you run along to the sewing room."

Seeing she was being dismissed and not wishing to prolong the distasteful conversation, Elinor swept past her mother-in-law and went directly upstairs. She was seething inside. Harriet Langford had set her mind against Elinor before she had ever met her. She was careful to treat Elinor with civility in Nicholas' presence, but Harriet's sharpest barbs were saved for when the two women were alone.

A mousy Janie Adkins gave a start as Elinor swept into the room. She had likely expected Harriet Langford. A look of relief washed over her. "Oh, it's you, Miss Elinor."

"I'm sorry I'm late, Janie. I hope you didn't have to wait long." Elinor didn't care what her mother-in-law said about apologizing to the hired help. She would not be rude to the wizened seamstress.

"Shucks, Miss, I've only been here a little while and I had

some hemming to do, so there's no harm done." The gray-haired woman grinned, showing the few teeth she had left.

Elinor stepped behind the screen and removed her gabardine skirt and linen blouse. Slipping the shimmering satin folds of the sapphire gown over her head, she stepped back out so Janie could help her with the hooks.

"All eyes will be on you, Miss, that's for sure. There ain't none that can hold a candle to you. Miss Geneva's nose will be out of joint, I expect." Probably realizing she had said too much, Janie's hand flew over her mouth. "I'm sorry, Miss Elinor, I spoke out of turn. Had no right to do that, at all."

"It's all right, Janie. It won't go any further. But I am sure you are wrong. Miss Geneva will look lovely in the red dress you made for her. She has no reason to be jealous of me."

"Yes'm, it is a pretty dress, if I do say so myself." Janie's face reddened as she swallowed hard and assumed her usual meek demeanor.

After removing the gown and getting dressed again, Elinor absentmindedly picked up a small discarded scrap of the blue satin material and rubbed it against her cheek. She then tucked it into her skirt pocket. Though she wanted the gown to be a surprise, it wouldn't hurt to let Nicholas see the color it was going to be.

After the fitting, Elinor went to her bedroom to lie down. Her head was throbbing and she felt nauseated. She had not been herself lately. Her usual robust health had given way to bouts of nausea and headaches. Her time of the month had just passed, so she knew that it had nothing to do with her hope to give Nicholas a son. Perhaps it was just as well. They were practically newlyweds and needed time to themselves. That was something they had precious little of in this house. Furthermore, when children did come along, Elinor did not want them born at Langford Manor.

Now that she and Nicholas were married, he was reluctant to talk about the westward move. When Elinor initiated the subject, he'd say, "Of course we will go, but there's some loose ends I have to tie up first."

Langford Manor was his ancestral home and it would be understandable if he wanted to remain and someday inherit the family business. But he had promised, saying that it was his dream, too.

Elinor knew instinctively that she and Nicholas had to get far away from the shadow of the Langfords. If they didn't, she sensed that their marriage would be doomed. Harriet Langford would stop at nothing to be rid of Elinor.

Trying to push the troubling thoughts from her mind, Elinor got up and went over to the wash bowl. It was an unusually warm day. The windows were open but there wasn't the slightest hint of a breeze. The scent of the lilacs in the bedside vase was blotted out by the musty odor of aged curtains and ancient furniture. Had Elinor planned on staying here, she would have put her foot down and insisted on new furnishings and decorations in this room. The entire house needed refurbishing, but Harriet Langford wouldn't hear of it. She liked things just as they were.

Elinor removed her skirt and blouse and dipped her monogrammed handkerchief in the bowl of tepid water on the chiffonier. After dabbing her arms and chest with the moist cloth, she squeezed the water from it and spread the handkerchief across the headboard of her bed to dry.

Her feet burned, and she could not resist the urge to free them from the hot, leather shoes. After undoing the numerous buttons, she pulled off her shoes and wriggled her toes. She loved going barefooted but to do so in this house was tantamount to high treason.

At last she sank down into the cushiony comfort of the large bed she shared with Nicholas. She plucked a bloom from the vase of lilacs and, holding it to her nose, breathed its sweet scent. Closing her eyes, she pushed aside her worries and thought back to the time when they had first met. Nicholas had rowed across the river bringing a bouquet of lilacs with him.

Wishing he were with her now, she pictured the way his dark eyes took on a glow when she came into the room. His lips had a habit of curling into a sensual smile imparting a message meant only for her. It was with these pleasant thoughts that Elinor drifted off to sleep.

The chirping of the birds was unusually loud as Emily gradually became aware of her surroundings. The sun's heat beat down on her face and her mattress felt as though it were made of stone. When something slithered across her hand, she opened her eyes and looked just in time to see the tail of a garter snake disappear in the tall weeds just beyond her outstretched hand.

Jerking away, she cried out and pushed herself into a sitting position. Since her body felt unusually heavy and lethargic, it was done with difficulty in spite of the rush of adrenaline. When she first looked about she didn't know where she was. Then, she realized she was sitting on the stone steps of Langford Manor. The last thing she remembered was standing by the door post and feeling lightheaded. She shivered again at the realization that she must have fainted.

Gooseflesh rose on her arms and her hair prickled at the back of her neck. An intense need to leave this place seized her. She scooted closer to the stone door post and, hanging onto it, she pulled herself to her feet.

Leaping down the stone steps on legs that felt as though they were partially asleep, she lost her footing and went sprawling in the dusty path. A greater sense of urgency took hold with what felt like the lingering pressure of someone's hand pushing her forward. Her elbows stung as she raised her face from the dirt and spit to rid herself of a mouthful of unwelcome earth. She quickly wiped her face with the back of her hand.

As she struggled to her feet once more, she heard a high-pitched laugh that turned her blood to ice. Looking about, she saw no one. On legs that suddenly found their strength, she broke into a run. She felt eyes watching her as the hot breath of an evil presence pressed against her back.

Emily cried out as she reached the car and quickly slid inside, locked the door and rolled up the window. Nothing seemed amiss when she looked toward the remains of Langford Manor. She scanned the entire area, looking beside and behind her, but there was no one.

Gripping the steering wheel with both hands and breathing a sigh of relief, she leaned forward and rested her head against her hands. What had ever possessed her to come alone to this isolated spot? She should have waited and had Becky come along.

Raising her head, she reached for the key which had been left in the ignition. She was comforted by the sound of the engine turning over. Steering her car to the left in the circular clearing, she aimed it in the direction of the lush tunnel that led back to the highway and freedom.

Freedom. It was an odd choice of words. She glanced in her rearview mirror for one last look at the old stone structure and her heart froze. She nearly lost control of the car as she stomped on the gas pedal. Reflected in the mirror was a new house with ornate black shutters and white columns in front.

Looking out of an upstairs window was a dark-haired matron. Her slightly graying hair was pulled severely into a knot on top of her head and she wore a black old-fashioned dress. Even at this distance, Emily could see the sharp features on the malevolent face. The woman's hawkish demeanor exuded hatred as an evil smile curled the cruel slit that was her mouth.

Lurching forward as Emily regained control of it, the car plunged into the leafy embrace of the tunneling trees. She kept her foot on the pedal, holding her breath as the green limbs reached menacingly out for her. She pressed on, suppressing an urge to scream. Finally, her car emerged from the near jungle-like vegetation and came to a stop at the edge of the highway. She took a deep breath to calm her racing heart and checked the highway for oncoming traffic. Seeing no cars, she pulled onto the road and headed home.

Chapter Fifteen

Emily gripped the steering wheel so tight her knuckles whitened. Glancing at the rear view mirror to see if she was being pursued, she gasped when she saw a large, black automobile following some two hundred yards behind. Her heart pounded wildly as she steered her car along the gray ribbon of road that sliced through the wilderness. She had been a fool to come here alone. Anxious, she scanned the distance, looking for the bridge.

"There it is!" she cried when she saw the steel girders jutting above the thick foliage seventy-five yards ahead. After rounding a sweeping curve and pulling next to the bridge, she made a quick left turn, screeching her tires. Hopefully, the inhabitants of the black car would not realize she had turned onto the bridge.

She pushed harder on the gas, propelling her blue compact across the narrow two lane span. Suddenly, a red, rusty pick-up truck was directly on front of her. She jerked the steering wheel just in time to avoid a collision with the oncoming vehicle. The startled driver cursed her and flipped her the finger. Any other time she would have been angry, but under the circumstances, she was delighted. The truck driver's reaction represented the normal, everyday world. Swallowing hard, she relaxed her foot on the gas pedal and finished crossing the bridge.

As she turned left onto the highway and headed for home, she took one last look behind her to reassure herself that she was not being followed. Seeing no one, she breathed a sigh of relief and glanced at her watch.

Twelve o'clock! How could that be? Somehow, she had lost time back there. One minute she had been standing by the door post, feeling light-headed and the next thing she knew, she was lying on the stone steps of the old house. She had assumed she had been out only a few minutes. A new shock wave coursed through her at the realization that she had been unconscious for two hours.

She recalled the new house and the cruel face in the window. It had seemed so real. Was she losing her mind, or did ghosts really exist?

By the time she pulled into her driveway, she was much calmer. After leaving her car, she couldn't resist a quick look across the river. As she suspected, there were stone ruins.

Mattie Devers was just leaving when Emily entered the kitchen. "I'm done for the day unless there's something else you'd like me to do?"

Concern washed over the old woman's face.

"I can't think of anything. Thanks, Mattie. I'll see you next week."

The cleaning lady started to say something, but apparently thought better of it and with a wave, she set out for home.

Emily was glad Mattie left. She didn't want to discuss the events of the morning. After washing her face and hands, she went to the refrigerator. She would re-heat the chicken and potatoes left over from the evening before. When she opened it, she found chicken, but instead of potatoes, there was rice.

"I didn't fix potatoes last night, I fixed rice. I knew that." Her hands shook slightly when she pulled the dishes from the shelf and placed them in the microwave. After pushing the appropriate buttons, she took a carton of milk from the refrigerator. As she poured it into the tall, crystal tumbler, the milk turned red, like blood. She gasped and dropped the carton, spilling white liquid on the counter and floor. The glass also slipped from her hands and shattered to pieces when it hit the floor.

Emily closed her eyes and remembered wine that had looked like blood when it was poured into tall crystal goblets. It had burned slightly when she drank it, but that was nothing compared to the burning of her lips as they anticipated a kiss that was to come. A kiss that would leave her lips bruised, yet wanting more.

The microwave rang, bringing her back to the present. She groaned at the sight of the spilled milk and broken glass. As she busied herself cleaning up the mess, the odd fantasy faded. By the time she finished washing the counter and floor, she had lost her appetite.

She went to the bedroom to comb her hair and put lotion on her hands. While studying her reflection in the dresser mirror, she noticed a patch of white on the carved oak headboard behind her. Walking over to her bed, she picked up the monogrammed handkerchief she had washed earlier. "I don't remember putting this here," she whispered.

She held the linen handkerchief to her face, and rubbed it against her cheek. She sniffed the lavender and lilac scent it gave off—certainly not the scent of the dishwashing soap. It belonged to another time, smelled of that earlier time.

Suddenly very tired, Emily stretched out on her bed. She thought about the handkerchief, the wine glass and the confusion between the potatoes and rice. There had also been the cut on her finger that had stung so in the shower that morning. She looked at her finger but could not find the small wound. No one healed that fast! Somehow, all of these things were connected with Langford Manor.

The ringing of the telephone broke into her thoughts. She arose, went into the hallway and picked up the receiver.

"Hello," she said, her voice guarded.

"Emily, it's so good to hear your voice again."

"Jeff?"

"I just heard of your grandmother's passing. I'm so sorry, sweetheart. I wanted to let you know that I am here for you."

For a fleeting moment, old feelings that Emily thought were dead began to resurface. Jeff had always been very supportive and affectionate. Then she remembered that his affections had been spread around a little too generously. She would not allow herself to be drawn back into his web of deceit.

"Thanks, but you really shouldn't have called. We have nothing to say to one another. It's all been said, so please do not call again."

As soon as she hung up the phone rang again. Jeff had never been one to take 'no' for an answer. "Damn," she said as she picked up the telephone receiver once more.

"Now look, Jeff..." There was static on the line. "Jeff, this isn't funny." The static grew louder. "I thought you were above making weird phone calls, but it looks like I underestimated you again."

Emily started to hang up the phone when the static lessened enough for her to hear a whisper.

"I need you, Elinor, come home."

Shrieking, she dropped the telephone as though it were a hot coal.

"Jeff! Stop it, stop it!" She put her hands over her ears. "Leave me alone." Her back to the wall, she slowly slipped down to the floor.

Swallowing hard, she choked back the tears that threatened to flow. Damn Jeff. He knew about her past fascination with Nicholas and Elinor. She never thought he'd be so cruel as to taunt her by pretending to be Nicholas."

She brought her knees up and rested her arms and face against them. Then she felt a reassuring hand on her shoulder and heard hushing tones meant to comfort her.

She should have jumped out of her skin, but strangely, she wasn't afraid. When she looked up there was no one there. "Nicholas," an inner voice whispered, "Nicholas."

The doorbell rang. Knowing she was visible through the antique glass panels of the front door, Emily knew she should answer it. Besides, she could see it was Becky.

Emily stood up and smoothed back her hair. Taking a deep breath and squaring her shoulders, she went to the door.

"Hi, Beck," she tried to sound cheerful when she opened it.

Becky stepped inside and gave Emily a hug. "Hey—how come you look so upset?"

An unwelcome tear slid down her cheek when she told Becky about Jeff's phone calls.

"But you are supposed to be over Jeff, remember?"

"Silly, isn't it?" Emily reached in her jeans pocket for a tissue, but instead, pulled out a scrap of blue satin. She frowned and muttered, "Where did I get this?"

"What did you say?" Becky stepped closer.

"Oh, I was just talking to myself, " Emily forced a smile as she stuffed the scrap of cloth back into the pocket.

"Well you don't have to talk to yourself anymore. I've come to treat you to dinner at a new Italian restaurant that opened in Charleston." Becky put her hands on her hips and struck a pose. "You know how determined I can be, Em, so you might as well go ahead and say yes right now."

"Beck, my stomach is kind of queasy and I know I won't be good company."

"I'll bet you haven't eaten much today. That's why you feel queasy.

You have to eat to keep up your strength, Em. We don't have to make an evening of it if you don't want to, but you can at least have dinner with me."

Emily saw her friend's concern. "All right, Beck, just let me change and freshen up."

Later at the restaurant, Emily managed to relax a little. She concluded that Becky had been right to urge her to go out.

"Em," Becky said in between bites of pasta, "What's the matter with you? I know you haven't told me everything. We've never kept really important things from one another. Are you in some sort of trouble?"

"Yeah, Beck," Emily forced a grin, "I just robbed a bank and the feds are after me."

Becky's mouth dropped open. "Now, Em, stop that! I am really worried about you."

"I know but there is no need to be concerned. Just look at my life, Becky. Everything has changed in a very short time. I'm just not handling it terribly well but I will survive." Emily toyed with the salad she had ordered.

"Em, I see you suffering and I want to help. Isn't there something I can do?"

"Just keep being my friend and accept me at my word."

Becky sighed and with a hurt look on her face said, "All right, Em, I will respect your wishes but just remember, I am your best friend and I'll always be here for you."

Emily smiled and patted Becky's hand. "I'll remember that, Beck."

When they returned to Emily's house, instead of inviting Becky in, Emily begged off saying she had a headache. Her friend looked skeptical but she didn't make an issue of it. Emily waved good-bye as Becky pulled out of the driveway and headed down the street.

Fumbling with her keys, Emily chastised herself for not leaving the porch light on, but it had been daylight when she left and she hadn't thought of it. Now she was standing in the darkness surrounded by the silence of the night, feeling utterly alone.

Finally she found the correct key and slipped it into the lock. As she did so, a strange sensation swept over her. It was as though an electrical current had passed from the key into her body. Her hair stood on end and her heart pounded loudly. A part of her wanted to run, get into her car and follow Becky home. Good, level-headed Becky. But how could Emily make Becky understand what was going on when she didn't understand it herself?

The scent of lilacs wafting on the breeze gave her a strange sense of comfort as she peered through the glass door. She could see nothing inside. Normally intimidated by the dark, her inhibitions fell away as she sensed her destiny beckoning her. Squaring her shoulders and taking a deep breath, she touched a trembling hand to the cool, smooth, doorknob and pushed the door open.

Chapter Sixteen

Emily slipped inside the blackened hallway and was immediately swallowed up by the velvety darkness. Closing the door, she stood with her back against it and listened. She knew she was not alone. As her eyes adjusted to the dark, she saw a tall form standing at the foot of the stairs.

"Nicholas?"

"Yes, my beloved."

Unafraid, she reached toward him and when their fingers touched, she felt a surge of electricity draw her to him.

"My Elinor," he murmured, his warm lips taking possession of hers as he folded her in an embrace. He stroked her hair and held her so tightly, she could scarcely breathe. When she did take a deep breath, the sweet scent of lilacs that surrounded Nicholas left Emily feeling slightly heady.

"I'm taking you home, dearest," he said, picking her up in his arms.

Emily clung to Nicholas as he carried her from the house to the waiting boat. She did not resist. She wanted to go with him. She now remembered another night when he had carried her away. The lilac scent had been strong then too. She had become confused and had thought herself to be Elinor. But how could any of this be happening? Nicholas had lived a hundred years ago.

If this was not a dream, then it was Elinor's life she was very willingly stepping into. Nicholas was Elinor's husband. Nicholas thought she, Emily, was Elinor. Was she? She was certain of one thing. She loved Nicholas above all else, even her own identity. She had always loved him. That love overshadowed all other considerations. Furthermore, this was not a ghost, but a flesh and blood man who carried her in his arms.

Nicholas settled her into the boat and she rested against velvet cushions. Emily gave herself over to the swishing and lapping of the waves and the shimmering trail of the starlight and crescent moon reflected upon the black waters. Awash with peace and contentment, she smiled. If Nicholas wanted her to be Elinor, then she would be Elinor. With that settled, she continued to gaze at the mesmerizing trail of silver reflected on the cool, dark river.

Suddenly the water convulsed and shuddered, turning into a brilliant jade and the sky became a lovely, tranquil blue. Elinor gasped, as though she had awakened from a dream. Shading her eyes from a western sun that had not yet dipped behind the mountains, she started to say something to Nicholas, but strangely could not remember what it was. In fact she did not remember getting into the boat with him. What was happening to her?

A chill swept over Elinor as she saw the magnificent columns and black shutters of Langford Manor just ahead. Then she looked into Nicholas' handsome face and her reluctance faded. As long as she was with him, she could face anyone or anything.

"You are so deep in thought, dearest. Is anything wrong?"

Elinor smiled. "I was just thinking about you, Nicholas, and how happy I am to be your wife."

He bent forward and took her hand. "Then promise me you will never go off alone like that again."

"Nicholas, it was only a small excursion across the river to see my mother. What harm could there be in that?"

"No harm, dearest, though I don't like being separated

overnight. This river is unpredictable. I will take you when you want to visit. You only have to ask."

"Very well, if it concerns you that much, I'll refrain from rowing across by myself. I would prefer having you accompany me anyway."

Elinor didn't tell him how overwhelmed she had felt at Langford Manor, that she had needed to get away for a short while. He had been working long hours and life at the manor house was only bearable when he was there. She did not want to burden him with such a revelation.

Convinced that his bride would keep her word, his look of concern faded. When the boat touched bottom, Nicholas jumped out and lifted Elinor onto shore.

"Dinner should be ready, we don't want to be late. You know Mother."

Elinor certainly did—probably better than Nicholas. Obviously her husband saw his mother in quite a different light. She and Nicholas had to get away if they were ever to be truly happy. She had not broached the subject in such strong terms, but she planned to very soon.

"Come, dearest," Nicholas slipped an arm around her waist to escort her into the house.

She took one last look over her shoulder at the home of her parents on the other side of the river.

"We will go again soon and visit your family. I know you miss them."

Once inside Langford Manor, Elinor changed into something more suitable and she and Nicholas entered the dining room just as the others were sitting down. Elinor's gaze immediately locked with Harriet Langford's. Had there been any doubt that her mother-in-law hated her, the look on the older woman's face dispelled it.

After taking her seat at the long mahogany table, Elinor scanned the high-ceilinged room. She had the strangest feeling that she was seeing the dark paneled walls and the worn red velvet draperies for the first time. The curtains drawn, as was the custom, the only light in the heavy, suffocating room was provided by kerosene lamps. The lamps were a luxury. In most of the rooms, Mother Langford insisted on the use of candles. She said candles were less expensive. Harriet Langford was ever vigilant when it came to keeping household expenses in check.

Elinor had a momentary stab of conscience when she remembered the lovely ball gown that was being made for her. Mother Langford had insisted on paying for it and she had spared no expense. But then, as she had so many times admonished when she and Elinor were alone, she wanted her son's wife to dress in a manner befitting the name of Langford. Elinor knew the Langford name was more feared than respected.

Elinor looked down at her green damask dress and at the wedding ring on her finger. Then she looked at her dinner companions. Other than Nicholas, they were still like strangers to her, cold and uncaring. Again, she was stabbed with the odd feeling that she was experiencing this situation for the first time. She leveled an assessing gaze at each of her dinner companions.

To her left, an arm's length away, sat Nicholas, so handsome in his stiff collar and black bow tie. His thick, dark hair was combed down but still curled at the edges. His perfect profile looked as though it was chiseled in fine stone with the tiny strawberry birthmark the only blemish.

At one end of the table sat Nicholas' mother, clad in her black taffeta dress. Her hair was pulled up into a tight knot on the top of her head, giving her dark eyes an upward slant and accentuating her high cheekbones. Her tight-lipped demeanor made her mouth look like a cruel slash.

Across the table, Geneva, a younger version of Harriet Langford, sat ramrod straight. Her lush, black hair was pulled back from her face and allowed to cascade down her back. She had her mother's thin-lipped mouth and dark piercing eyes. In spite of that, she might have been attractive had there been a touch of softness in her. Geneva's brittle stare told Elinor that any friendship between them was out of the question.

It's a pity, Elinor thought. Geneva could have been the sister Elinor never had, but Nicholas' sister was too much her mother's daughter to allow that to happen.

"Is something the matter, Elinor?" Tobias Langford boomed from the other end of the long dining room table. He sat slumped in his chair and raised a questioning eyebrow. His eyebrows were so like Nicholas' as were his full lips, but they did not smile in approval as did Nicholas'. Rather, the elder Langford had a perpetual mocking expression.

Why did they all hate her so?

"No, nothing is the matter, Mr. Langford." Elinor felt her cheeks redden under his intense gaze.

"You did have a rather sudden and I might say, overly long visit with your family. I thought perhaps you were not happy with us."

Elinor could not help but look at Tobias' strawberry birthmark. Unlike Nicholas', his was considerably larger and rested directly on his chin. Furthermore, it seemed to accentuate Tobias' perpetual sneer, thus detracting from his looks.

"Father," Nicholas interrupted, "Elinor had a touch of homesickness, but now she is here with us where she belongs."

Elinor was pleased by the way Nicolas jumped to her defense. She saw the determined set of his jaw. While Tobais did not back down, he said nothing further and instead demanded that dinner be served.

After the meal, Nicholas suggested they retire early and Elinor eagerly agreed. She wanted to be alone with him. She could put it off no longer. Tonight she would tell him they must leave Langford Manor now and make a home far away from the evil and hate that permeated this place. They would just have to make due with the funds they'd already saved. A year or two at this house would be an eternity. When children came, she wanted them born in a place of light and happiness, not darkness and shadow.

Chapter Seventeen

Elinor stood by the open window gazing at the lacy patterns of shimmering moonlight on the dark river. A faint light, winking from across the water, was all but swallowed up by the darkness cast by the hovering mountains. The light was coming from her house, she thought, as a new wave of homesickness enveloped her. No, she corrected herself, Langford Manor was her home now. But only Nicholas' love made the otherwise hate-filled house bearable.

As if he knew she was thinking about him, Nicholas stepped behind Elinor and, slipping his arms around her waist, pulled her against him. "Is my bride having another bout of homesickness?" He kissed the back of her neck and nuzzled against her ear.

"It isn't just a matter of homesickness, Nicholas. Your family hates me."

"They don't hate you, Elinor. They just need time. Our marriage was a shock to them. They had another life planned for me."

"Exactly, Nicholas, and you have disappointed them. They will never forgive me for interfering with those plans. Your mother would like nothing better than to see us part."

Nicholas turned Elinor around and cupped her chin in his hand. "No one will ever separate us. I have told you that before. I know Mother is difficult, but she will come around. You'll see."

Elinor had never wanted to make Nicholas choose. She

told herself that she had been married only three months, that she should give it more time. But she knew now that nothing was going to change. She would not live like this, even for a year or two.

"If you love me, Nicholas, you will take me away from here now. Darling, we can go out west, start all over. I have some money and I know you have accounts independent of your parents. We can make due on what we have."

Nicholas frowned and the stricken look on his face made Elinor almost wished she hadn't spoken. But the words had to be said and there would never be a good time to say them.

"Dearest," he whispered, "you're tired and homesick, you don't mean what you are saying."

Elinor stiffened and pulled back from him. She and Nicholas had never argued. Now, she looked at him as though he were someone she didn't know.

"If I were merely homesick, I would hardly suggest moving across the country away from *my* family. I am sick of the hate in this house! I will not bring a child into the world if it must be raised here."

"Elinor, are you saying—" He reached for her but she again pulled away.

"No, I'm not with child and I don't intend to be as long as we live here."

Apparently realizing the meaning behind her words, Nicholas fell silent for a moment.

It was one of the longest moments of Elinor's life. She wanted to take him in her arms, tell him she didn't mean it. But she knew she mustn't. She was doing this to save their marriage and preserve the family she hoped to have.

"Then there is only one thing to do," Nicholas whispered.

Elinor searched his face, but his guarded expression revealed nothing.

"We will leave in a month. That will give me time to wrap up my business affairs." His eyes filled with sadness, he managed a smile. "Did you think I would deny you anything?"

Elinor went into his arms. "I didn't know for sure. You do understand why we must go, don't you?"

"I understand that you are unhappy and I know that my family can seem remote at times." He held her close, kissing her forehead, cheeks, and eyelids. Lifting her up, he carried her to the four poster bed and unfastened the hooks and buttons of her dress.

As he slipped from his clothes, she studied him in the flickering candlelight. He looked like a god. She worshipped him almost as though he were. She wished he had seemed happier about the decision.

"I will never let anyone come between us, Elinor. You will be with me always." He slid in the bed next to her and took her in his arms. Holding her, he cradled her as one would a child. Then his lips began to burn a trail down her face and neck, her throat and breasts. His hands stroked and explored as he whispered over and over, "My love, my dearest love."

Elinor's body shook from the power of his touch. She wound her fingers in his long, dark hair as he slipped above her. Her eagerness matched his as he probed and searched the depths of her being. Waves of ecstasy washed over her, absorbing her in total oneness with the man she loved.

Suddenly, Nicholas jerked away from her and she became aware of her surroundings once more. Someone was knocking on the door.

"Nicholas, dear, I was just going to bed and I thought I heard a noise. Is anything wrong?" Harriet Langford's voice sounded from the other side of the door.

Before he could respond, the door opened and Harriet stepped inside. The candle she held gave off a flickering light that only accentuated the displeasure reflected in her hawkish features.

Nicholas quickly pulled the sheets over himself and Elinor. "Mother! I suggest you leave immediately."

"Has this slip of a girl besotted you so that you have no sense of decorum? A decent woman would not carry on in such a manner!"

"Enough, Mother! Elinor is my wife. Furthermore, a decent woman would not burst into her son's bedroom while he and his wife were making love."

Harriet Langford clutched her chest as though her heart had stopped beating and said in a voice that dripped of venom, "This is what this common tramp has led you to. You would never have talked in such a vulgar way before she got hold of you."

"This wonderful woman," Nicholas said, slipping his arm around Elinor, "has opened my eyes to the truth. You should be happy to know we will be leaving soon so you will not have to be annoyed by our love-making in the future."

"Nicholas, must you continue to speak to me in this vulgar manner? As far as your leaving here, huh! Where would you go? We've given you everything. Your father's business will be yours someday." She paused and stared at the ceiling for a moment. Then, with a determined set of her jaw, she returned her gaze to Nicholas.

"However, if you are foolish enough to leave, you won't get a penny. I'll see to that!"

"We are going out west, Mother, with or without your blessing. It's as simple as that."

Harriet's dark gaze rested on Elinor. "This is your doing, isn't it? You have filled his head with all of this nonsense. Well, we will see, we will see!" Harriet Langford left the room, slamming the door behind her.

Elinor shuddered. Though she was happy Nicholas had finally stood up to his mother, there was something very chilling about Harriet's words and expression. The woman would stop at nothing to keep her son at Langford Manor.

"You're shaking, darling, are you cold?" Nicholas pulled the sheets up under her chin and held her close. "Don't worry about her. She can't stop us, Elinor."

"I'm not so certain," Elinor whispered as she cuddled against her husband.

Nicholas was very reassuring the next morning before they went down for breakfast. "The month will go by very quickly, you'll see."

"Nicholas," Elinor began, "it will be a very long month indeed now that the fat is in the fire. Perhaps we should consider relocating temporarily. I am sure my parents would love to have us stay with them until we have made the necessary preparations."

"Dearest," a frown creased his brow, "I would prefer to stay here and stand my own ground. However," he sighed, "if Mother makes it unpleasant, we will, of course, make other arrangements. I won't have you subjected to the kind of insults she was hurling last night. But, I know my mother. She is probably very repentant this morning. She sometimes behaves in a totally unacceptable manner, but she always makes up for it."

His smile was indulgent, apologetic.

"Nicholas, your mother was just being herself last night." Dismay was evident in Elinor's voice. "When the two of us are alone, she always speaks that way to me. I never wanted to tell you about it but I feel I can no longer keep it to myself."

Nicholas recoiled as though she had slapped him. He turned and looked out the window. "I know how Mother can be. She means well for the most part. She is just too overprotective of me."

"How can you say that?" Fury blazed in Elinor's eyes. "She calls me a fallen woman and you say she is merely being overprotective?"

Nicholas went to Elinor and took her in his arms. "You are right, darling. It's just hard to accept. I do have some good memories of her from my childhood. She wasn't always so unreasonable." He sighed, "But she has made it impossible for us to remain here. Perhaps we should take a house in Charleston. I could remain in the family business. We don't have to leave the state to get away from my mother's interference. How would that suit you?"

Feeling as though she had been hit by a lightening bolt, she stiffened in his arms. She knew she had to get Nicholas completely away from his family's influence. It wouldn't be enough to just change residences. As long as he worked for his father, the Langfords would control Nicholas' life.

"It would not suit me, Nicholas. You promised me we would go out west. It is a promise I intend to hold you to." Elinor knew she had to take this unbending stance even though it went against the love she had for her husband. It was for the salvation of that love that she had to stand firm.

"Very well," he said, looking into her eyes, "I will keep my word. We will leave within the month and if Mother can't treat you with respect, we will stay elsewhere until our plans are complete."

Elinor had not taken Nicholas' predictions seriously so she was unprepared for the reception awaiting her at breakfast. Tobias smiled slightly and nodded his head when Elinor entered the dining room. Geneva said good morning without her usual sarcastic edge. Harriet Langford provided the greatest surprise of all.

"Nicholas, Elinor," she gushed, "my dears, I could not sleep a wink last night. I know I behaved dreadfully. Can you ever forgive me?" She swept over to them, her black skirts rustling like the beating wings of a flock of birds.

Standing between them, she slipped a cold, claw-like hand into Elinor's. "My dear daughter-in-law, you are very welcome in this house. We look upon you as a daughter, don't we Tobias?" She looked at her husband who had already sat down and was helping himself to a hot biscuit.

He lifted an eyebrow and started to say something but must have thought better of it. He only nodded his head and concentrated on his plate.

Elinor glanced at Nicholas and saw how relieved he looked. He winked at her as if to say, see, I told you so. Elinor's heart sank. In spite of Nicholas' promise to leave West Virginia, she knew his mother had a bag full of tricks and Harriet Langford would use every one of them to keep her son with her.

Harriet turned her dazzling smile on Elinor. "Dear, you will forgive your repentant mother-in-law, will you not?"

Her honeyed voice belied the coldness in her gaze. "I suppose I have forgotten what it's like to be young and in love." Smoothing her tightly wound knot of hair, Harriet threw a stony glance at Tobias, who ignored her and continued buttering his biscuit.

Returning her attention back to Elinor she said, "We both love Nicholas. Surely we can come to some sort of understanding. Nicholas' future is here with our family holdings. If he stays it will all be his someday and yours too since you are his wife. It is the birthright of your children. Surely you would not want to rob them of their inheritance any more than you would want to rob Nicholas of his."

All eyes were on Elinor. Harriet Langford's gaze was smug. Tobias looked at Elinor with a mixture of boredom and amusement. A smirk played at the corners of his mouth. Nicholas' gaze carried hope and love. He had clearly been impressed by his mother's contrite display.

"Well, dearest, what do you say?" Nicholas smiled, apparently thinking the crisis had passed. "Mother is asking our forgiveness."

Elinor looked into Nicholas' eyes in a silent plea for understanding and support. Then she looked at Harriet Langford. In a clear, steady voice, she said, "No, Mother Langford, I do not forgive you. Nicholas is not for sale and neither am I."

Chapter Eighteen

Disappointment clouded Nicholas' face and Elinor's heart broke for having put it there. She expected a sharp retort from Harriet Langford, but was once again surprised by the older woman.

"Perhaps in time, dear. I know I have offended you, but I am sure you would not disobey the Good Book. It speaks of forgiveness and turning the other cheek."

Elinor's skin crawled when Harriet patted her on the arm. "I think putting distance between us would be the best remedy, Mother Langford. That is why we are moving to the West Coast."

Harriet Langford looked at Nicholas. "Son, surely you do not mean to go through with this?"

"We are leaving in a month, Mother."

Relief washed over Elinor like a wave of cleansing water. She had seen him wavering, but he had not caved in.

Suddenly, Tobias Langford pushed his plate aside and stood up. "Nicholas, do you know what you are doing? If you leave, you'll not get a penny from me."

"I don't need your money, Father, I have my own. We will make it just fine without your help."

"Very well, as you wish. I have others who can take your place and share in the wealth. Just don't come crawling back in a year or two saying you have reconsidered. Once you close the door, it stays closed!"

Nicholas' eyes blazed with anger. "There's no danger of that, Father. I am quite capable of making my own way. In fact, I could arrange to take my leave today."

"Tobias!" Harriet shrieked, "you can't just let him go like that. He belongs here with us."

Tobias' weary gaze rested on his wife and it was apparent to Elinor that any love he might have had for Harriet had died long ago. "Harriet, he is a grown man—we can hardly stop him. It's his decision and he will have to live with it. But of course, he is welcome to stay here until his plans are finalized."

He turned to Nicholas. "There's no need to go charging out of here today. We can accommodate you until you are ready to leave."

Seeing she was getting nowhere with her husband, Harriet pulled a handkerchief from her pocket and dabbed at her eyes. "Son, please reconsider." She clutched her chest and grimaced. "I don't know how much longer I'll be on this earth. Surely you would not deny me the pleasure of my grandchildren in the time I have left?"

Heaving an impatient sigh, Tobias rolled his eyes and stalked out of the room.

Nicholas' expression softened. He put his arm around Harriet and said, "Mother, it's not good for you to become so upset. Come, let's have some breakfast. We will talk later."

He guided his mother to a chair while Elinor watched in dismay at the way her husband had been manipulated by the woman who had brought him into the world.

Nicholas went to the office right after breakfast so there was no chance to talk. What could Elinor have said anyway? She busied herself the rest of the morning by making a list of things to do in preparation for the westward move. When lunch time came, she avoided Harriet Langford and ate in the kitchen.

After lunch, Elinor went for a walk by the river. The sun beat down overhead and there wasn't ever a hint of a breeze. She unbuttoned the top of her blouse and removed her shoes and stockings. She loved wading at the water's edge. In fact, she was tempted to jump in the water fully clothed.

Looking across the river, Elinor gazed at the Foster house. It was only a short distance away, yet, it was in a different world. There she had lived in an atmosphere of love and acceptance. Though her parents liked Nicholas, they had warned that life at Langford Manor might be difficult for free-spirited Elinor. They had also suggested that she at least consider a longer engagement. A delicious shiver washed over Elinor. She could not have waited another minute to belong completely to her Nicholas.

Elinor glanced at the boat and thought momentarily of rowing across and visiting her mother. Nicholas had been upset the last time she had done so. He had asked her not to go alone again and she had agreed to his wishes.

Besides, it was only yesterday that she had seen her mother, wasn't it? She rubbed her forehead. Yesterday's events prior to her boat ride with Nicholas were a confusing blur. She must have told her mother of her plan to ask Nicholas to leave the state. Although she could not remember her mother's reaction, she was sure her parents would support any decision she and Nicholas might make.

Elinor knew she would miss them and her brothers terribly, but she felt she had no choice. She would also miss Celia, her life-long friend. It seemed ages since they had talked. Celia's bubbly personality had always kept Elinor laughing. Now, Celia was engaged and Elinor had been preoccupied at Langford Manor. She would be sure to see Celia before she and Nicholas left the state.

Elinor sat down on a wooden bench and gazed at the gentle lappings of the winding, green river. Until recently, she had been happy. Even her in-laws' cold reception had not dampened her enthusiasm. Now, everything had changed except her love for Nicholas. Something from deep within was urging her to leave Langford Manor. She could feel the unspoken threat in the air she breathed and in the creaks and settlings of the old house. They all whispered, "Leave, leave."

A gust of wind joined the chorus as dark clouds appeared

overhead, suggesting some much needed rain. Unlike anything she had ever seen, a thick fog rolled in and settled over the river. The wind whistled as it blew down the valley, and the former blue sky was suddenly gray and threatening. Elinor knew she should go in, but the breeze felt so good, she could not bear the thought of retreating inside the stuffy house. Pulling the pins from her hair, she let the breeze ruffle the long tawny strands. She stretched her arms out wide as if to embrace the wind and sky.

As she gazed across the river, the thick fog began to thin and what she saw on the other side made her knees grow weak. Her parents' home was there, but was it their home? She shaded her eyes for a better look. The varnished wood exterior had been replaced with yellow paint and the house seemed not to be as straight and tall as it had been a few moments before.

The eerie fog moved back in before she could study the house and she blinked, telling herself what she had seen must have been a trick of the sunlight. But there was no sun. It was the fog, then. The fog had only thinned, it had not cleared completely. Yes, that must be it. The thick mist had distorted her view of the house and had made it look as though it were painted yellow. How ridiculous, she thought, but somehow, she could not laugh. A cold shiver went up her back. Something was wrong, she could feel it. She did not understand it, but she knew it was there, suspended, waiting.

It was much like the dark mist that hung over the river, ominous, threatening and vague without clearly defined borders. She sensed that she was being propelled toward a precipice and that the only way to avoid the calamity that awaited was to go far away and never look back.

She felt a sudden urge to get in the boat and row across the river. She wanted to see her mother, and her friend, Celia. She had promised Nicholas, yet the desire was so strong. But the fog—she knew it could be dangerous.

As she stood up and walked toward the boat that was

being rocked and buffeting by the wind gusts, someone called her name. She turned around and saw Nicholas coming to meet her.

"Elinor, what are you doing out here? There is a storm brewing. You had better come inside."

"Not yet, Nicholas. You know how I love storms. I'll come inside before the rain starts."

Stopping in front of her, he reached over and brushed a strand of hair away from her cheek. "Are you still upset about last night?"

Going into his arms, then, she nuzzled against him, feeling the soothing warmth of his body. Her nose delighted in his familiar scent of sandalwood mingled with lye soap.

"Nicholas, truth known, I've been upset since I moved to this house. You have been wonderful and I love you with all of my heart. It is just that lately I have had this feeling of impending doom that I cannot shake. That's one of the reasons I want to leave. Every fiber of my being tells me that we are not safe here, that we must go far away and make a life for ourselves."

"Dearest, we are going to go. As I told you before, when I was a boy, I dreamed of going to California. It is time I struck out on my own. But as far as it not being safe here, don't you think you are being a bit fanciful? Have I married a soothsayer?" His teasing tone did not soften the impact of his words.

"I can't explain it, Nicholas, but I take it seriously. It is as though someone is trying to tell me something."

"I am trying to tell you something, dearest. I am telling you that I love you and that we are going to California to start a new life. Doesn't that make you happy?"

Elinor turned to him and smiled. "You have made me very happy. We will have a wonderful life together and God willing, we'll have lots and lots of little Langfords."

Nicholas kissed her sweetly on the lips and then held her to him as the breeze teased and swirled around them "Are you ready to go inside now?" he asked.

"May we stay a little longer? It's not raining yet."

Nicholas didn't answer. He gazed across the river at the area where the thick fog crouched like a large gray cat. "That certainly is odd. How long has it been there?"

"Just the last few minutes." Elinor hesitated for a moment. She started to tell him about the strange vision she had seen, but thought better of it.

Suddenly the mist thinned and Nicholas gasped. "Would you look at that! How could your parents' house have changed so in one day? The entire property looks different."

Elinor straightened and looked across the river at the yellow house she had seen earlier. There was no fog now and the sun had even come out from behind a cloud.

"Nicholas, that's not my parents' house. It can't be. We were just there yesterday. They couldn't have changed it that quickly. Yet it is standing where their house stands."

"I don't understand what is happening, Elinor. This doesn't make sense." His eyes scanned the opposite shore looking for his in-laws' home. Once again his gaze rested on the large, yellow house and then at something in the yard.

"Look, Elinor, standing at the back of the property. Who is that woman? Is she a relative of yours? Look how she's dressed! Her skirt is so short, half her leg is showing."

Elinor stared at the woman across the river. Her hair was like Elinor's own in color and length. It, too, was blowing in the breeze. Elinor could not see her face clearly and, like Nicholas, she noted the woman's short skirt.

She watched the young lady go and sit in the swing that Elinor's father had made. The woman pushed back with her feet and then lifted them. She dipped and soared and held her head back so that her long, sun-kissed hair touched the ground.

Elinor stood mesmerized watching each back and forth motion. "Oh, merciful Jesus," she whispered, "I think it's me. I don't know how it could be, but somehow that woman is me!"

Chapter Nineteen

Elinor watched. Finally, the young woman stopped swinging and stood up. She seemed to be as intrigued with them as they were with her.

"She looks like me, Nicholas," Elinor said, "though her clothes are different, she could have been me when I lived there. But how could that be?"

Nicholas stared across the river. "Yes, she is like you."

Suddenly the fog returned, blotting out the house and the young woman. Nicholas and Elinor stood and stared for another five minutes, still disbelieving what they had seen. As suddenly as it had settled in, the fog vanished again, revealing Elinor's childhood home.

Nicholas looked at his wife. "Dearest, are we dreaming? We both saw the woman, and the painted house, did we not?"

Elinor nodded. "Yes, very clearly, but I still can't believe it, nor will anyone else. We must keep this to ourselves. It is some sort of omen."

Nicholas pulled her close. "I don't understand any of this, but I think the sooner we leave this place the better. There is no need for us to wait a month. I will rush to wrap up my affairs. We could be ready to leave right after the Fourth of July festivities. In fact, that would be a nice send-off, almost like a going-away party."

"Oh yes, Nicholas, that would be wonderful and it's only two weeks away! I can pack and say all my good-byes by then. I'll admit I have been looking forward to wearing my new ball gown, especially after missing the ball last year. As you say, it will be like a going-away party." Elinor's voice grew serious, "Will we tell your parents right away?"

"I don't think my father cares now that he knows we are going. As for Mother—let's go tell her now."

"Nicholas," Elinor held him back for a moment, "you know she will say or do anything to stop us, don't you?"

"I know she will try to talk us out of it, but she can't. So, stop worrying." He gave Elinor a reassuring squeeze.

Elinor's step was a little lighter as she walked toward the house. She couldn't resist one last peek over her shoulder. Her parents' home was there where it belonged. She suppressed a shiver as the memory of the golden-haired girl flashed once again in her mind's eye.

Elinor carried her shoes and stockings in her hand and allowed her windblown hair to hang freely as she and Nicholas sought out his mother. Harriet Langford was in the parlor doing needlepoint. Elinor knew her state of disarray would annoy her mother-in-law, but she didn't care.

The look on the older woman's face told Elinor that she had hit her mark. Harriet's eyes narrowed and the corners of her mouth turned down as she tightened her lips. She wanted to chastise her daughter-in-law, but she dared not and Elinor knew it. It felt good to have the upper hand for once. Elinor had never been one to be spiteful or gloat but she couldn't help but smile and flaunt the small victory over this woman who hated her so.

"I see you have been walking on the beach." Harriet Langford made it sound like an accusation. "In my day—" She stopped short, apparently realizing that Nicholas was watching her. Forcing a smile she said, "Well, my dears, what is it you wish to speak to me about? Have you come to tell me you are staying after all?"

"Not at all, Mother. In fact, we don't like long good-byes. We will be leaving right after the Fourth of July celebration."

Mother Langford gasped and dropped her needlepoint. "That's so soon! I thought we were going to talk about this further before any decisions were made."

Elinor and I have talked about it, Mother," Nicholas said, a new confidence in his voice.

"I see." Harriet stood up, walked over to the window and gazed outside. "Will I ever see you again?"

"Of course, Mother. We will visit from time to time. We would not think of depriving you of knowing your grandchildren."

I would if I could, Elinor thought. She knew that Nicholas would not see it that way. She would have to settle for infrequent visits. A pang of conscience hit her. Perhaps Harriet Langford would be a much better grandmother than she was a mother-in-law. There were also Elinor's parents to be considered. They already had three grandchildren from Elinor's brothers. Her mother and father doted on the little ones.

"It's not very much time, but perhaps it will be enough." Harriet Langford turned around to face Elinor. "We do have some fence-mending to do, don't we dear?" The forced smile on the older woman's face accentuated the lines in her sallow skin.

Seeing the hopeful look in Nicholas' eyes, Elinor said, "Yes, Mother Langford, I suppose we do."

To Elinor's surprise, dinner was pleasant. She figured Harriet Langford would be on the offensive, but instead, she was gracious. Elinor wished she could trust her. It would be wonderful if she and Nicholas could leave the Langfords on a peaceful note. Even Tobias refrained from his usual sarcasm.

After dinner, the rain that had been threatening all afternoon finally came down in torrents. Elinor longed to throw the windows open and allow the breeze to cool off the humid house. But Mother Langford had insisted that all the windows be closed. Elinor would have escaped upstairs to her room but was detained by the family's unusual insistence that she play the piano for them.

Nicholas was clearly pleased that his family was eager to have his wife display her creative talents. Elinor knew the others were not sincere but Nicholas' eyes shone with pride when she took her place at the piano. She would play for him as she frequently did when the two of them were alone in the parlor.

She began with a rousing rendition of *Oh Dem Golden Slippers*. Nicholas grinned and winked at her. It was a private joke between them. He would sometimes sing a few bars of the bawdy song when Elinor kicked off her shoes and went barefooted. Even Tobias seemed faintly amused by the jaunty tune. Mother Langford registered her disapproval by raising an eyebrow and sticking out her lower lip.

Figuring she had tortured her mother-in-law long enough, Elinor changed to Chopin's lilting and wistful *Fantasie Impromtu*. The music calmed and soothed away her cares. Her last piece was Beethoven's *Moonlight Sonata*. It was her and Nicholas' favorite. Nicholas' eyes filled with pride and desire as he looked at Elinor. She could almost feel his heart beating as one with her own as their spirits soared to the hauntingly beautiful music.

The moment passed when Elinor glimpsed Harriet Langford looking at her in an unguarded moment. *Too bad Nicholas doesn't see you now,* Elinor thought. *Then he would see how much you really hate me.*

Clearly, Harriet was not going to give up without a fight. Her words and gestures had been for Nicholas' benefit and only served to hide her true feelings and motives.

At last, Elinor and Nicholas climbed the stairs to the privacy of their own room. Once inside, Elinor went to the the window and opened them. Mother Langford insisted that rain would come in on the rug and cause mildew and rot, but Elinor didn't care.

The wet drops sprayed against Elinor's face and shoulders as she slipped out of her dress. In a gesture of defiance, she tossed it on the floor not caring if it rained on her clothes, the floor or the furniture. She then peeled off her undergarments until she stood nude before the windows.

"It's a good thing I have not lighted the candle," Nicholas said as he came and stood behind her. "Otherwise, the people across the river would be getting a rare treat indeed."

He slipped his arms about her and cupped his hands over her breasts. Feeling his nakedness against her, she realized that he, too, had undressed. They stood for a few minutes peering out at the darkness. The water spray beaded on Elnior's skin, bringing blessed relief from the heat and with it a feeling of complete freedom.

"Are you cold, dearest?" Nicholas asked.

"Not at all, darling. This is wonderful. I couldn't wait to get up here and open the windows."

"Me, too, but I loved your music. I could hardly sit in the parlor and watch you without taking you into my arms. There is such passion in your playing."

"There was not so much passion until I met you, my love."

Nicholas' hands slipped from Elinor's breasts to her waist as he pulled her even tighter against him. "If we could see through the darkness and rain, I wonder what we would see across the river."

Elinor shivered at the memory though instinctively, she felt a kinship with the strange lady.

"Are you thinking about the woman we saw earlier?" Nicholas asked.

"Yes, how did you know?"

"I was thinking about her too. I still don't know how to explain it. I am sure the locals would say we are bewitched."

Elinor turned around and kissed her husband, "I don't care about the locals or strange ladies who wear short skirts. I only care about my husband and the feel of his body next to mine."

Nicholas laughed as he picked her up and carried her to the bed. Then, he went over to the door and put a chair under the handle. "We'll have no repeat performances of last night, at least not where my mother is concerned." Silently, he crossed the room. Pulling back the crisp sheets, he crawled in beside Elinor.

She went into his arms with the reckless abandon of the thunderstorm that pounded and flashed outside. Her hands explored his body as she tasted the sweetness of his lips. She delighted in the familiarity of his own special scent.

He in turn stroked and soothed her until she slid above him and they joined together as the thunder and lightening raged and flashed outside the open windows.

Nicholas had already left for the mining offices when Elior awoke at eight o'clock the next morning. She was sure her mother-in-law would have some remark about sloth being one of the deadly sins. She wouldn't be surprised if Harriet hadn't already had the breakfast food removed from the dining area.

Surprisingly, the eggs, ham and biscuits, along with assorted jellies and fruit, were still on the sideboard. Harriet was also there, lingering over a cup of black coffee.

"Good morning, dear," the older woman purred. She started to drum her talon-like fingernails on the table, but stopped herself.

So, she is going to try the nice approach, Elinor thought as she sat down with her food.

"Elinor," Harriet began as her daughter-in-law took a bite of scrambled egg, "you don't like me, do you?"

Elinor almost choked on her eggs. "Mother Langford, I wanted us to be close when I came here to live. I tried to be a good daughter-in-law, but you would have none of it. You insulted me and my family at every turn. You have made it impossible for me to feel any fondness for you."

"Well, this is the thanks I get for trying to be nice to you!"

"Look, Mother Langford, you can drop the pretense. Nicholas isn't here. We both know that you hated me before we even met."

Angry blotches of color mottled Harriet Langford's neck and crept up to her cheeks. "Yes, I did hate you and I always will! You are much too common for my son. He could have married an heiress from one of the old families of

Charleston, but you beguiled him by displaying you body in various states of undress. I saw him watching you across the river as you teased and taunted him until he could stand it no longer. Yes, my dear, you are common and you will always be common. You cannot make a silk purse out of a sow's ear!"

The satisfaction was apparent on the older woman's face as she pulled herself up, trying to display a dignity that she did not possess. Her tight lips contorted into a sour smile, having at last said what she must have been dying to say for months.

"Common, Mother Langford? I'll match my pedigree against yours anyday. But then, that's all a bunch of nonsense. I'll not try to deprive you of your misconceptions since you seem to take such pleasure in them. Just remember, Nicholas is my husband. He's no longer your little boy. My husband and I will be leaving soon and there's nothing you can do about it!"

Even as she heard herself utter the words, Elinor felt a shiver of apprehension. She did not underestimate the lengths to which this woman would go to hold on to what she perceived as being hers.

"Since we are speaking freely," Harriet said in a tight voice, "let me remind you that I still have two weeks. A great deal can happen in two weeks. You would do well to remember that."

Elinor stood up, leaving most of her food on her plate, and said, "I have suddenly lost my appetite."

She left the room feeling slightly nauseated, and went outside to sit by the river. The ham had tasted sour and she couldn't finish it. Perhaps it had more to do with the company. At least the battle lines were drawn now. There was no longer any pretense between the two women. She would have to be careful. Harriet Langford reminded her of a cornered rat eyeing a piece of cheese.

Elinor decided to keep her mother-in-law's threats to herself. If she told Nicholas and he confronted his mother,

Harriet would deny it or wheedle her way out of the situation by claiming that she had misunderstood her.

Elinor removed her shoes and socks before walking down to the waterfront. It was a pleasant morning, much less humid after the thunderstorms of the previous day. She sat on the wooden bench and gazed at the smooth surface of the placid river. Her thoughts kept returning to the unpleasant conversation she had just had with her mother-in-law.

It was ironic that Harriet Langford thought Elinor was not good enough for Nicholas. Harriet seemed to have some lofty notion about the Langfords being the cream of society. Nothing could have been further from the truth, at least not in the eyes of the townspeople. The old money class in Charleston considered Tobias Langford to be remote, vulgar and ruthless. However, he did own several coal mines, so he was a moneyed interest with whom to be reckoned. He had built Langford Manor on the far side of the river, away from the city, with no near neighbors. This suited Charleston's upper class just fine, but it only added to the family's reputation for being odd. The Langfords were dealt with but they were not liked or respected.

Unfortunately, Nicholas was judged by his family name and the fact that he worked for his father's companies. Few bothered to get to know him and he was not the type to press the issue. He was very passionate about Elinor and about his work, but he didn't seem to need society's approval.

Elinor's friends had warned her not to marry him. They said she would rue the day she went to live at Langford Manor and they had been right about that part of it. But they had been wrong about Nicholas. Elinor loved him now more than ever. Away from his family and the shadow of Langford Manor, he would learn to smile more easily and live life more fully.

Elinor's lips curled into a smile as she remember her friend Celia's wide-eyed warning. "There are those who say that Harriet Langford is a witch, Elinor. You dare not live under the same roof with her!"

If Elinor believed in witches as many of the superstitious mountain folk did, she would have had no trouble seeing Harriet Langford as one.

When Elinor's gaze traveled across the river, she saw someone waving at her from her parent's backyard. She shielded her eyes and recognized the diminutive figure of her best friend, Celia. She motioned for Elinor to row across.

Elinor though about her promise to Nicholas, but it had been a long time since she had seen her friend. Nicholas was going to be so busy he might not get an opportunity to take her to see Celia.

Elinor stood up and waved back. She went to where the boat was moored and untied it. Pushing the boat into deeper water, she waded after it, soaking her skirts in the process. There would be dry clothes for her to change into once she got to her mother's house. She looked over her shoulder at Langford Manor. Perhaps she should leave a note for Nicholas. But then, she would probably be back before he got home. Besides, her dripping skirts would not be welcome on Mother Langford's rug.

A great sense of freedom washed over Elinor as she rowed away from shore. There was only a slight breeze on the water and it teased and kissed her face. Just as she thought about how perfect the weather was, it suddenly changed. A thick blanket of fog settled around her, blocking out the sunshine.

She tried to quell the rising panic as she was reminded of the fog she and Nicholas had seen on the river yesterday. She tried to keep her sense of direction as she continued rowing in what she hoped was a straight line.

"Be calm," she told herself, "there's nothing to be afraid of." Celia would be waiting on the other side, her dear, funny friend. What if it wasn't Celia? What if the house was painted yellow and that strange woman with the short dress was there swinging in Elinor's childhood swing?

There was no turning back now. Elinor steeled herself for whatever lay ahead as the fog thinned and the rays of the brilliant sun temporarily blinded her view of the shore.

Chapter Twenty

Emily squinted her eyes in the bright sunlight as she guided the boat towards land. What had ever possessed her to take a boat ride today? She hadn't rowed in years.

She could see Becky standing on the shore waving madly, motioning for her to hurry. Becky's fiery curls bounced as she paced back and forth.

Emily's shoulders felt taut and sore as she rowed the final strokes before hitting shallow water. Stepping out of the craft, she nearly lost her balance on the slippery rocks. Righting herself, she grabbed the rope to the moorings and tied the craft securely before wading to shore.

"Emily Foster, where have you been?" Becky put her hands on her hips and eyed Emily as her friend stepped onto dry land. "I have been calling you for the last two days and you haven't been answering your phone. Now I come here and find you out in a boat that probably hasn't been used in ages. I'll bet you didn't have it checked to see if it was sea worthy before taking it out, did you?"

"You're right, Beck, I didn't." At least she didn't think she had. "What do you mean you have been trying to reach me for two days? We just had dinner last night at that new Italian restaurant, didn't we?"

Becky's face paled. "Em! What's the matter with you? That was two nights ago, not last night!"

"Really?" Emily frowned. "But I—" She stopped and rubbed her forehead. What did she remember of the last two days—or of today for that matter?

"Em, what is it, what's wrong?" Becky's voice was gentle as she put her arm around her friend and guided her to the house. Inside, she made Emily sit down at the kitchen table while she made her cup of tea. Becky rummaged around in the cupboards and came up with a can of tuna. She made tuna salad sandwiches for both of them and joined Emily at the table.

"I ran over on my lunch hour to see you, so I sort of invited myself to lunch. Anyway, Em, here, eat. You look like you have lost weight and you didn't need to. While you are eating you can tell me what's troubling you."

"Yes, Mother Hen," Emily said, forcing a smile as she bit into her sandwich. "This does taste good, Beck. Maybe I'm just tired of my own cooking. You always did make a mean tuna sandwich."

Becky rolled her eyes. "You're not going to get off the hook by flattering me, Em. It's time to 'fess up."

"If I understood it myself, I would tell you," Emily replied.

"Then tell me what it is you don't understand." A look of recognition came over Becky's face. "Say, does this have anything to do with that Langford business?"

"Now why would you say that, Beck?"

"Because I know you, that's why."

Emily could no longer put her best friend off. She hadn't wanted to worry her, but it was clear that she was already very worried.

"Yes, I think this does have something to do with Langford Manor. But before I go any further, I want you to give me your word that you will be calm and keep an open mind."

"All right, I promise." Becky sounded apprehensive.

Emily told Becky about the time lapses and the strange sensations she had experienced. She went into detail about the handkerchief, the glass of milk that had looked like blood and the confusion about the rice and potatoes. She also told her about the man on the phone who had called her Elinor.

Becky checked her watch. "Hold on, Em, I have to call

the school and see if someone can take my afternoon class. Why I signed up to teach summer school, I'll never know. Anyway, you and I have to talk."

"Now, Beck, you are doing exactly what I didn't want you do. Don't call the school. I'll be fine. You wanted me to tell you and I did."

"All right, I won't call the school but when my class is over I'm coming back here. Will you be okay until then?"

"Of course I will. You promised you wouldn't overreact, remember?"

A look of contrition washed over Becky's face. "I'm sorry, Em, but I would like to come by after school so we can talk more. Is that all right with you?"

That will be fine, Beck. I feel better already just from what I've told you so far."

"You mean there's more?" Becky's eyes grew large.

"Yes, but it can wait until you come back this afternoon."

After Becky left, Emily went to her room and changed into a shirt and jeans and slipped on her socks and loafers. There was a chill in the air again today, unusual weather for late June. She asked herself why she had worn a skirt and gone shoeless earlier. The obvious answer was that she would likely have gotten her shoes and jean bottoms wet getting in and out of the boat.

Emily went into the living room, sat down at the old piano and flipped open the lid. She thought back to the piano lessons she had as a girl. Grams had provided her with dancing lessons, too. That had proved valuable to Emily when she was auditioning for parts in plays. But Emily never played the piano except when she came home to visit Grams. Her grandmother had loved the old church hymns and would lean back in her rocking chair and close her eyes as her granddaughter played.

Now Emily put her fingers to the keys and began playing *Amazing Grace* and *How Great Thou Art*. She was surprised at how easily the melody flowed even after all this time. She closed her eyes and marveled at the effortless way her fingers ran over the keys. It was as though she had been practicing every day.

She launched into the classic, *Fantasie Impromptu*, giving herself over to the sense of abandon that seemed to accompany the music. She followed the Chopin piece with her favorite, Tchaikovsky's *Moonlight Sonata*. The hauntingly beautiful stains infused her soul with a wistful longing.

She pictured the handsome Nicholas Langford as he looked in the dream. She was in his arms, swaying to the beautiful melody. Then she was reclining on a boat with velvet cushions to comfort her. He was standing above her looking down with only the starlight and crescent moon to guide the way. "Elinor," he said, "promise you will never leave me."

Thunderstruck, Emily stopped playing and opened her eyes. It wasn't just a dream or fantasy, it had really happened to her, Emily! He had called her Elinor and she had not protested. "No, this is impossible! It just cannot be."

Her longing intensified as she stood up and walked over to the sofa. The breeze coming through the window caused the curtain to billow out. It touched her face and suddenly Emily recalled how she had gone outside and looked at the man across the river, Nicholas Langford. Again, she felt the pressure of his lips, the warmth of his body next to hers.

She leaned back on the sofa and closed her eyes trying to force a memory that was just beyond her reach. She thought of the music she had played and she could again feel herself swaying to its lilting melody. She saw blue—yards and yards of sapphire blue satin, swishing and twirling as it clung to her body. A lovely blue gown made just for her.

"Blue satin!" she said, springing up from the sofa. She ran downstairs to the clothes hamper in the basement and searched until she found the blue jeans she had worn the other day, though to her it had only been yesterday.

"Yes!" she cried, as she took them from the hamper. She plunged her hand into the pocket. Her fingers recognized the silky scrap of material even before she pulled it out. It was blue satin.

"From my ball gown, from Elinor's ball gown."

She held the scrap in her hand, rubbing it with her fingers as if by doing so she would learn all of its secrets. Then she held it to her nose and sniffed the distinct lilac perfume, the same scent that lingered on the lace handkerchief that had belonged to Elinor Foster.

Someone had made Elinor a dress out of this material, only she, Emily, had also been there. She had tried the dress on and had taken a scrap of the material.

Later, when Becky returned, Emily held the piece of cloth out for inspection. "Remember when I started to show you this last night, or that is, the other evening?"

"I can't say that I do, Em. Why? Is it important?"

Emily didn't answer. Instead, she asked, "Beck, do you believe time travel is possible?"

"You promised you would keep an open mind, Beck. So just answer the question."

"I've never thought so in the past, but I have heard Fred mention it a few times. In his line of work I guess it is natural to be open to such things."

"Beck, I think I have somehow stepped back in time. That would account for the time lapses. It would explain a lot, in fact. But I wasn't me. I was someone else."

Becky rolled her eyes. "I know I'm going to regret this. Who were you, Em, if you were not yourself?"

"I think I was Elinor Langford."

"Why am I not surprised? You've always had this obsession with Nicholas Langford and his beloved Elinor."

"Becky, I need you to be understanding about this, not sarcastic. If you can't be, then I have nothing further to say to you on the subject."

Becky flinched at her friend's unusually sharp tone. "I'm sorry, Em. You're right. We need to talk this out. Obviously you believe what you just told me. Do you want me to tell you what I think?"

"Now, I am the one who is going to be sorry for asking. Okay, tell me what you think."

Becky took a deep breath and exhaled. "All right. Now keep in mind I am just suggesting this as a possibility. I am also not rejecting your theory outright. But, Em, isn't it possible that the strain you have been under is getting to you? You don't look as though you are sleeping. You have dark circles under your eyes and I know you are not eating. Honey, your system is overloading and I think these strange happenings are merely symptoms."

Emily sat back in her chair and fell silent for a moment. "So, you think I'm cracking up, is that it?" she finally said.

"I didn't say that. I just think you need to see a doctor. He can give you something to make you feel better and get you through this bad time."

"Are you saying that I need to see a shrink?" Emily couldn't hold back the disappointment in her voice. She had hoped that Becky would understand what she was going through.

"No, Em, I am just suggesting you see Dr. Wilson, that's all. It can't hurt and it might help. Let me call and see if he can see you this evening. I'll go with you."

"No! If my best friend doesn't believe me, the doctor is sure to think I'm looney."

"Look, you only tell him what you feel comfortable telling him. You have certainly had enough to make you depressed. It's not unusual to go through such periods when you've lost a loved one. Dr. Wilson will understand that. If he can't help, then you and I will sit down and we will examine this time travel thing more thoroughly. Won't you at least try? It's not like he's a stranger. Dr. Wilson's been taking care of both of our families for years. Please, let me call him."

Emily sighed, "All right, go ahead and make the call."

Two hours later they left Dr. Wilson's office. He had listened to Emily tell him about her lack of appetite and her sleeplessness. She said nothing about the time lapses and odd flashes of memory. He prescribed a mild sleeping pill, a multi-vitamin and he gave her a B-12 shot.

When the Lilacs Bloom

It was Friday and Becky insisted on spending the night in the guest room so she could watch over Emily. Emily doubted the sedative would make any difference, but it was worth a try. A good night's sleep couldn't hurt, so she took one of the pills.

For the first time in many days, Emily slept very well. She awoke to the aroma of coffee perking and bacon sizzling in the kitchen. For a moment she thought she was home and Grams was cooking breakfast, but then she remembered that Grams had passed away.

"I'll bet Becky is making one of her famous breakfasts," she thought, arising from the bed. Emily stepped into the shower and reveled in the cleansing beads of water beating against her skin. It felt like clean, rejuvenating rain, after a long humid day.

She slipped into jeans and a sunny yellow shirt and headed downstairs, realizing that for the first time in days, she was very hungry. Was Becky right after all? Was lack of sleep the main culprit behind the weird feelings she'd been experiencing?

All the shadowy thoughts vanished when she strolled into the kitchen.

"There she is," Becky exclaimed, "now you sit down in the place of honor and get ready to be pampered—and to add a few pounds, too."

Emily smiled at her friend who had obviously gone to great lengths to make her feel better. "What about your diet, Beck?"

"You let me worry about that, you just feast your eyes on this." Becky set a plate before Emily piled high with eggs, hash brown potatoes, bacon and homemade biscuits and jam. Next to it was freshly squeezed orange juice, a steaming cup of black coffee and a vitamin pill.

"You look better already, Em."

"I feel much better, Beck, but I don't think I can eat all of this."

Becky sat down before a plate that was equal to Emily's.

"If you don't want to make me look like a pig, you will try to at least eat some of it."

Laughing, they dug into the delicious food.

After breakfast, Emily waved off Becky's protest and helped clear the table. "Maybe you were right about everything, Beck. I feel so much better today. I suppose the mind can play tricks on you when you are run down."

Becky squealed and gave Emily a big hug. "You are going to be fine, Em. I'm going to see to it. For openers, I'm staying here the rest of the weekend."

Emily washed the dishes and Becky dried them. "Maybe we can do something today, Beck," she said, "like go to the park or have a picnic."

"Sure, a picnic sounds great, and we could take in an Alley Cat's baseball game later. Fred and I talked about going. The game doesn't start until four o'clock, so we'll have plenty of time. The Alley Cats are doing great this year. They're first in their division."

"Sounds like fun," Emily said, looking up from the sudsy water. She glanced out of the window above the sink. Today, there was only sunshine and chirping birds. "I'm going to be all right, Beck. I can feel it in my bones!"

"I know you will be. I'm going to keep you busy! The Fourth of July falls on a Thursday this year, so I have a four day week-end off and we will make the most of it. "Omigosh!" Becky said, smacking her forehead with the heel of her palm, "I almost forgot the reason I came here in the first place yesterday. I am going to fix you up with a friend of Fred's."

"I don't think so, Beck, I'm not ready to get involved with anyone."

"Who's talking involved? I am merely talking a date. Actually, he hasn't arrived in town yet, so I haven't met him. He'll be joining the faculty at Kanawha State University as a professor of Anthropology. He and Fred were fraternity brothers at USC."

"I don't know, Beck. I haven't had too much luck with blind dates."

"Come on, Em. His name is Travis Whittaker and I hear he is handsome, so we don't have to worry about him being a dog, at least not in the looks department. Anyway, you would be doing Fred a big favor. Travis will be arriving at the end of June. Since the Fourth of July Festival and Ball are among our oldest traditions, Fred thought the four of us could take in the festivities together. It will be a good way for Professor Whittaker to get aquainted with the area.

Emily felt a sudden chill at the mention of the ball. It was on that evening one hundred years ago that Langford Manor had burned and Nicholas and Elinor died. She knew she must not dwell on such thoughts. She must push them from her mind and stop living in the past.

"All right, Beck, I wouldn't want to disappoint Fred. Besides, it's two weeks away. A lot can happen in two weeks."

Chapter Twenty-one

Emily and Becky went grocery shopping and afterward prepared a picnic lunch. Arriving at Daniel Boone Park around one o'clock, they found a table near a shady tree by the river. Stealing a glance across the river, Emily noted that the ruins of Langford Manor were not visible from this distance downstream. She was glad. It could not watch her. She chided herself for having such a foolish thought. Yet, she did feel a new sense of freedom.

After eating a generous lunch, Emily reclined in one of the lounge chairs they had brought with them. Warming rays of the sun caressed her skin and the wafting breeze, laden with a floral scent, delighted her senses. "This is wonderful, Beck. Just like old times. Remember when your parents used to bring us here?"

"I remember. I can't believe it was so long ago." Becky stretched out in her own lounge chair.

Suddenly, Emily heard shouting and thumping footsteps followed by a loud, 'whack'. She jumped up and nearly collided with a yellow dog that was intent on retrieving the red frisbee that had hit the back of Emily's chair.

A sandy-haired man in his late twenties jogged toward the dog. "Here, Cap, here boy!" An apologetic grin flashed across his tanned, handsome face.

When he stopped in front of Emily, a look of recognition registered in his hazel eyes and his grin widened. "Emily?"

"Mitch Ames! It's been a long time, but you haven't changed a bit."

Mitch gave her a hug. "I hope Cap didn't scare you.

Actually, it was my fault. He was only chasing after the frisbee that I threw."

"There's no harm done." Emily said.

Becky stood up. "Why don't you join us for awhile? We're just having a little picnic and there's plenty to share. That is if you are alone."

Mitch smiled, "All right! Thanks. There's just me and Cap here. He needed a good run. I moved to a townhouse recently that allows me to have Cap but there's no suitable place for him to get enough exercise."

Cap, the yellow labrador, sat at Emily's feet and allowed her to pat his head.

"I see he's made a new friend." Mitch said.

"I heard you and Jenny split up. I didn't realize you had moved from the house at Burning Springs though." Becky persisted, much to Emily's chagrin.

"Jenny has the house, I have the dog. The divorce was final yesterday. I guess you could say I am celebrating today." He smiled, but Emily sensed his pain.

Even though she and Jeff had not been married, she still identified with the feelings involved. Emily could imagine the little wheels turning in Becky's brain. She flashed her red-headed friend a warning which Becky promptly ignored.

"Mitch," Becky began, a huge grin dimpling her freckled face, "why don't you come with us to Alley Cat's game later. I know you're a baseball fan. Fred will be meeting us at Watt Powell Park. How about it?"

Mitch looked at Emily to see how she felt about the invitation.

"Of course, you are very welcome to join us," she said.

"In that case, I accept."

When Mitch wasn't looking, Emily shot Becky a *"stop your match-making"* look. She and Mitch had been friends in high school and she had no objections to being friends now, but beyond that she really wasn't interested.

Mitch turned out to be good company. He enjoyed the plate of food Becky fixed for him. Emily, in turn, put together some meat and cheese for Cap. She had always loved animals and had had a dog when she was a child. But, it had gotten old and died.

Emily could have killed Becky when she suggested that Mitch and Emily take Cap for a walk along the river while she packed the picnic basket and chairs in the car. They, however, insisted on helping, so she agreed to wait until after their walk before packing up.

"I'm game if you are," Mitch said to Emily, as he extended his hand to help her from her lounge chair.

She accepted. She would deal with Becky later. There was no need to be rude to Mitch. They walked over to the water's edge and Cap took his place beside them. Mitch picked up a stick and threw it ahead. Cap broke into a run to retrieve it.

"I must apologize for Beck," Emily said, when they were out of earshot. "Being a born matchmaker, she can't help but try to shove us together."

Mitch smiled but said nothing as he waited for Cap to bring the stick back to him. He then took it from the dog's mouth and threw it back into the water. Cap jumped in and swam to it and was soon on the way back with the stick.

"I guess Becky was being pretty obvious, wasn't she?"

Mitch said, "I hope it didn't make you too uncomfortable. Personally, I think it's sweet of her."

"Perhaps, but misguided," Emily replied. "Your divorce is just final and I have barely recovered from a long term relationship. Neither of us is ready to be pushed into a new romance, even by a well-meaning friend."

Cap, seeing his master had other things to do besides tossing a stick for him to retrieve, fell into step along side Emily and Mitch.

"We were friends in high school. I see no reason why we can't be friends now, do you?"

"No, I guess I don't, Mitch."

When they reached a large boat ramp, they turned around and headed back.

Mitch had to take Cap home but agreed to meet the two

women at the main gate of the stadium at three forty-five. Emily and Becky decided to take their picnic goods home and freshen up before heading for the ballpark.

"Mitch is really nice and available," Becky said as soon as they got into the car.

"Now look, Beck, this is twice in one day that you have tried to fix me up. This morning you asked me to do Fred a favor and attend the Fourth of July festivities with his friend, Professor What's His Name. Now, when we join Fred, I will be with Mitch."

"Professor Whittaker is not in town yet. Why should you twiddle your thumbs until then? He doesn't own you. You need to get out and mingle. It's not good to stay cooped up in that big house all alone."

Emily sighed, "I appreciate your concern, Beck, but from now on, you've got to stop the matchmaking. You embarrassed me this afternoon. Mitch and I are old friends. You didn't need to push the way you did, Neither Mitch nor I are emotionally ready for someone else in our lives and when we are, I doubt that either of us would choose the other."

"I'm sorry, Em," Becky's freckled face turned crimson. "I guess I was a bit pushy. I'll stop—scout's honor. You're still going to be Professor Whitaker's date for the Fourth of July aren't you?"

"Yes, Beck, I will do that, but I hope you don't expect too much."

Later at the stadium, the two women met Mitch, who was right on time. Fred was another matter. He was late. When he finally arrived, the short, studious archeologist was very apologetic.

Emily picked up on the devotion between Becky and Fred as Becky teased him for his lateness. Emily hoped someday she would know the same kind of love. Suddenly a picture came to mind. It was a vision of Nicholas Langford, and Emily knew that had she lived one hundred years ago, Nicholas would have been the love of her life. What of Elinor?

Emily shivered. If *she* had been Elinor, she would have died in the fire along with Nicholas and their young love would have been unfulfilled. Emily pushed the disturbing thoughts from her mind and concentrated on the baseball game.

The remainder of the afternoon went by pleasantly. Mitch and Fred got along very well. After the game, the four of them went out for pizza.

The next morning, Emily and Becky decided to go to church. Grams had taken Emily to Sunday school and church every week while she was growing up. Emily had gotten out of the habit when she moved away from home.

The congregation at the Benson Community Church gave Emily a warm welcome. Becky was a member and she beamed as she sat next to the local celebrity.

Emily didn't feel at all like one, but she soon realized that was her status when the minister announced her presence and asked her to stand. She wished he hadn't called attention to her. Once it was past, she settled back and enjoyed the choir.

The preacher soon launched into his sermon and Emily was surprised at the subject matter. "If there are soothsayers among us, let them repent!" His eyes blazed with fury as he leveled his gaze at the back corner of the room.

Emily became aware of the congregation turning around and looking behind them, so she did the same.

All eyes were on Mattie Devers, Emily's part-time housekeeper. At first Mattie appeared to shrink in her seat, then a look of defiance came over her and she sat up and looked straight ahead.

The minister's voice boomed, "The devil has a foothold in you, sister. Repent! Give up your evil idolatry. The Lord is forgiving."

Mattie's face drained of color and Emily's heart went out to her. Finally when the old woman had had enough, she stood up and with all the dignity she could muster, she walked out.

Emily sat for a moment with a hollow feeling in the pit of her stomach as the minister continued his harangue. She realized her silence implied approval of his condemnation of the harmless old woman. Emily stood up.

The preacher's jaw dropped and he stopped in mid-sentence as Emily excused herself and made her way from the middle of the pew. Once in the aisle, she ignored the stares and whispers as she walked down the aisle and left the church.

She heard footsteps behind her but did not turn around until she stepped outside into the fresh air and sunshine.

"Imagine the nerve of that man! He's only been here two months and he has already ruined what used to be a fine place to worship." Becky stepped next to Emily.

"I'm sorry, Beck, I know it's your church, but I just couldn't sit still for that kind of witch hunt."

"Correction, Em. *Was* my church. I can't be part of that kind of personal attack either."

They both looked up at the same time and saw Mattie walking down the dusty path. Her shoulders seemed more stooped than usual and from the way they shook, they knew she was crying.

Emily and Becky ran to catch up with her. "Come on, Mattie, we're giving you a ride home." Emily said.

Mattie looked up, surprised. She wiped away the tears from her sallow, wrinkled skin with a wadded up white handkerchief. You young ladies shouldn't miss church on account of me."

"Mattie, what was going on in there was anything but a worship service. We couldn't be a part of it." Emily put her arm around the old woman's waist. "Now, come on. Becky and I are taking you to brunch. Right, Beck?"

"We most certainly are!" Becky patted Mattie's shoulder.

"Oh, I couldn't let you do that, you've done too much already." Mattie looked away. "Every now and then, I take it into my head to go to church. I knew there was a new preacher. I just thought I'd stop by and pay my respects. I know they don't believe in my ways, but none of them ministers ever singled me out like that before. Some of my ways are different but I read the Good Book. Yes, I do. I read it most every day. That's where my power comes from." She pointed a bony finger upward. "Up there," she said.

Her gaze returned to Emily. "Don't you see, you two will be asking for a lot of gossip and trouble if you are seen with me. It's enough, Miss Emily, that you let me work for you."

"Nonsense, Mattie," impatience tinged Emily's voice, "my grandmother was a member of the church and well respected by the community. She was also your friend and never tried to hide it. For me to do any less would dishonor her memory. You are having brunch with us and that is that!"

A crooked smile, revealing several missing teeth, broke across Mattie's face. "Very well, young ladies. Ol' Mattie will never forget your kindness. Maybe someday I can return the favor." Her gaze lingered on Emily.

Emily shivered. Though Grams wasn't superstitious she did say that Mattie had the gift of second sight and that many of the townspeople didn't accept her. As people usually do, they condemned what they did not understand.

The old lady's eyes gleamed when she stood before the delicious buffet at the Riverside Inn. "Well look at all of this, would you. I think I'll have a little dab of everything!"

As they prepared to leave once the meal was over, Mattie took Emily's hand and stroked it with her dried, bony fingers. Then she turned Emily's hand over and looked at her palm.

For the second time that day, Emily say Mattie's face grow pale. She let go of Emily's hand and turned away.

"I have to get home. I have to feed my animals."

"Wait," Emily took Mattie's arm. "What frightened you? What did you see?"

"Now, Miss Emily," Mattie emitted a nervous laugh, "I know you don't put no stock in fortune telling. I was only having fun with you. I didn't see nothin'."

Emily didn't believe her but she let the subject drop.

Besides, Mattie was right, she didn't believe in fortune telling.

Later that afternoon, Emily and Becky rehashed the events of the morning.

"I imagine my celebrity status has been rescinded," Emily joked.

"And I no longer fit the profile of pillar of the community." Becky added. "You know, Em, you are quickly becoming your old self. I was proud to be your friend when you stood up and walked out of the services like that. Why ol' Preacher Roscoe nearly swallowed his upper plate." Becky chuckled. "I don't know if I would have had the courage if you hadn't done it first. Now we will both be pariahs."

"Yeah, think about it, Beck, we took a stand, we made our mark."

"Yeah, think about it, Em," Becky wiggled her eyebrows like Groucho Marx, "we have to live in this town."

Later that evening, Becky headed for home, assured that her friend was well on the road to recovery. Emily had promised that she would take her sleeping sedative that night.

It had been the best weekend Emily had spent in a long time. She was feeling alive again. Two good nights of sleep in a row had done wonders for her. It was true that she had occasionally fallen into thoughts of Langford Manor and Nicholas, but she knew it was only a fantasy. Time travel was an interesting concept, but very unrealistic.

Even as she scoffed at the idea, a feathery chill settled at the tip of her spine and slid up her back causing her to shiver. She wanted to be well, to banish the unhealthy thoughts. Becky was right, all the strange thoughts had probably been due to stress and lack of sleep. Emily was grateful for her friend's intervention. She didn't feel so alone now.

The sun was just setting and Emily felt restless. She tried reading, but could not concentrate. Putting the book aside, she got up and went to the hallway and climbed the stairs. Since there were three bedrooms on the main floor, the upstairs had been closed off for several years.

Once inside the long hallway of the second level, Emily opened a door that led to the attic. After switching on the lights for the attic, she mounted the narrow stairs. She didn't know why she had this sudden urge to explore. She told herself it wasn't exactly a healthy pursuit since the attic storage area was filled with the possessions of long-dead Fosters.

Undaunted, she stepped on the upper landing and looked about. Dress forms, numerous trunks and discarded furniture littered the open space. Along with a myriad of cobwebs, a thick layer of dust had settled onto everything that wasn't covered by a sheet.

A violent fit of sneezing reminded Emily of her allergy to household dust. She needed to set aside a day for cleaning the attic. Even though she didn't use it, the large vaulted ceilings and familiar objects held many good memories of her childhood. The musty place definitely needed to be cleaned and aired out. Perhaps she'd have Mattie Devers help her. Mattie could likely use the extra money.

Emily walked over to the small casement windows and opened the one with a screen on it. From her vantage point, she could look straight across the river at Langford Manor. The gathering shadows of night made it impossible to make out much detail. She could see the manor's dark form against the backdrop of the encroaching mountains. As she gazed at the forlorn scene, she noticed a light on the other side of the river. It bobbed up and down as though someone were walking with it along the shore. Who would be in that deserted place at this time of evening?

A numbing chill washed over her as she watched. She recalled her visit to the ruins when the sun was shining. Terror, perhaps brought on by her overactive imagination, had driven her from the place. She couldn't fathom being there at nightfall.

Suddenly the light stopped in one spot and began moving across the river. Whoever held it must have gotten into a boat and was now moving rapidly in Emily's direction. It got closer and closer until the light flashed in her eyes and filled the room, surrounding Emily and bathing her in its glow.

Chapter Twenty-two

Emily tried not to look at the brilliant light that encircled her. She held up her hand to shield her eyes, but she could not get away from the hypnotic pull. She could feel a metamorphosis creeping over her, like an electric eel slithering up her body and winding around her head. Along with the sensation came the memory of other times when her identity had become infused with someone else's. It was like a flash of a forgotten dream suddenly remembered. The very act of recalling it seemed to break down her final defenses and she surrendered to the invading force.

"Elinor, remember when we used to play with these old dolls?"

Slowly Elinor raised her head and looked up into the smiling face of her best friend. Celia's blonde curls bounced as she thrust the china dolls outward for Elinor's inspection.

You have so many things stored up here, but I doubt that you can take them all to California. Oh, Elinor, I am going to miss you so!"

Elinor stood up after pulling a fresh garment from the trunk. Her extra clothes had been stored in the attic after her marriage to Nicholas. "This should do nicely." She slipped out of her wet petticoats and skirt and put on a dry, gingham-print skirt.

"Let's go downstairs. I want to hang this out on the line to dry. Of course I'll only get it wet again when I go back across the river. Mother Langford will have a fit when my wet skirts drip on her rugs."

"Not that it should bother you," Celia teased as they started down the narrow steps, "but if it does, perhaps you should wait and have Nicholas row across and pick you up."

"I'll have to go back before he gets home. I promised him I wouldn't cross the river by myself. I don't like breaking my word, but when I saw you, I couldn't resist."

Celia smiled showing her deep dimples. "I'm sure he won't mind. You and I have been best friends since we were children and now you are moving far away. When Jonathan and I are married, we will come and visit you. Who knows, if we like it we may settle in California too."

"Oh, Celia, do you mean it? It would be so wonderful."

The two young women entered the main floor and headed down the hallway. "I'm sorry I won't be here for your wedding. I hope you don't think I'm letting you down. I was looking forward to being your Matron of Honor but I don't think Nicholas and I will be coming back for a visit so soon."

"It's all right, Elinor. Of course, I would love you to be my Matron of Honor. But the sooner you get away from that old witch, the better. You can bet she is up to no good."

"I agree with Celia," Elinor's mother said as the two young women entered the kitchen. Mary Foster was standing by the table stirring a pitcher of lemonade and had apparently overheard the comments.

Elinor planted a kiss on her mother's cheek. "You'll not get any arguments from me. I don't see how such a spiteful woman could have given birth to someone so wonderful as my Nicholas."

Mary patted her daughter's hand. "That's all the more reason to take the steps you are taking." Her lovely blue eyes moistened and she blinked several times. "Lord knows I'll miss you terribly, but I won't worry nearly as much about you. Take care these next few days, daughter. I don't trust that Harriet Langford."

Elinor saw the fear in her mother's eyes and it further ignited her own sense of urgency about leaving. "Don't worry, Mother, I'll be careful. I'm not going to let that woman spoil my happiness."

After hanging her wet skirts on the clothes line, Elinor and Celia sat down on the ground at the top of the slope and looked across the water.

"That place looks menacing. It always has." Celia gazed at Langford Manor. "I don't blame you for wanting to get away from there."

"The house wouldn't be so bad if all the people in it were normal, happy people. But that isn't the case. There is a constant undercurrent that lurks in the shadows, waiting for the right time to pounce."

Celia looked at Elinor and frowned. "You are frightened, aren't you? You should tell Nicholas that you want to leave Langford Manor immediately."

"It's not that easy, Celia. He's given me so much already. I know he would leave now if I insisted, but I don't want to demand anymore from him. I believe he would much prefer to stay at the Manor for the remaining days."

Celia sighed, "I can see your point but if the old crow makes life impossible you will have to tell Nicholas."

"Old crow? Elinor raised an eyebrow and smiled, "what a clever description, and well deserved, I might add." Elinor's smile faded. "I suppose I should be ashamed for talking so disrespectfully about my husband's mother. Nicholas loves her and I have tried, but she makes it impossible."

"I'm glad Jonathan's mother likes me. I can see where it could make things very difficult if she didn't." Celia's voice was gentle. "California will solve the problem."

"Celia, would you consider spending some time with me at Langford Manor before we leave? It would make the remaining time easier to get through if you were my guest for a few days."

Celia's hazel eyes reflected her surprise. "Elinor, I'd love to spend some time with you, but at Langford Manor? That place is scary and I swear that old woman is a witch!"

"Just try it for one day and night and if you are uncomfortable, you can leave. Who knows, Mother Langford doesn't usually have guests and since you are marrying Jonathan Wilkes, she might treat you like royalty. She's always trying to impress Charleston society and the Wilkes' certainly represent the old money class."

Celia giggled. "That's funny, Elinor. Me, a link to society? Do you really think she would be on good behavior?"

"I can't promise anything, Celia. Harriet Langford is unpredictable. The fact that you are my guest would be a strike against you, but her desire to prove she knows how to entertain a future member of the elite Wilkes family might well whip her into line. Please Celia, it would mean so much to me."

Celia patted Elinor's hand. "I'll do it, though I'll probably not sleep a wink. I just know that scary ol' house has to be haunted, if not by ghosts, then certainly by its resident witch." Celia sighed. "You have put up with Langford Manor for three months, I suppose I can tolerate it for two or three days."

"That's wonderful!" Elinor smiled and hugged her friend. "When can you come?"

Celia thought for a moment. "How about this weekend?"

The two young women made their plans. Jonathan and Celia would ferry across the river at Malden and he would bring her to Langford Manor by carriage.

"I thought you girls might be hungry." Mary Foster, tray in hand, walked over to the river overlook where Elinor and Celia were sitting. "Cheese sandwiches and lemonade, just like old times," she said, placing the tray on the ground between them.

Mary Foster wiped a tear from her eye with the corner of her apron. Elinor felt a twinge of guilt. Leaving wasn't going to be quite as simple as she had thought. Still, it had to be done. Her mother had said so herself.

"Mother, Celia is going to spend some time with me at Langford Manor before I leave."

"Oh, Celia, I think that's marvelous." Mary Foster flashed a smile. "You two girls have always been so close."

Elinor caught the wariness in her mother's lovely blue eyes. Did everyone have the same apprehensive feelings about Langford Manor?

Elinor and Celia spent the rest of the afternoon making plans. Soon it would be time for Elinor to leave. She had thoroughly enjoyed the afternoon and found herself wishing she didn't have to go. The strain of living at Langford Manor had melted away and she felt like her old self again. The shadows of the manor house did not touch her here. If it were not for her deep love for Nicholas, she would never set foot in that gloomy house again.

As Elinor rose to retrieve her dried skirts from the clothesline, a sharp stabbing pain, followed by a wave of nausea, stopped her in her tracks. She stood for a moment, fighting the accompanying lightheadedness. Swaying against the clothes line pole, she grabbed on to keep from falling. Bitter vomit erupted forth, pouring from her mouth and nose.

"My God, Elinor, what on earth?" Celia jumped to Elinor's side and grabbed her at the waist to keep her from falling. "Mrs. Foster!" Celia cried, "Elinor's sick, come quick!"

Mary Foster ran from the kitchen and joined Celia at Elinor's side. Finally, the retching stopped and they led Elinor into the house. They steered Elinor towards the parlor and settled her on the settee. Mary left the room and returned with a bowl of water and two cloths. She plunged the cloths into the water and, after wringing them out, placed one on Elinor's forehead and the other across her throat.

Elinor's mother left the room again and returned with a pail for Elinor to use, should she vomit again.

"Daughter, did this just come on you suddenly?"

"I don't know, Mother," she murmured. "I think I felt a little sick this morning right after breakfast."

Mary smiled, "Is it possible that you could be with child?"

Elinor glanced at her mother. "I don't think so. I bled last month. I am due again soon."

"That could be it. You do have the look in the eye. But I suppose it could also be something you ate. I know the cheese sandwich and lemonade I gave you were all right. Celia and I had the same thing and we're fine."

"The ham I had for breakfast tasted a bit sour. I thought it was just my taste."

"It could be. If you're expecting, it will affect your taste, especially where meat is concerned."

"Oh, Mother! Do you really think it's possible that I am going to have a baby?" Elinor smoothed her hand over her abdomen.

"Yes, dear, I think it is very possible. But you mustn't get your hopes up too much. If you are with child, the ill feeling should pass shortly. If you have gotten hold of a bad piece of ham, you will be sick for several hours to come. In any case, you must stay the night and let me look after you. I'll send word to Nicholas."

Elinor tried to raise up but the nausea swept over her again. "I need to go home to Nicholas," she protested just before retching and vomiting again. When she finished, she rested back against the cushions. "He told me not to come alone and now he'll know."

Mary Foster wrung out a cloth and placed in once again on Elinor's forehead. "Nicholas loves you, Elinor. He'll understand."

It will give his mother time to work on him, Elinor thought. Harriet would do all she could to persuade him against Elinor and the westward move. What if Elinor was with child? Mother Langford would use it as an excuse to postpone or even cancel the move to California. Even Nicholas would be reluctant to leave now if Elinor was carrying his baby.

"Mother," Elinor seized Mary's hand, "you mustn't tell

Nicholas that I might be with child. Tell him it is food poisoning, which it probably is anyway."

Mary gazed at her daughter. "Elinor, he has a right to know, but it would not be my place to tell him. Now stop worrying and let me take care of you. It will all work out, dear, don't fret so."

Elinor looked up into her mother's serene face that was still pretty, in spite of a few lines and creases that Elinor had never paid much attention to before. She closed her eyes as her mother's soft hand caressed her forehead. That touch always made everything all right when she was a small child. Even racked with nausea, she felt safe and good to once again be in her mother's care.

Elinor looked at Celia, who stood silently at the foot of the sofa. "Give me your word that you will say nothing about a child to anyone, especially Nicholas."

Celia nodded. "Very well, Elinor, I will say nothing."

Elinor sank back into the cushions and closed her eyes. After vomiting several more times, it became obvious that she was suffering from food poisoning or possibly a bout of the stomach flu.

If she had to be sick, she was grateful to have been at her mother's house when it hit her. She shuddered to think of being ministered to by Mother Langford. Elinor didn't like to admit it, but to some extent, she did fear the woman when Nicholas was not around.

As another wave of nausea hit Elinor. So did a nagging suspicion that she had been trying to ignore. Contrary to her usual custom, Mother Langford had waited that morning for Elinor to come down for breakfast. She'd had a strange look on her face and seemed particularly interested in Elinor's plate. No, Elinor thought, I mustn't think so viciously. Even Harriet Langford wouldn't be so vile as to try to poison her son's wife.

Chapter Twenty-three

The next morning, Emily awoke on the sofa and did not remember how she had gotten there. She pushed herself up on one elbow and looked about, at first not recognizing her surroundings.

The grandfather clock struck nine times. "Goodness," she said, shaking her head to get rid of the cobwebs, "I guess those sleeping pills do work. I didn't even make it to the bedroom."

An odd chill swept over Emily. She didn't remember taking the pill last night. She concentrated, trying to recall the events of the evening before. She remembered going upstairs to the attic after Becky left. She had gone over to the window and looked out at the ruins of Langford Manor.

Then a wave of nausea and a clammy sensation had swept over her. There had been a light on the water and it had seemed awfully bright. But what had happened after that? Emily pressed her fingertips to her temple as though she could force a memory. Nothing.

Obviously she had come downstairs and, stopping to rest on the sofa, had fallen asleep. She did not remember doing it. "It's happening again," she groaned

Becky had been something of a guardian angel. Everything had been fine when she was there. When she left, the memory lapses returned. Am I going crazy? Emily asked herself.

Whatever it was, she had been much better in the positive atmosphere of Becky's presence. She must not give in to negative thoughts. The past drew her. Becky was right. Emily had been too preoccupied with the lives of people who had lived a century ago. Their lives were over. Hers was still ahead and she must make the most of it. Grams would be the first to tell her to not sit and brood.

Convinced that the lure of the past was directly connected to the time lapses, Emily resolved to start living again. She would start today.

The phone rang just as Emily was getting out of the shower. She wrapped herself in a towel and ran to answer it.

"Emily, it's Mitch. I wanted to tell you how much I enjoyed seeing you again."

"I had a real good time, Mitch. It was great seeing you again too."

Mitch hesitated. "Emily, I know we agreed to be friends. But, there's nothing that says a friend can't take another friend out to dinner and maybe even a little dancing, is there?"

"I think that would be fun."

"Well, in that case, I realize this is short notice, but, are you free this evening?"

"Yes, I am free and I would enjoy spending the evening with you."

Emily kept busy the rest of the day, tidying the house, and weeding and watering Grams' flower garden. It was the least she could do for her grandmother's beloved plants. She'd ask Mitch for his professional advice since he was part owner of his family's greenhouse and nursery business.

Becky stopped by for a short visit after school. "Go girl! Keep this up and you'll make the cover of one of those fancy home magazines." Becky flashed her contagious smile. "If I weren't in my schoolmarm digs, I'd join you. It's good exercise. Say, you know what, Em? We should start exercising. We could jog or go biking. Maybe we could even join an exercise class. What do you think?"

"It sounds like a winner to me. I definitely feel out of shape." Emily turned off the hose and sat down in a lawn chair next to Becky.

"Well, all right! Why don't we start this evening?"

"I can't tonight, Beck. I have a date."

"Em! You have a date? Who with?" Becky's freckles danced. "You let me sit here and rattle on about exercise when all the while you had some juicy news like that?"

"Come on, Beck. It's not as though I've never had a date before."

"Now don't you be coy with me, Emily Foster. Who's the lucky guy?" Without waiting for an answer, Becky chattered on, "I'll bet it's Mitch. It is Mitch, isn't it?" She grinned. "I knew he was interested. I saw the way he looked at you."

"Beck, I told you Mitch and I are just friends. You said you wouldn't push. Remember?"

"Yeah, I suppose I did make such a foolish promise. I made it under duress." She wiggled her eyebrows like Groucho Marx. "Okay, Em. I'll behave, but you must tell me everything that happens."

Emily cast a knowing glance and a funny little smile curled her lips. "Come on, Beck, everything?"

Becky giggled. "Well, almost everything."

At five o'clock, Emily stepped into the shower. The water soothed her tired muscles and washed away the soil and grime of the flower beds. She was grateful for having such normal feelings. The work had been therapeutic. She had enjoyed the day. Now she would spend the rest of the evening with an old friend.

Old friend or not, she thought later as she looked into the bedroom mirror, *I want to look nice.* She slipped into a clingy, pink silk dress and pinned her hair up, allowing a few wisps to cascade down the sides and back.

Mitch rang the doorbell at seven o'clock sharp. His gaze showed his appreciation of the extra care Emily had taken in preparing for their evening.

"I thought we would go to the Connover House Inn," he said as he opened the car door for Emily. "It's a bed and breakfast inn, but their dining room is open to the public for dinner, by reservation only. You usually have to book at least a day or two in advance. I called today and they had a cancellation."

"It sounds great, Mitch. I remember the old Connover mansion on the other side of Charleston. I didn't realize they had turned it into a bed and breakfast inn."

"Yes, they opened a couple of years ago and business has been great."

"I've often thought it would be fun to operate an inn."

"If you're serious about it, your old Victorian would make a perfect one. The atmosphere is all there and having a Broadway star as proprietor would certainly be a drawing card. Naturally, Ames Nursery would see to your gardens and provide fresh flowers daily. We'd give you the best deal in town." He flashed a smile as he started the engine of his dark blue sports car and eased it out of the driveway and onto the road.

"Believe me, Mitch, the name of Emily Foster is not a household word. But I do have friends in New York who would enjoy getting away from it all. They in turn have many friends. It is something to think about. Right now everything is up in the air."

"Does this mean you are thinking of giving up your acting career?"

"Nothing is certain, Mitch. Right now, I don't feel that I ever want to go back to it. The joy has gone out of it for me. It can be a very cut-throat business and I just don't want to be in that rat race anymore." Emily sighed. "I really don't know what the future holds at this point. My feelings may change in the coming weeks and I might once again get that itch to be onstage. There was a time when it was the most important thing in my life. Now it seems so shallow. I could have spent that time with Grams."

Mitch reached over and patted her hand. "It sounds like your grief over the loss of your grandmother is clouding your judgment. Give it some time and don't be so hard on yourself. It would not have been healthy for you to have stayed home and denied yourself a career just to be with your grandmother. I'm sure she wouldn't have wanted you to do that."

"That's what Becky said. I know you're both right. Grams wanted me to be happy, fulfilled. The years just went by so fast. I wish there could have been more of them."

The inn was everything Mitch had promised. Dining by candlelight, they ordered filet mignon and it was the best Emily had ever tasted.

"This place is loaded with atmosphere—it would be pretty tough to compete with," Emily said, over the delicious strawberry shortcake.

Mitch leaned toward her. "Should you decide to open your own bed and breakfast, the Connover is far enough away from you so that you really wouldn't be in competition with it."

"There's a lot to think about." Concern flashed across Emily's face. "I haven't exactly given up on the idea of marriage and family. A bed and breakfast inn seems better suited for someone whose family has grown and left the nest."

Mitch's blue eyes took on an extra glow. "So you haven't sworn off domesticity? I wasn't sure after some of the things you said."

"I haven't ruled anything in or out, Mitch. I'm not ready to get involved at this time, that's all. As I told you, I am just getting over a shattered long-term relationship. Because of your recent divorce, I'd say we are pretty much in the same boat."

Mitch flashed an easy smile. "Oh, I don't know. If the right person came along, it might turn my head." He reached across the table and took Emily's hand.

She wasn't immune to a handsome face and romantic candlelight. But, it was the wrong face. The man across from her should have jet-black hair that curled around his ears and his eyes should be liquid pools of ebony heat. A strawberry birthmark would rest just beneath the tip of his chin.

A chill rippled up Emily's arm. She was glad the dimly-lit room prevented Mitch from seeing the color she felt rising in her cheeks. She wanted to pull her hand away, but she didn't. She had to live in the real world and stop thinking about the shadowy, phantom lover that could never be hers. Mitch was handsome, had a secure future and he was good company.

She smiled and looked into his eyes.

It was all the encouragement he needed. He leaned over the small expanse of the table and kissed her lightly on the lips.

Later, he slipped his arm around Emily as they were leaving the inn. "Would you like to go dancing? There's a nice club with a piano bar and dance floor a couple of miles from here."

Emily started to decline, but Mitch's expectant smile won her over. "Sounds like fun, Mitch. I'd love to."

Several couples were enjoying a slow dance when Mitch and Emily entered the club. Mitch chose an out-of-the-way table and ordered a bottle of champagne.

The music seemed to reverberate in Emily's soul as she sipped the champagne. When Mitch asked her to dance, she went into his arms. She could visualize blue satin as she twirled to the melody of a Viennese waltz on the dance floor. It seemed an odd selection for the piano player to have made. Probably a private request, she thought.

The music slowed down its pace and changed to, *I'm Always Chasing Rainbows*. "*Fantasie Impromptu*," Emily murmured as a chill swept over her.

There was a timeless quality to music. The dancers held one another close and swirled to the marvelous refrain. Emily could not get the swishing sound and brilliant blue satin out of her mind. It was as though she were in a different time and place. She closed her eyes and allowed her feet to follow her partner's lead.

The music's tempo seemed to pick up and its sound became distorted as though it were echoing from far away. Faster and faster, Emily's partner twirled her until she was lightheaded.

She could see dark eyes looking at her with adoration as she glided across the floor. Her feet followed the music as she grew increasingly dizzy. Suddenly, the pace slowed and the melody no longer came from a piano. A deep male voice hummed melodious strains of *Fantasie Impromptu* as familiar arms held her close and guided her in the dance.

Elinor opened her eyes as Nicholas twirled her around the bedroom. When they got near the bed, he dipped sharply causing both of them to lose their balance and fall sideways onto the goose down mattress.

"My beautiful Elinor," he rested on one elbow and looked down at her, "nothing can ever separate us. We will be together always."

Reaching up and caressing his cheek, Elinor pulled Nicholas to her until their lips touched, igniting a heat in her veins that spread to the center of her being. His hands slid down her back, unfastening the hooks on her dress. His lips, all the while, continued to leave patches of liquid fire wherever they touched.

Suddenly the music returned. Though sounding very far away, it drew Elinor's attention. It pulled at her irresistibly, so that even Nicholas' burning kisses could not draw Elinor away from it. The music grew louder and louder as it echoed inside of her body and soul.

When the music stopped, Emily was clinging to Mitch in a seductive embrace. His lips were on her neck and his hands had wandered possessively down her back.

She opened her eyes, at first confused. When she realized where she was, she pulled away from him, rejecting the familiarity of his touch.

"Please take me home," she said, turning and heading toward their table.

Mitch looked as though she had slapped him. "I'm sorry,

Emily." He followed her to the table. "But you have to admit you do send mixed signals."

Emily was shaken. Were her fantasies taking over her life?

Once they were in the car and on the way back to Emily's home, she apologized to Mitch. "I've been going through a very confusing time lately. As you said before, my grandmother's loss has clouded my judgment. I wasn't being fair on the dance floor. I can't excuse my behavior, I can only ask that you forgive me."

Mitch didn't say anything until he pulled into Emily's driveway and turned off the ignition.

Even in the darkness, she could see his easy smile. "Please don't spoil it by apologizing. I enjoyed every minute of it. We are both lonely and needed to feel close to someone. What's wrong with that? I'm here for you, Emily, in whatever capacity you choose. If you insist keeping it platonic, I can handle that." He hesitated for a moment, glancing out the window, weighing his words carefully. Then he looked into her eyes. "But if you want to be lovers, I wouldn't mind one bit."

He leaned over and kissed her gently on the lips. "I say that with the utmost respect."

Oh Mitch, she thought, *it would be so nice to be held by you for just a little while.* She didn't want to be alone tonight. It would be so easy. She could forget all the pain, the confusing thoughts and just be with this very nice man. A good, decent man, but one that she did not love. Morning would come and she would not like herself very much. If she allowed this to happen she would only be using Mitch as a substitute. Even if he were willing to be used, she could not do it. If she ever made love to Mitch, it should be because she loved and wanted him, not the phantom lover who haunted her soul and stroked the flames of her desire.

"I'm sorry, Mitch. In spite of the signals on the dance floor, I'm not ready to take this step."

"I've got all the time in the world, Emily. I'm a patient

man," he said, nodding. "Meanwhile, I hope you are not going to feel awkward about this. I meant what I said about wanting to be your friend and helping you with your flower garden."

Emily smiled, grateful for his good grace. "I want us to be friends, too, and I'll appreciate any help you can give me with Grams' plants."

After saying he would call her and they'd go out again sometime soon, Mitch planted a chaste kiss on her cheek and said goodnight at the door.

Once inside, she went to the living room and without turning on the lamp, she sank down on the sofa and leaned back to close her eyes. "That was a close call," she sighed, "I don't understand what is happening to me."

There was electricity in her veins and she felt consumed with unfulfilled desire. Maybe she should have invited Mitch in. But, she didn't want Mitch. She wanted Nicholas. A sob caught in her throat as she again realized that she was in love with someone she could never have. Yet her lips had somehow known his kiss, her body had reveled in their lovemaking.

"Nicholas," she whispered, "Where are you my darling, Nicholas?"

"I am here, my love," a deep resonant voice answered from the shadows of the darkened room.

Chapter Twenty-four

"I am here, Elinor." The words sounded far away as a new wave of nausea enveloped Elinor. Slowly, she opened her eyes and looked into the concerned faces of her husband and her mother.

The oil lamps had been lit to dispel the darkening shadows that had gathered in the parlor. The muted light further accentuated the worry lines on Nicholas' face.

Celia spoke from the other side of the room. "Granny Akers sent over some ginger root tea. She says it will help."

"I think we should wait for the doctor," Nicholas said.

Elinor heard a commotion as her father came into the room. "Doc Landers has gone to the other side of town to birth a baby and the other doctor is visiting his in-laws in Kentucky." Jacob walked over to his daughter and bent down to speak to her. "How're you feeling, Ellie?"

A frown creased his brow and Elinor noticed how much older he looked. He had always seemed so formidable when she was a child. Now she would be leaving West Virginia and might never see him again.

"I'll be all right, Papa, you mustn't worry about me."

Mary Foster looked at Nicholas. "We'll have to use the ginger root tea. It can't hurt. I've used it plenty of times myself." Mary wrung out a wet cloth and placed it on her daughter's head. She looked at Nicholas again and he nodded, bowing to her wishes.

"You know best, Mother Foster. I know we have to do something. She is so ill."

Seeing the grave concern on his face, Elinor reached out to him. "I'll be all right, Nicholas. Just stay with me."

"Oh course, dearest. I will be by your side until you are well." He knelt down on one knee and kissed her fingertips. "You mustn't worry about anything. We will stay here until you're better."

Blessed relief flooded over Elinor. She was in a home where she felt completely safe. She hadn't known that feeling since moving to Langford Manor.

She and Nicholas would spend the night in Elinor's former bedroom. It seemed strange to be sharing the frilly, canopy bed with him. He wanted to sit by her side all night, but she insisted that he join her in the bed instead.

When she awoke the next morning her stomach was more settled, but she was not fully recovered. She had a headache and the sunlight streaming through the white lace curtains hurt her eyes.

Nicholas, seeing her squint and shield her eyes, arose and pulled the draperies across the windows. "You must stay in bed and rest today, dearest. You have had quite a bout of the stomach flu."

"Is that what it is? I though perhaps I had eaten some bad ham yesterday morning. It did have an off-taste."

"I had ham for breakfast yesterday and I'm fine, so that wasn't it. You were probably coming down with the flu and that's why the ham tasted strangely to you." Nicholas placed his hand on her forehead.

Elinor smiled up at him. "I really am feeling better today. You have taken good care of me, darling."

Relief washed over Nicholas' face. "You had me worried for a while there. I suppose that ginger tea is pretty potent. Granny Akers turned out to be an angel of mercy."

Elinor looked away for a moment, her smile fading. "Nicholas?"

"Yes, dearest?"

"I'm sorry I didn't keep my word to you about not rowing across the river by myself."

Nicholas bent down and kissed Elinor's forehead. "There was no harm done. Celia explained. I know you've missed seeing your best friend."

"Celia agreed to spend a few days at Langford Manor. I assumed it was all right for me to invite her. Do you suppose your mother will mind?"

"Not at all. I think it's a splendid idea!" Nicholas got up from where he had been sitting on the side of the bed and walked over to the window. "Do you feel well enough for me to leave you with your mother while I go to the office?"

Elinor felt a twinge of disappointment but she reminded herself that Nicholas had a great deal of work to attend to before they left for California. She did not want to do anything that might delay their departure. "I'll be fine, darling. You go ahead. Mother will be here with me and Celia will stop by, so we can visit some more."

As if to prove that she was better, Elinor pushed herself up to a sitting position and swung her legs over the side of the bed. She didn't tell Nicholas about the sudden dizziness that swept over her.

"I'm still a little weak," she admitted as he rushed to her side to help her stand.

"Dearest, you shouldn't be getting up. It's too soon."

"Just help me to the chair. I'd like to sit up for awhile."

Elinor rested in her room for the better part of the day. Her mother and Celia passed the time with her. She was able to keep down tea and a little toasted bread. With each hour she grew stronger and her mood lightened. It was such a relief to be away from Langford Manor.

As the evening shadows fell, Elinor sat by her bedroom window and gazed at the dark river. The frogs and crickets had begun their evening chorus and a hint of lilac wafted on the breeze that blew through the open window and kissed her face.

Elinor could see the manor house. All the windows were dark, except those in the kitchen and dining room. The family would be having supper now. She was glad she and Nicholas were not with them.

She wondered what Mother Langford was making of Elinor and Nicholas' absence. Elinor could almost hear her mother-in-law saying, "That foolish girl should never have gone off like that by herself. If she's sick, it serves her right!"

Nicholas, my dearest Nicholas, how sad that you had to be brought up in such a family, she thought. Elinor had been blessed with a loving home where people laughed and loved whole-heartedly. That Nicholas had not been so fortunate only made her love him all the more.

Hearing the door opening behind her, Elinor looked over her shoulder. The lantern had not yet been lit and the room was now enveloped in shadows. All the same, she had no trouble recognizing her tall, handsome husband.

"How's my sweetheart?" he asked. He walked over to where she sat. Bending down, he kissed her cheek. "Your mother said you are feeling considerably better."

"I am, darling. I am still a little weak, but I'm feeling much better than I did at this time yesterday."

"That's my girl," he said softly as he pulled up a chair next to hers. "Perhaps tomorrow you will feel well enough to return to Langford Manor."

A chill slithered up Elinor's back, bringing with it a sense of dread. "I'm not ready yet, Nicholas. As I said, I am still weak. I'll need at least another day."

"Of course, dearest. I didn't mean to rush you."

Elinor felt ashamed. She wasn't being completely honest with him. "Actually, I thought we could stay here until the weekend. I'd like some extra time with my parents before we leave for California. Also, as I mentioned, Celia is coming back to Langford Manor with me to spend a few days. It will be such fun!"

She couldn't see his face but Elinor wondered if Nicholas was disappointed that she would not be returning to the manor house sooner. "You will stay here at night with me, won't you darling?" she asked.

"Just try to keep me away," Nicholas reached for her and wrapped her in an embrace.

That night, Elinor knew from the way her body responded to her husband's touch that she was definitely on the mend.

The room hinted of lilacs and lavender borne on a breeze that caused the lace curtains to flap gently. The sparkling light of the half moon created sharp outlines in the room. Elinor felt strange to be with her husband in the bed that had been hers when she was growing up.

The cool night air danced lightly across Elinor's skin, leaving a tingling sensation. She removed her modest nightgown and slipped in between the crisp, cool sheets and cuddled up to Nicholas.

She nuzzled her head in the crook of his arm and he pulled her closer. He held her and stroked the long silken strands of her hair.

"We shouldn't rush you. You haven't had time to fully recover," he whispered.

"We'll see about that," Elinor challenged as she slowly moved her hand across his chest and down his abdomen. She felt his body respond as he shuddered. Resting on one elbow, she kissed his forehead, his cheeks, and the strawberry birthmark.

She flicked her tongue across his lips then traveled downward with light touches against his neck and shoulders.

His breathing quickened as her hands and lips spread magic over his body. He groaned when she at last slipped above him. He guided her, seeking her body with his hands and lips until they cried out from the explosive force of their love-making.

Afterward, Elinor lay awake listening to the sound of her husband's breathing as he slept beside her. When she had lain in this very bed a little over a year ago, she had tried to imagine the husband she would someday have. Nothing in her virginal mind and body could have comprehended the passion she and Nicholas shared.

Feeling safe and completely contented, Elinor fell asleep.

Chapter Twenty-five

Emily awoke the next morning with the sun streaming through the open window. She breathed deeply of the floral laden breeze that sweetened the room. Her eyes still closed, she languished in the comfort of her bed. She reached over and touched the empty space beside her. It felt warm. As though someone had been sleeping there and had just gotten up. She opened her eyes and looked at the pillow. It bore an indentation.

She told herself that she had probably been on that side of the bed just before waking and had shifted to her present side only moments ago. The logic of it did not dispel the sudden sensation of being abandoned and very much alone.

Turning on her side, she hugged the extra pillow and, resting it against her cheek, she breathed its essence. The scent of lilacs delighted her senses and left her feeling lightheaded.

When she put the pillow aside, she noticed something out of the corner of her eye—something that bothered her because it didn't belong. It was so small she could easily have missed it.

Emily raised up on one elbow and with great care, lifted the single strand of hair from the pillow. She knew right away it was not from her head. She had light, sun-streaked hair. This one was as black as a raven's wing.

Where had it come from? Emily stared at it for a moment before depositing it on the night stand. A chill crept over her. Surely she had not had a stranger in her bed! Even in a time lapse she couldn't imagine herself getting involved in that kind of situation.

Maybe she had carried it in on a piece of clothing. Or perhaps one of Mattie's dark hairs had gotten on the linens when she was folding them and this one had remained. But, Mattie's hair was mostly gray where it had once been black.

Suddenly a strange peacefulness settled over her as she pictured Nicholas Langford, his black hair combed down, but curling around his ears all the same. His dark eyes smiled at her and his lips sent a message of desire that set off a reaction inside of Emily. She could feel his kisses burning her lips.

"Stop it," she told herself aloud, "you can't allow yourself to fall into these wild fantasies." It was crazy to think that the hair could have been from Nicholas Langford's head. Yet, he was the man of her recurring dream, the phantom lover who seemed so real she could almost reach out and touch him.

She closed her eyes and breathed the sweet scent of lilacs as she tried to recall the sequence of events of the night before. She knew that Mitch had left her at the door. It was after she stepped inside that things became unclear. Emily sensed that Nicholas had been waiting for her. But how was that possible?

She picked up the strand once more, carried it over to the waste basket and dropped it in. She had to stop this insane behavior. She had her whole life ahead of her. It lay in the future, not in the past.

As Emily prepared scrambled eggs, Mattie Devers came to the kitchen door and let herself in. Emily had forgotten that it was Mattie's day to work.

"Good morning, Miss Emily. It's a fine day today, it surely is." She placed her hands on her hips and smiled. "Is there anything special you would like me to do?"

Remembering the sorry state of the attic, Emily replied, "There is something, Mattie, but not today. If you have tomorrow free, I could use some help cleaning the attic. I was up there the other day and it really needs it."

"I'd be happy to help, Miss Emily. I'll get here bright and early and we'll whip it into shape in no time."

Emily made sure she took her vitamin. Deciding to pamper herself, she put on a bikini and after applying sun blocker, she went outside to the deck with her radio, cordless phone and book. She gazed across the river at the stone ruins of Langford Manor. She got a chill every time she thought about the new house she had seen. It had been so real. She had a hard time believing she had only imagined it.

Emily stretched out on the chaise lounge and allowed the warming rays of the sun to work their therapeutic magic on her taut nerves. Tuning the radio to an FM station that played classical, the smooth, melodic strains further soothed her tension.

Her thoughts traveled back to last night. She just couldn't remember anything after she had come inside the house. Had she taken her sleeping sedative? She didn't recall. One thing was certain, when she had taken it last weekend the medication had helped dispel the weird thoughts and fantasies that had been plaguing her.

She realized that she was becoming obsessed with Nicholas Langford. As a child, she had been intensely interested in Nicholas and Elinor, and there had been the dreams. But this was different. Nicholas Langford was touching her life. She didn't know how or why.

She imagined a warm, masculine hand on her shoulder, speaking to her in soft, loving tones. She felt bathed in the love she received from the man whose face was framed by black hair and whose dark-winged eyebrows seemed to be questioning, watching. His searching lips could set-off a thousand fires in her soul. She could see him now beckoning her.

"Elinor, come to me."

Emily opened her eyes and she was back on her deck, alone. There was no Nicholas with her, yet he had seemed so close, so real.

Was that how the time lapses happened? Was she

involved in some sort of self-induced hypnotic state in which her fantasies became so real, she felt she was actually experiencing them?

In spite of herself, Emily's heart gladdened at having known Nicholas Langford, even in this strange hypnotic way. What of the monogrammed handkerchief? The blue scrap of material and the single strand of hair? She wondered if one's wish fulfillment could be so strong that actual objects materialized?

Emily shook her head. It was just too weird to comprehend. Again, she resolved to put the past behind her. Nicholas Langford was part of it and as such, he could never share her future. She must try to concentrate on other things, other people, to live for today.

The ringing telephone interrupted her thoughts.

"Hello."

"Hi, Em, it's Becky. I'm on my lunch hour and I thought I'd stop by after class if you're going to be home."

"Sure, Beck, I'll be here. Right now I'm stretched out soaking up some sun. Aren't you sorry, you're stuck in class?" Emily teased.

"Thanks a heap, Em. Actually, I would pass on the sun anyway. The last thing I need is more freckles."

"I'll see you later, then." Emily pushed the off button on the phone and in an effort to clear her mind, she picked up the book she had brought outside with her and began reading. Soon, she became tired and closed her eyes. She listened to the soothing music on the FM station.

The hauntingly beautiful strains of *Moonlight Sonata* washed over Emily lulling her into an irresistible sleep. Carried along by the lilting melody, she felt as though she were floating. Deeper and deeper she slipped until the music sounded far away. The floating sensation became more pronounced and the melodic stains changed into a swooshing and slapping sound.

* * *

Elinor opened her eyes and was almost blinded by the force of the sunlight. She quickly reached for her folded parasol and chided herself for not wearing a hat.

Celia wore her bonnet and had a parasol, too. She smiled at Elinor as the boat jostled from side to side.

"I'm so glad you're going to spend some time with me, Celia."

"I couldn't let my best friend go off to California without visiting her once more."

Elinor's gaze traveled past Celia to Nicholas whose loving smile sent a pleasant shiver through her. She silently prayed that it would always be this way between them.

"It's good to see the roses back in your cheek, dearest," he said.

"I certainly felt ill, but you were very good medicine for me."

A private look passing between them, recalling their love-making, caused Elinor's cheeks to color even more at the arousing memory. Apparently reading her thoughts, Nicholas' smile widened.

"I'm glad I decided to come across in the boat. It's much faster this way." Celia broke in.

"We're going to have fun, just like in the old days," Elinor turned her attention to Celia. "We can walk along the river, have a picnic, even swim, though some in the household might frown on it."

Elinor stole a glance at Nicholas but he seemed not to have noticed the remark. She was glad. She did not want to constantly remind him of the hostility between her and his family. It was enough that he was willing to take her to California to start a new life.

The stones of Langford Manor loomed ahead and Elinor realized her expression must have changed because Celia looked at her strangely before turning around to check out the surroundings.

"Nicholas," Celia began in her usual bubbly manner, "you do live in a spooky looking house. What was it like growing up there?"

Nicholas smiled at Celia. "The house isn't so bad. It holds numerous hiding places. That worked to my advantage when I was a young boy and had fallen into disfavor with my mother."

"Did that happen often?" A look of concern creased Celia's brow. Good-natured, fun-loving Celia was always the soul of compassion.

"All too often, I'm afraid. You know how little boys can be." Nicholas replied.

"I suppose we do, don't we, Elinor?" Celia drew her friend into the conversation. "We both grew up with older brothers."

Elinor smiled and nodded, but her heart felt a chill. She had never heard much about Nicholas' childhood. She knew his mother had been strict in the upbringing of her son, but Nicholas had always added that there were good memories too. She never realized things were so bad he had to hide from his mother on a regular basis.

Harriet was difficult now. She must have been a real tyrant in her younger days. Yet, she seemed to dote on her son, and he was clearly devoted to her. It was all very confusing. Elinor did not understand the kind of twisted, possessive love that characterized Harriet Langford.

Mother Langford. Elinor had enjoyed the time away from her. The woman was like a viper ready to strike when you least expected it.

She was even worse now that the gauntlet had been thrown down. *I wish I never had to lay eyes on her again*, Elinor thought. A feeling of dread and impending doom again settled over Elinor as the boat nosed its way to the moorings of Langford Manor.

Nicholas pulled the boat up on the riverbank and helped the young women out of it. His arms lingering around, Elinor, he pulled her to him and held her.

"Mother has been very worried about you. She's happy that you are recovered and back home." He smiled, apparently to reassure Elinor, but it would have taken even more than Nicholas' smile to make her feel happy about returning to Langford Manor. She did not look forward to being welcomed by the mother-in-law who hated her.

Nicholas retrieved Celia's valise and guided the ladies toward the house.

Elinor's apprehension grew with each step they took. Her reluctance was not lost on Celia.

"Maybe I should have had you spend some time at my house," Celia offered meekly.

She feels it too, Elinor thought. The very air at Langford Manor seemed stale and dank. There was no floral-scented breeze today, only a fish-like odor from the river that made Elinor gag. She had never before noticed it being so pronounced.

Even the steep mountains behind the house looked threatening, as though they were ready to swoop down and swallow up the manor and everyone in it.

Elinor swayed against Nicholas as a wave of vertigo gripped her.

"Dearest, are you ill again? Perhaps this trip was too much for you."

"It'll be all right, Nicholas. It's just this oppressive heat. If only there was a breeze."

"I'm sure that's all it is," Celia added, putting her hand on Elinor's arm. "Let's get you inside and into bed, you're still not fully recovered."

"But I was feeling so much better. I don't want to be an invalid while you're visiting, Celia. I wanted us to have fun."

"Now don't be silly," she said, "this is just for today. I'm sure you will be fine tomorrow."

"Perhaps you're right, Celia. I'm so glad you are here." she smiled at her kind-hearted friend.

Elinor held onto Nicholas' arm as she approached the entrance of Langford Manor. Her feet felt heavier with each step as her sense of dread increased.

The door opened and Harriet Langford stood there, ramrod straight, in her customary black dress. Celia was right, Elinor thought, she does look like a witch, an evil, old hate-filled crone.

Elinor leveled her gaze at the malevolent face of Mother Langford.

Her black taffeta dress, rustling like the beating of wings, Harriet Langford reached for Elinor to enfold her in an embrace.

Elinor backed away.

"Elinor isn't feeling well after the boat ride, Mother," Nicholas said. "She'll be going right up to her room."

"I'm so sorry to hear that," Harriet cooed like a roosting pigeon. She reached out with her claw-like hand and placed it on Elinor's shoulder. "You come inside, dear, Mother is going to take very good care of you."

Chapter Twenty-six

"Miss Emily, Miss Emily, wake-up…"

Emily recoiled at the pressure of the older woman's hand on her shoulder.

"No, let go of me!" Struggling to open her eyes, she pulled away from the unwelcome touch.

"What's the matter, Miss Emily? Were you having a bad dream?"

Looking into the sun, all Emily could make out was a woman's dark silhouette. She shrank back further until she realized it was Mattie's reassuring voice that she heard.

"It's me, Miss Emily. You don't have to be scared of ol' Mattie."

Emily, responding to the kindness in the older woman's voice, remembered where she was and regained her composure.

"I didn't mean to be harsh with you, Mattie. I must have been having a nightmare."

"I'm sorry I woke you up. I thought maybe you had fallen asleep and might be gettin' too much sun. Don't trust those sun-blockers. Can't see how they can keep you from burnin'. Anyway, I brought you a nice glass of iced tea." Mattie pointed to the chairside table.

"No need to apologize, Mattie, something tells me I was in a dream I didn't want to be in, so you did me a favor. And," she added, "I do believe I have had enough of the sun." Emily rose from the chair and moved it over in the shade of the maple tree. "Thanks for the tea, Mattie. I'm dying of thirst."

Mattie stood with her hands on her hips and watched as Emily took a long drink. "Miss Emily," she said when Emily set the glass down, "is there something wrong? You can tell ol' Mattie, you know. I might even be able to help you."

Emily returned the old woman's gaze. Could Mattie possibly have an understanding of what she was going through? She quickly rejected the notion. She would only confuse and perhaps frighten her. It wasn't right to unburden herself at Mattie's expense.

Forcing a smile, Emily said, "No, Mattie, there's really nothing you can help me with. I've just been a bit distracted lately."

The housekeeper continued to stare as though pondering whether or not to say anything further. After a moment she turned and went back into the house.

Emily looked over the placid, green river and the stones of Langford Manor. She knew she had to stop dwelling on the place and the people who lived and died there. She needed to concentrate instead on her own life and what she wanted to do with it.

A promising career awaited her in New York if she chose to go back to it. She had worked hard to get as far as she had. It seemed foolish to throw it all away now. Yet, there was a strong pull to remain in West Virginia. She didn't understand it, but something was urging her to stay.

The ringing of her cordless phone broke into her thoughts.

"Hello."

"Hi, Em, it's Becky again. I just had a great idea. How about having a cook out tonight at my place or yours? We could invite Fred and Mitch."

Emily chuckled, "Oh, Beck, you're impossible. You just never give up, do you?"

"What kind of friend would I be if I did?"

"I guess you wouldn't be Becky, would you? Anyway, I'd

be happy to have a cook-out here, but isn't it rather late notice for the guys?"

"Not really," Becky replied, "I had already planned to see Fred tonight. We didn't have anything specific in mind. Why don't you give Mitch a call and see if he can make it. I'll call you back in fifteen minutes. I'm in a hurry; otherwise, I'd be asking about your date last night."

When Emily called Mitch at the greenhouse, he readily accepted. He seemed relieved that things were not going to be awkward between the two of them.

When Becky called she was thrilled that Mitch could make it. She said she'd be by after school to help with the preparations and to get all the details on Emily's date with Mitch.

Emily went grocery shopping after lunch and bought steaks and all the trimmings for the barbecue. Later, she carried two glasses of iced tea outside and relaxed on the front porch swing while waiting for Becky's arrival.

A short time later, a grateful and thirsty Becky plopped down on the swing and took a long drink of the icy liquid. "You're a doll, Em, this tea hits the spot. It's really been humid today."

"Yes, but it's nice and shady here on the porch."

"I must say, the view is an improvement. We don't have to look at those gloomy old ruins across the river."

"I know. I'm finished with all of that, Beck. I have been dwelling on the past too much. Maybe it was a fantasy my mind created to escape the reality of Grams' death. The point is, it has to stop. I am living my life for today, not for someone or something that existed a hundred years ago."

"Oh, Em, I am so happy to hear you say that! You have a wonderful life, you just need to open your eyes and look at it. Take Mitch for instance. How was your date?" Becky's eyes sparkled and her dimples creased with her impish grin. "Tell me *everything*."

"It was very nice, Beck."

"Nice?" Becky rolled her eyes. "Is that all you can say?"

Emily pondered on whether or not to tell Becky about the strange sensations on the dance floor last night and the memory lapses after she had returned home. She decided against it. Since she had come to a decision, there was no point in going into it.

"There really isn't a whole lot to tell. He took me to the Connover House Inn for dinner and afterwards we went to a local club with a piano bar and danced. He brought me home and we said goodnight at the door."

Becky's freckles drooped and her dimples relaxed. "That's all?"

"What else did you expect, Beck? I told you Mitch and I are friends. There couldn't be anything more at this point. I'm not going to rush into anything."

"I know you're right. I just get carried away because I've got Fred. I want my best friend to have someone too."

"In due time, Beck. Some things just can't be rushed. As you said, I have a wonderful life. I have a future, but it is not necessary for me to live it all right this very minute."

"Speaking of the future, Fred spoke with Professor Whittaker last night. He's eager to meet you. He said he saw you in a New York play the last time he was there."

"And he remembered me? I must say I'm flattered."

"That's all well and good, but meanwhile there's Mitch to keep you company until Travis Whittaker sweeps you off your feet." Becky giggled.

Before she went home to shower and change, Becky prepared the tossed salad while Emily put together a luscious tropical fruit salad. After putting the steaks in a marinade and scrubbing the potatoes and wrapping them in foil, the food preparations were complete.

When Becky returned she brought a string of Chinese lanterns she'd found in her parents' basement. "We used to hang these when we had evening cook-outs. I'll have Fred string them up when he gets here. They'll add to the romantic atmosphere." Becky wriggled her eyebrows and giggled.

Emily was excited about the upcoming evening. She knew Grams was smiling down on her. She'd always encouraged Emily to invite friends over.

Catching a glimpse of herself in the hallway mirror, Emily liked the way she looked. There was more color in her cheeks. She'd chosen a gauze floral print skirt and a white off the shoulder blouse in the same cool material. She whirled around and as she did so, her blood turned to ice. A light shadow in a long white dress superimposed itself over her image.

She gasped as it quickly faded.

"What is it, Em?" Becky must have heard her all the way from the kitchen.

Emily was shaking by the time Becky reached her side. "I was doing it again, Beck. It wasn't a conscious thing, but I just saw something in the mirror. It was just a flash, but it was like me in a dress from another era. I must have been daydreaming."

Becky took Emily by the shoulders and looked her straight in the eye. "You caught it and stopped it this time, Em. That's good! Don't let it shake you. You are in control. I think that's wonderful progress, don't you?"

Emily smiled and tilted her chin. "Yes, I suppose you are right, Beck. I'm not going to give into this thing. I will conquer it."

"Atta girl!"

Fred arrived before Mitch and dutifully hung the lanterns and got the barbecue grill going.

A short time later Mitch arrive with two bottles of wine and a bouquet of flowers which Emily promptly put in water and set on the picnic table as a centerpiece.

The evening went well. The steaks were delicious and the wine helped Emily relax. The creepy feelings were all but gone. She ignored Langford Manor and concentrated on her guests.

Mitch suggested building a fire down by the edge of the water. It sounded like fun, but Emily and Becky were not properly dressed for such a trek down the steep bank. So, while Fred and Mitch got the fire going, Becky went home and Emily went inside to change into jeans.

The stars had already come out and the half moon shone over head by the time the women were ready to rejoin Mitch and Fred. Going down the steep embankment during the day was one thing, but at night, it was treacherous.

Emily was beginning to think she had been foolish to agree to having the fire by the river.

"Wait up!" Mitch called from below. "We'll come up and help you ladies down. The footing can be tricky."

"I hope there aren't any rattlesnakes slithering about," Becky said. "Whose crazy idea was this anyway?"

"I believe we have Mitch to thank."

"Remind me to do just that when he gets up here." Becky replied.

Mitch was all smiles when he slipped his arm around Emily to help her down the slope. "We have wine and glasses down by the fire. It's really great by the water."

Fred and Becky started the slope first, with Becky chattering all the way. "What's that over there? It's not a snake is it?"

"No, Rebecca," Fred replied, "it's only a stick. Mitch and I have everything under control."

"Ready?" Mitch asked, nudging Emily onward.

Suddenly, Emily thought of a man with dark eyes and hair beckoning her to follow him. "No," she murmured under her breath, as she pushed away the unwelcome memory.

"What did you say?"

"It was nothing, Mitch," she smiled at him, "I was just talking to myself."

About halfway down the rock-strewn pathway, Emily's foot slipped. Mitch caught her and held her to him for a moment. It felt good to be in someone's arms again. But it was not like the arms of.... *No, I must not think of Nicholas. He is only an aberration.*

The fire warmed the chill that had crept into the night air. It was always damp by the river and the lush foilage released so much oxygen, nights were seldom hot. Emily listened to the frogs' mournful song as it broke the ethereal stillness. The insistent chatter of the crickets blended to create a unique chorus. How she had missed this in the city!

The gentle lapping of the dark waters touched a wistful note in Emily's soul and between that and the wine, she began to feel at ease.

She avoided looking directly across the river. She must not think about the ruins that stood silently watching. It was nothing to her.

Becky started humming the tune of the *What Do You do With A Drunken Sailor* and soon the four of them were laughing and singing. Emily thought they sounded pretty good. Fred had a fine tenor voice and Mitch's mellow tones rounded out the harmony.

They slowed down their tempo and launched into some old songs appropriate for a campfire. *Danny Boy* always brought a lump to Emily's throat. For some reason it reminded her of the loss of her parents. She had never told that to anyone, not even Becky.

Emily joined in the singing of the bittersweet song, but it saddened her. Tears brimmed in her eyes and she looked away from the fire so no one would see.

Mitch, whose arm rested loosely around her waist, pulled Emily closer as if he sensed her melancholy. She leaned her head against his shoulder and closed her eyes. For the moment she felt safe. He had been a good friend in the past. Solid and true, Mitch was someone who could be counted on.

"Well, would you look at that!" Fred said. "Where do you suppose that is coming from?"

Emily looked up to see what the commotion was about.

"It seems to be coming from the old Langford place." Mitch answered.

Her heart lurching at the mention of the place, Emily

looked across the dark waters. There was a light, a soft flickering one, blinking from Langford Manor.

"It's probably some high school kids exploring the old place. Langford Manor is one of their favorite spots." Becky's voice was matter-of-fact.

Now Emily's heart pounded wildly. Somehow the old house found a way to pull at her, in spite of her resolve.

"I don't know, that doesn't look as though it's coming from a flashlight. It seems to be shining from an upstairs window. I thought the upper floor had been completely destroyed in the fire." Mitch said.

"Maybe someone climbed up to the top and is signaling or just plain wants to show off," sensible Becky quipped.

Emily saw Becky looking at her and she knew that for her sake, her friend wanted to quickly dispel any suggestion of mysterious goings on at Langford Manor.

"I don't know, Rebecca," Fred joined in, "that is an unusual looking light. It flickers much the way a candle or possibly a lantern would do. My guess is that it is a candle. Someone has lit a candle in an upstairs window. Perhaps they saw our fire and are trying to signal us."

Becky gave Fred a light poke with her elbow. "Well thank you, professor, for your scientific explanation!"

"Fred might be right. Maybe there is someone over there and they are signaling us because they saw our fire."

Mitch stood up and walked to the edge of the water. Cupping his hands around his mouth, he called out, "Hello over there! Can you hear me?"

Emily held her breath as she stared across the dark lapping waters at the flickering light.

"Hello!" Fred stood up and called.

Becky and Emily exchanged glances. Emily saw Becky's concern.

"Would the two of you sit down and stop acting like fools!" Becky tugged on Fred's pant leg.

Suddenly from across the river, came a voice that was

barely discernable, but Emily understood every word. Her hair stood on end and the gooseflesh rose on her arms as she listened to the plaintive cry, "Elinor, come home to me!"

Chapter Twenty-seven

Even in the dim light of the campfire, Emily saw Becky's face grow pale.

"Who is Elinor?" Fred asked.

"You heard it too?" Emily looked at Fred.

"So did I," Mitch added, "I guess the high school kids are playing their little ghost games." He turned to Emily, "Remember Crazy Charlie and all the fun we had with him?"

"Yes, I sure do." Emily tried to sound casual though her heart was pounding out of her chest. "Beck and I were just talking about him the other day, weren't we, Beck?"

"Yes, just the other day," Becky chuckled, but not too convincingly, "We sure had our share of fun."

Emily tried to ignore the sound as the feeble voice called out once again, "Elinor, come home."

Suddenly the flickering light went out and an eerie silence settled over the dark side of the river.

"I suppose they got tired of the fun and games," Mitch said.

"Speaking of tired," Becky stood up, "I have to teach school tomorrow. It's time for me to get going."

"But who is Elinor?" Fred asked again, "and who is Crazy Charlie?"

"Come on, Fred, let's go. I'll tell you all about them later."

Still shaken, Emily was glad to see the evening end. She knew Becky had read her mind and had come to the rescue.

Fred and Mitch carried the empty bottles and glasses and, at the same time, managed to guide the ladies up the steep hill.

"Once they reached the top, Becky and Fred said good night and left. Emily and Mitch stood by the front porch and waved goodbye to them as they left in separate cars.

"Can we sit on the porch for awhile?" Mitch asked.

"Maybe for a few minutes."

They walked over to the swing and sat down. She felt better in the front area of the property where she didn't have to look at the river and what lay on the other side.

"Shall I give you a hand with the cleaning up?" Mitch asked.

"Thanks, but no, Becky and I took care of that while you and Fred were building the bonfire."

Mitch draped his arm loosely on the back of the swing behind Emily. "That voice from across the river was a bit eerie, wasn't it?"

"Yes, it was, Mitch, but I'd rather not talk about it."

"Sorry, I guess it was a bit unnerving. Anyway, there are more interesting things to talk about. I'd like to see you again, Emily. After I get back, that is. I'm going out of town on business tomorrow and I won't be back until Monday, or Tuesday."

"Why don't you give me a call when you return, then."

"Definitely will. Since it's only a little more than a week away, I thought I should ask you now if you have any plans for the Fourth of July? My family always has a big picnic and we take in the fireworks. I'd love you to be my date and meet the clan."

The very mention of the Fourth sent an odd chill up Emily's spine. "Mitch, I'm sorry, I already have plans."

Emily sensed his disappointment. "I made plans with Becky and I need to follow through."

"Sure, I understand. Another time, then?" he leaned over and kissed Emily lightly on the lips.

"Yes, Mitch, another time."

He stood up and helped Emily to her feet. "It's getting late. I'll call you when I get back."

After watching him leave, Emily stepped inside the shadowy hallway. A lamp, shining from the kitchen at the opposite end of the house, provided enough light for her to see where she was going. Making her way to the bathroom, she undressed and stepped into the shower.

Afterwards, she went into the kitchen and took her sleeping sedative. Glancing out the window above the sink, she looked into the backyard. She was grateful that her view of Langford Manor was blocked. Pushing the thought of the old house from her mind, she went to her room and crawled into bed. The warm shower and sedative did their work and she was soon asleep.

The next morning Mattie showed up as Emily was finishing breakfast.

"How about having a cup of coffee with me before we get started?" Emily asked.

"Don't mind if I do."

"Have a seat, Mattie." Emily pulled out a chair and gestured for the older woman to sit. "Would you like something to eat," she asked as she poured Mattie's coffee.

"No thank you, Miss Emily, I just had a big plate of bacon and eggs before I came here."

"Mattie, I wish you would call me 'Emily'. You've know me since I was a little girl. We're friends. So the 'Miss Emily' really isn't necessary."

The old woman tucked her head down. "It just don't seem right, Miss. I'm used to talkin' this way and it's hard to change, I reckon."

Emily reached across the table and patted the old woman's hand. "I don't want you to feel uncomfortable, so, you may call me whatever you like."

"Thank you, Miss. You always were a sweet child. Now you've grown up into a fine lady."

After they finished their coffee, the two women gathered various items needed for the project and headed for the attic.

"I'm glad we have electricity up here," Emily said as she stepped into the vast upper area. "At least we can see what we're doing."

"Do you think we should bring up the vacuum cleaner, Miss? I believe it would better than a broom."

"You're right, Mattie. I'll go get it."

As Emily opened the closet door in the main floor hallway she caught a glimpse of herself in the mirror. The eerie image of the young woman in the old fashioned dress appeared again as it had the night before.

It was only a flash, and in the blinking of an eye it was gone. "I didn't see that, I refuse to see it," Emily said aloud in a controlled voice. "I'll not let these fantasies take over my life."

She figured being in the attic had prompted the unwelcome vision. She used to play up there as a child. The Langfords had been uppermost in her thoughts at that time. So, her conscious mind must be recreating the fantasies she had lived as a child.

With a new resolve, she picked up the vacuum cleaner and headed for the attic.

Mattie was busy knocking down cobwebs when Emily joined her. She had tied a scarf around her nose and mouth to protect against the dust and Emily did the same.

"We look like a couple of bank robbers, Mattie," Emily joked.

The old woman chuckled, "I reckon we do, Miss."

The work went by uneventfully at first. Then Emily decided to push the trunks and various pieces of furniture back against the walls. "That way we can clean under them and have an open space in the middle of the floor. That seems neater to me. Some of it might be heavy though. I'll have Mitch help if we can't manage it ourselves," she said.

"I believe we can handle most of it, Miss Emily. Ol' Mattie is stronger than you think."

Mattie was right. Emily was surprised at the strength the old woman displayed. The last thing they attempted to move was a giant trunk that held most of the Foster memorabilia. As children, Emily and Becky had gone through it dozens of times, trying on long dresses and frilly bonnets. Now the chest wouldn't budge.

"We'll just leave it, Mattie. It's too heavy."

"We can get it, Miss. I'll tell you what, let's empty it. That's bound to make it easier to move."

Emily lifted the lid and a flood of memories washed over her. The clothing inside was not neatly folded. She and Becky had always been in too much of a hurry trying on the various outfits. They had tossed things back inside in a haphazard manner.

Emily pulled out hats, high-buttoned shoes, and a beaded reticule. "Maybe I should keep this out and use it as an evening bag. They're definitely back in style."

She set the small purse aside and dug in further, trying to be unemotional about it. Each article brought back a memory of the good times she had when she was a little girl. Again, she felt Grams' loss anew.

Emily knew she couldn't allow herself to get sidetracked by her emotions. There was a job to be done. Finally, she reached the bottom of the trunk.

"Whoa! That was a job. Now let's see if we can move it."

Pushing with all of their might, the two women managed to shove the trunk against the wall.

"Here, let me help you put the things back." Mattie said, lifting the trunk lid. Glancing inside, she stepped back and scrutinized the front of the trunk. Then she looked inside again.

"What are you doing, Mattie?" Emily noted the old woman's odd behavior.

Mattie didn't say anything. She leaned over the edge of the chest and started pulling.

"What is it?" Emily said, approaching the trunk.

"What is it?" Emily said, approaching the trunk.

"Just as I thought," Mattie beamed as she stood upright with a wide, flat piece of thin wood in her and. "Did you know there was a false bottom in this trunk?"

"No, I never dreamed."

Mattie set the piece of wood aside and both women checked to see if anything was in the hidden compartment.

"Looky-here," Mattie displayed her near-toothless grin as she lifted a large Bible from the secret drawer. Beside the Bible were two framed pictures that lay flat, one on top of the other.

A violent chill shook Emily when she lifted them from the trunk. Staring at her from an aged photo was a face very much like her own. The young woman was wearing a white lace dress. She clutched a bouquet of flowers. The radiant smile on her face was evident, even in the old, yellow print.

Emily though about the vision in the mirror. At the bottom of the photo was written, "Elinor-1900".

"Elinor," Emily whispered, her hands beginning to shake. She stared at the face that was so like her own.

Then, hugging the picture to her bosom, she picked up the second photo. The lighting wasn't so good in the attic but she could see it was a group picture. As Emily drew it closer, she saw Elinor standing in the center, wearing the same dress she had worn in the photo. She was also holding the same bouquet of flowers. Might this have been taken on her wedding day?

Emily took her breath in sharply when she saw the man standing next to Elinor. His hair was as dark as a raven's wing and his smile reached out through the ages. His eyes captured Emily. They looked straight at her, pulling her into his world.

"Nicholas," she whispered, tracing her finger across the old photo. Her heart pounded and her mouth went dry. The sultry attic felt oppressive and the room began to spin.

"What's wrong, Miss Emily?" Mattie's voice sounded far away.

Emily felt the older woman tugging at her arm, pulling her away from the trunk.

Come over here and sit down. You're as white as a sheet." Mattie took the pictures from Emily's hands and, setting them aside, she guided Emily to a chair by the window.

"You need some air." Mattie pushed the window open further. Then she picked up one of the old photos and fanned Emily with it.

"Something scared the wits out of you, Miss Emily. Now tell ol' Mattie what it is. I told you before, I might be able to help you."

"Please give me the pictures, Mattie. I can't run from this thing. I have to face it."

Looking at her strangely, Mattie picked up the other picture and handed both of them to Emily.

"I'm not going to be drawn into it," Emily said as she forced herself to look at the group picture again. She shivered, but remained in control.

"Had I lived then, he would have been the love of my life, Mattie." Emily pointed to Nicholas. "This is Nicholas Langford. He was married to my distant cousin, Elinor, one hundred years ago. They died in the fire that burned Langford Manor. I feel sad when I think about it. Sometimes I feel so drawn into it that I think I am actually there, living back then. Yet, when I am myself again, I can't remember much about it. Does that make sense, Mattie?"

"Maybe more than you realize, Miss Emily."

"It does? Then you don't think I'm crazy? Oh Mattie, I have been so confused about this and I was afraid to tell anyone. I did talk to Beck. She took me to the doctor for vitamins and sleeping pills."

"There, there, child." The old woman put her bony arms around Emily and hugged her. "Ol' Mattie doesn't think you're crazy. I don't reckon vitamins will hurt and neither will sleeping medicine, if you're not resting. But if you are being called from the other side, pills aren't going to stop them. They are contacting you for a reason, Miss Emily. We have to figure out what it is."

"No, Mattie, I don't want to find out. I just want them to leave me alone and let me live my life!" Emily sobbed, tears stinging her eyes.

"It's all right, child, don't you worry none. I'll get to the bottom of this. Let me see those pictures."

Emily handed the photos to Mattie who first studied the one of Elinor.

"She was a pretty young thing, looked a lot like you, Miss Emily." Setting it aside, Mattie studied the group picture. "There's no doubt he was a handsome fella. This is a weddin' picture. I reckon these others here are the parents of the bride and groom. This woman looks like the girl, so that was probably her mother. Wait a minute—"

Emily watched Mattie's face grow pale, "What is it, Mattie, what do you see?"

Mattie turned to Emily. "I know who we are dealing with now, yes I do." The older woman pointed an arthritic finger at a woman dressed in black.

Emily had been so distracted by Nicholas' image that she had not paid much attention to anyone else. Now, when she looked at the woman, Emily trembled. "My God," she gasped.

Staring out from the photograph, looking very much like a giant crow, was a tall woman with a pinched face. A face only too familiar to Emily. It was the malevolent face she had seen in the window at Langford Manor when she visited the ruins last week.

"You know who she is, Mattie?"

"I know what she is, Miss Emily, and that's what's important.

Chapter Twenty-eight

"You recognize it too, don't you?" Mattie looked at Emily. "Evil, Miss Emily, you are looking at evil. That woman has blackness in her soul. I can see it even in this old picture."

"I saw her another time, Mattie. When I went to Langford Manor last week. I felt dizzy and I must have fainted. I lost two hours there that I can't account for. When I was leaving, I saw her in the window of a new mansion where the ruins stand."

"Oh my, Miss Emily! You shouldn't have gone there alone. You put yourself in danger. This crow woman will harm you if she can."

Emily shivered. "That's not going to happen because I'm not going to let it. I have put it all behind me. I'll not allow myself to be drawn back anymore. I think I somehow activate it when I think about the Langfords. I just have to keep these thoughts out of my mind."

"I hope you're right but it may not be that simple. You must promise that you'll tell ol' Mattie if there are any other strange occurrences. I have my potions and spells, too. I'll find a way to help you."

From the light that shone in Mattie's eyes, Emily almost believed her. She placed the Bible and pictures back in the trunk and closed the lid. Someday, when she was sure she could deal with them, she might bring the Bible and pictures out and display them downstairs. For now, it was out of the question.

By lunch time, the two women had finished cleaning the attic. "I'm glad that's finally over. Now, Mattie, you are going to have lunch with me. I won't take 'no' for an answer. I've got lots of fruit salad and there's also tossed salad left from yesterday. We'll just add something to that and we will have an instant lunch."

The old woman chuckled. "That fruit salad sure sounds good. I reckon I'll accept your invitation." She studied Emily. "You won't forget what I told you, will you?"

"I won't forget, Mattie, but I don't want you to worry. I've been controlling it instead of letting it control me."

Later, over lunch, Mattie quizzed Emily. "Can I ask you another question about those spells you've been having."

"I suppose so, Mattie, but I really don't want to dwell on it."

"How do you feel when you come to, after having one of them? Are you scared or is it something else you feel?"

Emily thought for a moment. "That's an interesting question. Sometimes I feel pretty jumpy because I'm aware that something has happened and I can't remember it. But mostly, I feel a warmth, like someone who has been loved."

Mattie's eyes lit up. "Well now, this is getting more interesting. Maybe it isn't the crow woman who is calling you back. Maybe it's the girl or the man. But the crow woman doesn't like it, of that I am sure."

"I have seen flashes of Elinor when I look in the mirror, Mattie, and I sense that I've looked into Nicholas' dark eyes. I have fantasized about being in his arms." Emily felt herself blushing. "Then there was the strange phone call I had last week, and the man's voice that Becky, Fred, Mitch and I heard from across the river as we were sitting around the campfire last night. Both times the voice said, 'Elinor, come home to me'."

"Well now, this is getting more and more curious. A man's voice you say? I could put you in a trance and take you back to one hundred years ago. I'll bet we could get to the bottom of things, but I must warn you, there are risks."

"No, Mattie!" I want to be done with this. I don't want to fall back into those delusions again. The past will have to take care of itself."

The old woman nodded. "You're quite right, miss. Taking you back might cause you to lose your identity if someone else was wanting to come through bad enough. It probably wouldn't be permanent but I couldn't guarantee it."

Mattie shook her head. "I really shouldn't have mentioned it. I wouldn't want to do anything to harm you, Miss Emily. You and your grandma have always been so kind to me. Now some of the others in this town—well, that's a different story."

Mattie chuckled, showing her missing teeth. Then she stopped, growing serious again. "Still, Miss Emily, sometimes them that's on the other side won't be denied. There's usually a reason for them to make contact in the first place. They don't always give up too easy."

"But isn't it true that they need a weak person to use or possess?" There, she'd said the word she'd been avoiding—possess—possession.

"The weaker, the better, that's true. If you're determined enough, maybe they will leave you alone."

After Mattie left, Emily went out to the porch swing and just as she was sitting down, the phone ran. She scurried back inside and picked up the receiver.

"Hello, Emily, it's Mitch. My trip was delayed and I won't be leaving until tomorrow afternoon. Cap and I thought we'd come and visit this evening if you're free. Cap says he misses you."

Emily's lips curled into a smile at the memory of the yellow Labrador. "I've missed Cap, too. Tell him it's okay if he brings you along."

"How about if I show up around seven with a pizza?"

"Sounds like a winner, Mitch. I'll see you then."

Becky stopped by after school. She looked closely at Emily before saying anything. "Are you all right, Em?"

"Now, why wouldn't I be?"

"After last night and that spooky voice, I was afraid it might have weakened your resolve."

"It only made me more determined, Beck. Besides, we all know that it must have been kids trying to scare somebody."

"Yeah, I know, that has to be it." Becky didn't look totally convinced. "Anyway, I came by to tell you that Fred and I are going to the Greenbrier Resort for the weekend. Isn't that neat?" Becky's face brightened.

"Beck, it sounds wonderful. How did you manage to tear him away from the Indian burial mound digs?"

"I just used my feminine wiles on him." Becky giggled. "Actually, it was Fred's idea." Becky, lowered her voice to a whisper, "I think he's going to pop the question."

"What? Beck, do you mean it?"

"I'm almost positive. He's been dropping hints lately."

Emily smiled, "Are you sure you're not the one who's been dropping the hints?"

Becky flashed a dimpled grin and her eyes sparkled. "If you're saying that I am the kind of woman who throws herself at the man she loves, you're absolutely right!"

"Oh, Beck? I'm so happy for you." Emily gave Becky a hug.

"Of course, nothing is official yet. So if I come back with a ring and show it to you in Fred's presence, you must act surprised."

"Well, of course, we girls have to stick together."

"Naturally, when I get married, I want you to be my Maid of Honor."

"I'd love to, Beck. Oh, this is so exciting!"

Becky's gaze softened. "It will happen for you too, Em, and when it does, I will be your Maid of Honor. That is, if you want me to." Becky grinned.

"Consider it a standing invitation, Becky. I can't imagine having anyone else. The only problem is I don't have a bridegroom." Emily's voice grew wistful.

"That isn't exactly true, Em. Just open your eyes and look right under your nose. It's obvious that Mitch is smitten with you and Professor Whittaker is already a fan and he hasn't even met you yet."

"Fans don't usually make good husbands, Beck, and Mitch is just a friend. Incidentally, his business trip was postponed for a day, so he's coming by this evening with Cap."

"Trip. What trip?"

"I don't know that much about it but he told me last night he was going out of the town today. He called me a little while ago and said it had been postponed until tomorrow."

"He just can't stay away, can he?" Becky's freckles danced.

"He's just a friend, Beck—how many times do I have to say it?"

"All right, all right, I'll stop. Anyway, I've gotta go. I have to shop for the weekend."

Emily had showered and put on a fresh skirt and blouse by the time Mitch arrived. Cap ran to meet her and barked a greeting before favoring her with a sloppy lick on the hand.

"I told you he wanted to see you," Mitch said, as he joined Emily and Cap. He bent forward and kissed Emily on the cheek while balancing a pizza carton in his hand.

"Hungry?"

"I'm starved." Emily smiled. "Shall we go inside or do you want to use the picnic table on the back deck?"

"How about the deck?" Mitch responded, "that'll give Cap an opportunity for a good run in your yard and along the river. He loves to explore."

As if he understood every word his master said, Cap barked and took off down the river bank.

"Don't worry, he'll come back," Mitch reassured, anticipating Emily's question of whether or not Cap would get lost. "I'm glad my trip was delayed. I have to meet with some suppliers in Georgia but hopefully our business will be concluded by Monday or Tuesday."

Emily and Mitch munched on the tasty pizza and drank iced tea while watching Cap jump and play at the water's edge. After a while, the dog tired and came up the embankment to beg for food.

"Would you like to go for a walk in the neighborhood?" Mitch asked when they were finished.

Emily readily accepted and Cap seemed to like the idea as well. They waved at several neighbors who happened to be sitting on their porches, enjoying the hushed sounds and dewy coolness of twilight.

"The old neighborhood hasn't changed that much since Beck and I used to ride our bikes up and down it. This place is like a different world. The mountains seem to shield and protect it from what's outside."

"Sort of like Brigadoon?" Mitch teased.

"Oh, I wouldn't go that far," Emily responded, as Cap trotted ahead of them. "But it is a special place I've always kept in my heart. More and more, I believe this is where I belong."

Mitch slipped his arm around Emily's waist. "I'm very happy to hear you say that."

Emily felt a stab of conscience. She didn't mean to lead him on. She hoped she had made her feelings clear enough to him. It wasn't because of Jeff. She had relegated him to the distant past, well before returning to West Virginia. It was because of Nicholas. *Stop it*, she told herself, *just stop it. For you, Nicholas Langford does not exist.*

Mitch suggested they sit in the swing for awhile after their walk. Saying that sounded agreeable, Emily went inside to get them some more iced tea.

She had to admit that she enjoyed spending time with Mitch. Perhaps this was the stuff that true love was made of. Maybe the pulsating, all consuming variety was pure fiction. *No*, she thought, *I have known that kind of love, somewhere, on another plane. It does exist.*

Emily and Mitch spent the next hour talking about old friends, the weather, politics and religion. Cap entertained himself by exploring the yard and riverbank.

Suddenly, Mitch and Emily heard Cap giving a shrill bark and then a strange yelp. They jumped up and ran to the back of the house and then to the edge of the embankment.

Cap was running and jumping excitedly at a huge, black shadow that circled overhead.

"What's that?" Emily cried, grabbing Mitch's arm.

"I suppose it's a bat I never saw one that big! Come here, Cap, get up here, boy." Mitch whistled for his dog.

Responding to his owner, the yellow Labrador gave up the chase and begun his climb up the embankment. However, the large dark, winged creature did not give up. It circled the dog menacingly and swooped down and pecked at Cap when he was halfway up the hill.

"My God!" Mitch cried as he started down the incline when he heard his dog yelp

"Don't," Emily called out, "it could be a rabid bat." She felt so helpless standing there. She was afraid the flying menace would attack Mitch. She didn't' feel too safe herself but she wasn't going to desert her friends.

Suddenly the black-winged creature did a sharp turn and headed toward the darkening shadows over the river. All was quiet as Mitch and Cap made their way up the hill.

Emily bent down and patted the excited dog, noting the blood on top of his head. "I'll get the first aid kit and have a look at this." She looked up at Mitch. "Are you all right? I was afraid that bat was going to attack you too."

"I'm fine. I can tell you one thing though. That was no bat. I know it sounds crazy, but that was a large, black crow."

Chapter Twenty-nine

The wound on Cap's head wasn't deep. Emily cleaned and disinfected it. She wondered if Mitch was mistaken and that what they had actually seen in the darkness was an unusually large bat, probably a rabid one, judging from the viciousness of its attack. She was relieved to learn that Cap's rabies' shots were up to date. Emily shivered. Bats gave her the creeps.

"Cap, I think you had better stay away from that river bank, especially at night." Emily gently scratched the dog's ear.

"I'll say," Mitch added, shaking his head. "I've never seen anything like that before. It looked like the 'Crow from Hell'." He grinned. "Thanks for taking care of my dog, Nurse Emily. Do you take care of humans just as well?"

"Only those attacked by the 'Crow from Hell'," she teased. Inside, she felt very uneasy about the entire incident. The fact that Mitch thought the attacker was a crow was not lost on Emily. She remembered Mattie's comments about the evil of the crow woman. Was the other side reaching out, trying to pull Emily in?

"Cap and I have to be going. I'll call you when I get back in town." Mitch kissed Emily on her upturned cheek and then on the lips, sweetly and non-demanding.

Later, as Emily prepared for bed, she kept thinking about the attack on the dog. She believed it was uncharacteristic of a crow to behave in such a way, especially at night. That was the province of bats and owls. She closed her eyes and tried to visualize what she had seen, but it had been dark and she could not be sure. The logical explanation was that it was a large, possibly rabid, bat.

She made sure she took her sleeping sedative before going to bed. Evenso, she tossed and turned and was unable to sleep. She felt the way she did when she was a child and had been terrified of the dark. Grams had helped her through those difficult times.

Now, she found herself peering at the shadows in the corner of the room. The breeze had picked up outside causing the curtains to move. Emily watched the dancing shadows telling herself that they were just that, shadows, and nothing more.

After an hour, she got up to have some milk and turn on the television. Perhaps that would help her relax and think of other things. Around midnight the phone rang and startled her so she nearly dropped the glass of milk. There was something unnerving about a telephone ringing late at night.

The first thing that came to Emily's mind was that it was a prank call. Then, she thought, what if it is some sort of emergency? She went to the phone and picked up the receiver.

"Elinor, Elinor…"

"No!" she screamed, throwing down the telephone. "No, I won't listen to you."

She could still hear the voice coming from the ear piece, "Elinor, come home, I need you. Elinor…"

"Stop it, stop it." Emily sobbed, covering her ears. She sank down in a chair. "I won't let you take over my life. I won't! You must leave me alone, Nicholas!"

The room began to spin and Emily felt as though she were being lifted up out of her body. All sounds faded and she had the sense that she was flying. Then she felt a calming hand on her shoulder and the turmoil ceased. She was back in her body, but who was she?

* * *

"Elinor, dearest, are you all right?"

"Yes," she heard herself answering, "It was a momentary dizziness, but it has passed."

Elinor opened her eyes and looked up into the face of her husband, Nicholas.

"That stomach flu certainly had a hold on you. I think you should have some more of that ginger tea Granny Akers prepared."

"That's a very good idea, I'll got fetch some." Celia volunteered. She rose from her parlor chair and headed for the kitchen.

Looking directly across the room, Elinor's gaze locked with Mother Langford's. The old woman was eyeing Elinor as though her daughter-in-law were a piece of meat.

When Nicholas looked in his mother's direction, her demeanor quickly changed.

"My poor, dear, Elinor," she pursed her lips and cooed. "I still think we should send for the doctor. He should be back by now. I don't trust this Granny Akers or whatever her name is. It sounds as though she's little more than a witch doctor!"

"I'm fine, really, and I have faith in Granny Akers. Many of the draughts the doctors treat with come from the same herbs and plants that she uses."

Celia returned with a cup of the tea. "If you feel up to it later, we'll take a walk by the river. If you're not strong enough, we can just sit. I think the air will do you good." Celia threw a challenging glance at Harriet Langford.

"That's a ridiculous notion!" Harriet stood up and went over to the parlor windows and jerked on the draperies that had been opened. "There," she said, thrusting her chin forward, after having closed out the morning sunlight, "that's better! The last thing you need, young lady, is that damp river air. Besides, the sun will freckle your skin."

Ignoring her mother-in-law, Elinor turned to Celia, "I think it's a fine idea. Maybe we could go swimming and have a picnic by the water."

Nicholas smiled. "If I didn't have to be at the office, I'd join you. It's a lovely day and I think Celia's right. You should get out and enjoy the fresh air." Nicholas ignored his mother's indignant gasp.

Harriet's slit of a mouth drew into an even tighter line that bend downward at the corners. She rose from her chair and marched from the room, her black skirts rustling.

"I will see you when I return," Nicholas bent down and kissed Elinor.

After he was gone, Celia and Elinor looked at one another and grinned.

"Old crow!" Celia whispered.

Instead of making Elinor laugh as intended, it alarmed her. Suddenly, she remembered the menacing crow from the past. Harriet, with her long, black skirts, reminded Elinor of a large black bird. But surely, there could be no real connection between the crow and Mother Langford. Elinor was not one to believe in witchcraft and black magic, but she had to admit that the strange crow had first appeared on the very day she and Nicholas met.

Celia, seeing the serious look on her friend's face, stood up and mimicked Harriet Langford as she went over to the window and pulled open the curtains.

That did make Elinor laugh and Celia joined in.

"I don't know what's so funny." Mother Langford stood in the doorway. Her gaze came to rest on the open curtains. "I though I closed those draperies! Has no one any respect for the mistress of this house?" She rustled her way over to the window and jerked the draperies shut.

"You young ladies will kindly respect my wishes in the future and leave them closed." She glared at Celia and Elinor. "The sun fades the rug—and that river air can give one consumption. Mind what I say, Missy!"

"We certainly wouldn't want to fade your rug," Celia

replied, "After all, it is very expensive to replace. Mrs. Wilkes has all of her draperies open. She doesn't care if the rug fades. Of course, Mrs. Wilkes can afford to replace her area rugs as needed."

It was all Elinor could do not to laugh.

"I could afford to replace mine too, if I wanted!" Harriet's eyes snapped with hatred. "I was brought up to believe that waste is sinful. 'Waste not, want not'. Further more, these rugs are family heirlooms. They belonged to my mother."

"I was brought up by the golden rule, 'Do unto others…' As far as being family heirlooms, well, I can easily see that. They do have a well-worn look." Celia smiled sweetly, knowing she had won that round of verbal jousting.

When Mother Langford again took a hasty departure from the room, Elinor turned to Celia.

"You were brilliant, but it doesn't pay to make an enemy of that woman. I know first hand."

Celia laughed. "Did you see the old crow's face when I mentioned Mrs. Wilkes? I don't know what my future mother-in-law's views of sun, verses, no sun on the rug, might be. It is all so ridiculous! Come on, Elinor, we are going to put on our swimming suits and have ourselves a dip in the river."

As they were leaving the parlor, Harriet Langford intercepted them in the hallway. She turned to Celia. Smiling sweetly, she patted her on the shoulder.

Elinor saw her friend cringe at the older woman's touch.

"Dear, Celia," Harriet began, "I must apologize to you. I just don't know what gets into me sometimes. I am afraid I was rather short with you this morning. I get that way on occasion. Elinor can tell you." Harriet shot a glance at Elinor as she was talking. "I certainly wouldn't want to offend the future daughter-in-law of my close friend, Mrs. Wilkes. I am sure the dear lady would find it most ungracious of me. Please say you will forgive my *faux pas*. That's French, you know."

"*Oui, Madame, je comprendez. Parlez-vous francais?*

Red splotches appeared on Harriet's face and neck and her jaw tightened into granite. "Quite so, yes," she stammered. "Well I must get into the kitchen and give Cook instructions. She will dawdle without my direction."

Harriet Langford tilted her chin and stomped off down the hallway.

Elinor and Celia laughed all the way upstairs. When they reached the upper landing, Elinor stopped Celia. "You are so clever, but take care, I'm not sure what she's capable of if she is pushed too far."

Celia pretended to shiver. "I know what you mean. I should keep my mouth shut but with all of her pretentiousness, she makes such an easy target. I can't stand pomposity."

"I understand. I'm just concerned about you. I sometimes share your view and think she is a witch. That's why it best not to make her too angry."

"Well, enough of her," Celia said, "after we get our swimming suits on, let's ask Cook to prepare us a picnic lunch for later. That is allowed here, isn't it?"

"We can always ask,' Elinor replied.

A short time later, the young women were heading for the back door on their way to the river. They passed Mother Langford in the hallway. Her raised eyebrows registered her disapproval when she saw the girls in what she clearly considered immodest clothing.

"Young ladies would never have dressed that way in my day." She couldn't resist the verbal jab. "What is this world coming to? With all sorts of body parts exposed, it's no wonder that men no longer respect women."

"Dear Mrs. Langford, your day was so long ago. If a woman has to look like a crow in order to be respected by a man, then who needs him?" Celia tossed the insult back.

Harriet's face drained of color and her eyes blazed with

unbridled hatred. "Mind your tongue, Missy!" She turned crisply, and walked away.

"Oh, Celia, I don't know if you should have said that. Did you see her face?"

"I certainly did," Celia giggled, "it was priceless."

"I think it would be best if we avoid these confrontations, Celia. I want my leave taking to go as smoothly as possible. Let's just ignore her remarks."

After making arrangements with the cook, the two young women walked outside and strolled over to the lapping, green river. It was a muggy day and in spite of the fishy smell that was so prominent today, the cool water felt soothing to their bare feet as they waded in.

Celia looked at Elinor. "I'm sorry, Elinor I don't mean to make things more difficult for you. I suppose handling the old woman with humor is my way of tolerating her. If she weren't so funny with all her pompous ways, she'd be very scary."

"It's all right, Celia," Elinor smiled at her friend. "Nicholas and I will be leaving in a few days. There's nothing she can do to stop us now." Elinor tried to sound convincing but there was a knot of fear in her stomach that seemed to grow each day. She knew that Harriet Langford was at the center of that fear.

Elinor and Celia were good swimmers so they lost no time in wading out into the deeper water. The cool, jade river melted Elinor's tension as she and Celia laughed and splashed like carefree children.

Around noon, one of the house girls brought a small picnic basket and a pitcher of lemonade out to the water's edge.

After thanking the shy, young woman, Elinor spread the feast on the ground on top of the table cloth that had been provided. "Cook thought of everything," she said, as she peered into the basket.

A loaf of crusty bread, cheese, cold chicken, apples and little sugar cakes, made for a delicious meal.

"I wonder if Mother Langford is aware that Cook prepared this sumptous feast. I should think the old crow would consider it wasted on the likes of us," Celia said.

After eating their fill, Elinor and Celia stretched out on a blanket they had brought outside with them, and warmed themselves in the sun. After a while, the sun became too warm and they decided to go back into the water.

Noticing Harriet Langford watching from the parlor window, the two girls abandoned all pretense of being ladylike. They ran headlong into the river and dived in. Knowing she would consider their behavior scandalous, they enjoyed it all the more.

"I don't see her at the window now," Celia said, glancing over her shoulder.

The two women swam out to the middle of the river. "We'd better turn back now. There are some undercurrents here that could be dangerous. Nicholas has warned me about them many times."

"If you insist, but you know what? I think we could swim to your mother's house if we set our mind to it."

"No, Celia! Let's go back now." An uneasiness, a sense of foreboding swept over Elinor. It was something more than just a reaction to her friend's reckless behavior.

Suddenly both young women became aware of a dark shadow reflecting on the water from above their heads. They both looked up at the same time.

A large crow circled overhead. "Caw, caw!" The shrill sound unnerved Elinor.

"Celia, come on!" Elinor screamed. "Let's head back to shore."

Celia's face drained of color. "It's her, it's her, Elinor," she shrieked as they turned around and swam in the direction of Langford Manor.

Elinor heard the bird's incessant cawing and the beating of its wings as it looped back and forth, getting closer to the water's surface with each pass. The shadow it cast grew larger each time as it dropped perilously close to the swimmers.

At one point, Elinor looked up and actually saw the dead blackness of the bird's eye as it swooped past.

"Elinor!" Celia screamed, "I have a cramp. I'm not going to make it."

"Yes you are!" Elinor grabbed her friend under the chin. "We're both going to make it. Just relax and let me help you."

"The crow is after us, Elinor, look!"

Suddenly the crow swooped down so close, Elinor felt it's wing brush her cheek. At the same time she heard Celia cry out.

A red gash just above Celia's eye quickly filled with blood as the bird circled back and readied itself for another pass.

Elinor waited until just before it struck. Then she quickly pulled herself and Celia under water.

In shock, Celia struggled with her friend and they both came to the surface. "Are you trying to drown me?" Celia screamed as blood oozed from the ugly wound.

"No, Celia, I was trying to get us away from the crow! See?"

Elinor pointed upward as the black-winged menace made still another circle.

Again it dipped down, aiming for the two women. They ducked beneath the water.

This time when they came back up, there was no sign of the menacing bird and the turbulent waters had returned to a placid state.

Elinor and Celia swam as fast as they could. They did not want to take a chance on the crow returning. Emily could not believe what had happened. Crows didn't attack people! They were shy of humans. The fact that the attack had taken place in water was even stranger. Crows were land scavengers.

The going was rather slow, particularly since Elinor's stamina hadn't fully returned after her bout of stomach flu.

Finally, they reached shore and she and Celia hastily scrambled out of the water.

"I've got to get you inside and take care of that wound, Celia."

"Does my head look very bad?" she asked, half-dazed.

Elinor studied the gash that was just over Celia's eye.

"It's not too bad, but it does need immediate attention."

Elinor looked over at the parlor window as she and Celia made their way to the house. Mother Langford stood there, her black taffeta dress glistening as the sunlight hit it. Elinor shivered as she noted the resemblance between Harriet and the menacing crow that had just attacked them.

Chapter Thirty

When Elinor and Celia entered the house, Harriet Langford rushed to the hallway and played the dutiful hostess.

"Bring her in here," she ordered, indicating that Elinor should lead Celia to the parlor.

"Don't just stand there, girl!" Harriet barked at one of the servants. "Go get a pail of water and bandages. Tell Cook what has happened. She'll know what is needed."

"Not on the settee!" Mother Langford shouted as Elinor guided Celia toward it. "Those wet clothes will ruin the fabric. You should never have been out gallivanting around in the first place. I knew no good would come of it. Here, she can sit on this." Harriet indicated the wooden chair next to the library table.

Elinor glared at her mother-in-law, but complied with her wishes. "You're going to be all right, Celia. That cut really isn't as deep as I thought. Once we get it cleaned and bandaged, you'll feel much better."

"Just keep that witch away from me," Celia said through clenched teeth, "and send for Jonathan. I'm not staying in this house another night." She grabbed Elinor's arm. "Please, send for him now."

Elinor's heart sank. This was only Celia's second day. She had hoped her friend would stay at least two more, but she understood Celia's feelings. "Of course, Celia. I'll take care of it right away."

When the cleaning girl came in with goods needed to

tend Celia's wound, Mother Langford rushed forward to grab them.

"I'll take that," Elinor said, stepping forward and taking the pan of water and the bottles and bandages from the frightened girl's hands. "Dotty," she spoke to the servant, "go fetch Jake, and tell him to ride to Malden and get word to Mr. Jonathan Wilkes that Miss Celia needs him immediately and that he is to bring the carriage."

"Well, it looks as though I am not needed here. You certainly seem to know how to take over as mistress of the manor." Harriet Langford scowled.

"Celia is my friend, Mother Langford. It is best that I take care of her. Celia feels she would be more comfortable in her own residence, so I have sent word for Jonathan to fetch her. Was there something more that you wanted to add?"

Harriet stepped forward, meeting Elinor's gaze. "Only that I am truly sorry that such a mishap occurred to the future Mrs. Jonathan Wilkes on my property. I saw what happened from the window. I have never seen such a shocking attack in all my days!"

In spite of Mother Langford's words, Elinor could see the excitement in her eyes. Celia had pushed the woman too far and now Harriet Langford reveled in seeing the young woman injured and her confidence shaken.

Elinor turned her back on her mother-in-law and began cleaning the narrow gash on Celia's forehead. The bleeding hadn't been too profuse once they left the river and came inside. *So, there's no need to apologize to Harriet for bleeding on her area rug*, Elinor thought, with not a little sarcasm.

Seeing that she was being totally ignored, Mother Langford left the room, her rustling skirts sounding her departure.

"She was involved with this," Celia said. "I told you she is a witch. She probably turned herself into a crow! She looks enough like one."

"Oh come now, Celia, you can't really believe that. I

know she is unscrupulous, but I don't believe she actually has the power to transform herself into a menacing bird!"

All the same, Elinor felt uneasy as she recalled the sheen on Mother Langford's dress as she stood in the window following the bird attack. It had looked very much like the smoothed feathers of a large black crow, glistening in the sun.

"Elinor," Celia's voice broke into Elinor's thoughts. "You have to get away from here too. Come with me now. You can stay at my house or Jonathan can take you on to your mother's. You're not safe here."

"I'm sorry, Celia, I can't do that to Nicholas. A long as he is with me, I'm safe. You mustn't worry about me, Celia. I'll be fine."

"That's just it, you are not safe here. I am sure Nicholas would understand."

"Understand that his mother is a witch who changes into a crow and attacks people? I can hardly ask him to acceptthat."

Elinor walked over to the window and looked outside. The skies were clear and the still, green waters of the river glistened lazily in the sunshine. "There's no sign of a crow there now."

"Of course not," Celia interjected, impatience tinging her voice, "she's upstairs in her bedroom, molting."

Both young women couldn't help but laugh at that.

"Come on," Elinor said, "We'd better go upstairs and get out of these wet clothes. You'll want to look nice when Jonathan arrives."

Later that afternoon, Elinor waved good-bye to her friend. Celia had again asked her to come with her. "I can't," Elinor had replied, "but I'll see you at the Fourth of July festivities."

The sun was just dipping behind the mountains when Elinor stepped back inside and shut the door. Harriet Langford, who had stayed in the background during Celia's departure, emerged from the shadows. Her eyes glowed with satisfaction.

"Too bad your little friend had to depart so soon. I do hope her future mother-in-law doesn't blame me for the girl's injury. Clearly the young woman behaved imprudently. After all, I did urge the two of you not to go into the water. It was the young lady's own foolhardiness that put her in harm's way."

"I doubt that you would want to hear what Celia will tell Mrs. Wilkes, Mother Langford. But if I were you, I would start wearing another color besides black."

Harriet's jaw dropped and a quizzical expression knitted her dark eyebrows.

Elinor turned and started up the stairs.

"Wait! Explain yourself, young lady, just what do you mean by that?"

Elinor ignored her mother-in-law and continued upstairs to her room. She would wait there for Nicholas. She'd had enough of Mother Langford for one day. Once inside her bedroom, she slammed the door shut and, after lighting a candle, went over to the long windows.

A rosy hue settled over the twilight sky. It was just the setting Elinor enjoyed sharing with Nicholas. They would find new horizons and sunsets to share out West. There, they'd be free of the oppressive atmosphere at Langford Manor.

A smile crossed Elinor's lips as she remembered her parting remark to Harriet Langford. She must remember to share it with Celia when she saw her again at the Fourth of July celebration.

She shivered as she thought of how serious Celia was in comparing Mother Langford to a crow. Perhaps her mother-in-law was some sort of witch, at least in her own mind. Elinor could acknowledge that, but changing into a crow or even controlling the actions of one was totally bizarre.

After the Fourth of July, it wouldn't matter anyway.

Elinor went to the armoire and took out her ball gown. It was beautiful. She held it up against her and looked in the mirror. Her blue eyes sparkled in the dim candlelight, perfectly matching the color of her lovely dress. Four more days. After that, she and Nicholas would leave this cursed placed for good.

She put the gown away as she heard Nicholas' voice calling to her from the stairway. Rushing our to greet him, she told him what had happened.

"Dearest, is Celia going to be all right? I feel terrible that such a thing has happened to your friend."

"The wound wasn't serious, but she did receive quite a fright. I think she'll do much better now that she is back home. She found Langford Manor a bit intimidating."

"She did?" Nicholas seemed surprised.

Elinor didn't want to tell him that his mother was to blame. Instead she said, "Celia's very bubbly and outgoing. We are so isolated here. You must admit, the house is rather gloomy."

"I suppose it is. I forget how other people perceive it. After growing up here, I'm used to the old house and rather fond of it. What about you? You probably feel the same way Celia does, don't you?"

Elinor felt a pang of conscience. Nicholas loved his home, but he was willingly giving it up for her. Yet, she knew it was for his own good, even if he didn't realize it now.

"I won't lie to you, Nicholas. Sometimes, when you are not here, I feel so cut off from everyone and everything."

"In four more days, it won't matter. We will be on our way to a new life."

Later, at the dinner table, Mother Langford mentioned the crow attack to Tobias.

"That's ridiculous," he scoffed, "it must have been something else. At any rate, it is hardly our responsibility if two young women behave in a foolhardy manner."

"Father, Elinor and I will be leaving in four days. Can we not have peace at dinner time? I would like to carry positive memories with me when we take our leave."

Tobias glared at Nicholas, but for once, he said nothing more.

Later, when Elinor and Nicholas climbed the stairway to prepare for bed, Elinor could not shake the impending sense of doom. She had tried to make light of it today, but it still nagged her.

She felt safe in Nicholas' arms, but she was afraid that even he was not strong enough to fight off all the forces that seemed to be against them.

Everything that had happened up until now seemed to be some sort of warning, but of what? She knew she must be wary of Mother Langford, but beyond that, she did not know. She would have to be very careful and keep busy preparing for her journey. There were also the festivities and the ball, her opportunity to say good-bye to all her friends. She must focus on that, not on the evil forces that lurked at Langford Manor, threatening to swallow her up.

After undressing and putting on her nightgown, Elinor stood by the window and gazed at the river and at her parents' home on the other side. So close, yet so very far away. She wished she could reach out and clutch it to her breast so that she might feel safe again.

She was a married woman now, and she must put aside the things of her childhood and accept adult responsibilities.

Besides, there was Nicholas. He more than made up for the loneliness and insecurity she felt at Langford Manor. Even in her present state of melancholy, her heart brimmed with hope when she thought of their new beginning. She only had to get through the next four days and all would be well.

Nicholas joined her by the window and planted a kiss on her temple. The headache that had been threatening her all afternoon seemed to subside from his mere touch. He was her strength and as long as they were together, they could face anything.

However, even in Nicholas' arms, sleep eluded Elinor that night. She kept reliving the crow attack. She kept remembering the look of death in its eye as it passed by, close enough to brush her with its wing. She shivered as she recalled how the feathery touch had chilled her soul. The crow seemed to be a creature straight from hell, bent on evil.

When she finally slept, Elinor dreamed of huge black wings beating and flapping in the sunlight and of rustling, black skirts flying and circling. Suddenly, she was in her room, lying alone on her bed. She wanted to wake up but could not.

A feeling of terror was upon her and she was paralyzed, the way one frequently is in a nightmare. Her eyes were closed but she could still see everything in the room. A candle flickered in the doorway and a woman resembling a giant crow entered the room, her face filled with hate. Then her arms turned into giant flapping wings as she moved closer to Elinor.

Chapter Thirty-one

Emily screamed and flailed her arms to ward off the black wings and sharp beak of the attacking bird. The giant crow turned and swooped down again close enough for her to see the death and destruction in its vacant eye.

"Stop it!" she screamed, sitting upright in bed. The morning sun streamed through the window with blinding force, adding to the pain that throbbed in her temple. She was in a cold, clammy sweat that left her thin nightgown clinging to her body.

"Oh no," she moaned as memories of the eerie dream came flooding back, "it's happening again."

Then she though about Cap and the dark bird or bat that had attacked him. It was no wonder she had dreamed about flapping wings and a constant rustling sound.

She heard the church bells ringing in the distance as she shuffled off to the shower. The warm water soothed her aching head. Feeling like someone who had been drugged, she returned to her bedroom to get dressed. The sleeping sedative had never left her feeling hung over before.

He stomach rumbled, reminding he that she was hungry. As she combed her hair and tied it back with a ribbon, the church bells sounded again. She looked at herself in the mirror as the color drained from her face.

Church bells rang on Sunday. Today was Friday. Why were they ringing? She raced down the hallway and threw open the front door. Three newspapers lay on the porch.

She picked them up. The last one was a thick Sunday edition dated June 30.

She had lost two days! Her knees turned to jelly and the papers slipped from her hands. Sinking down onto the porch swing, Emily stared straight ahead. She must think, try to remember what she had done during the last two days.

She buried her head in her hands and closed her eyes. The blackbird, the beating wings and the rustling sounds. That was all associated with the attack on Cap, wasn't it? She thought back, trying to remember every detail of the night the dog was injured.

For some reason the rustling noise in the background took on a special significance because she sensed it wasn't directly connected with the dog's injury.

A feeling of impending doom seized Emily. She had to fight it and not let it take over. She had been in control, but then it had slipped and she had not been thinking about the Langfords! Perhaps she had been so unnerved by the attack on Cap that her defenses were down. Possibly that, coupled with the vulnerable state of sleep, had allowed those other forces to influence her again.

What should I do now, she wondered? *Leave and go back to New York?* That might solve the problem but it would mean leaving the lovely old family home where she had shared so many happy years with Grams.

Yet, if that's what it took to be free of this obsession, then at she would have to do it. She would rent or sell the house and go back to Broadway where she'd throw herself into furthering her career. She'd be so busy there wouldn't be time to think about Nicholas.

Her stomach again let her know she was hungry. She got up from the swing and headed for the kitchen. Feeling good about the decision she had made, she pulled the bacon and eggs from the refrigerator. She would fix a good country breakfast for herself.

As Emily put the bread in the toaster, the phone rang. It was Becky.

"Oh, Em, I just had to call you. The Greenbrier Resort is lovely, but there is something even lovelier on my third finger, left hand."

"Beck! Fred proposed? That's wonderful."

"It is, isn't it? I couldn't wait until we got home to call you. I just had to tell you now. I gotta go, Em, Fred and I are going down for brunch. See you when we get back."

Emily was happy for her friend. She and Becky had become even closer, if that was possible, since she had returned to Benson. Now, she was leaving again. Running was more like it. She had already started putting down roots here. Now she was going back to Jeff's world, though Jeff would definitely not be a part of hers anymore.

She thought of Mitch. He was a fine, decent man. Who knows where their friendship might have gone, had she decided to stray? She corrected herself. No use in having any illusions. She and Mitch would never have been more than friends. Emily looked about the cozy kitchen. In many ways, leaving would be difficult. Maybe she should just stop thinking about it and go ahead and book a flight to New York.

There, she would forget the crazy thoughts. Nicholas would be relegated to the past where he belonged. There would be no more crows that attacked people and skirts that rustled.

Skirts! That was the background noise she had heard in her dream! The sound of long skirts, made of a stiff, silky fabric, rustling when the wearer walked. Somehow the rustling had become interspersed with the beating of the bird's wings. Now that she had identified the sound, what did it mean?

The crow. The crow woman. A chill raced up Emily's spine. She thought about what Mattie had said. Someone on the other side wanted something of Emily. Would that someone or something really leave her alone if she went back to New York?

She thought again of Becky and experienced another pang of guilt. Her friend had been so excited when Emily told her she was thinking of staying. Now she would have to tell her that the plans had changed. But, Becky had Fred and she would be starting a new life with him. Emily would see her friend often. She always had over the years and she would definitely be Becky's Maid of Honor.

Emily's thoughts moved ahead to the Fourth of July. "Beck will kill me!" she groaned. She had promised to be that professor from Colorado's date for the festival. Emily hoped she could make Becky understand.

Emily knew she wasn't being fair. She had promised and now she was leaving Becky and Fred in a lurch. Suddenly she wasn't sure of anything. The urge to run to New York was strong, but her life there had not been all that satisfying.

Perhaps she should stay here and face whatever it was that was plaguing her. At the very least, she should postpone her decision until after the Fourth of July and keep her promise to Becky.

Emily shivered at the mere thought of the Fourth. It was the day Nicholas and Elinor had perished in the fire. In fact, this would be the one hundredth anniversary of their deaths.

The realization hit like a lightening bolt. Something was going to happen on that day! She could feel it. It included her. If she stayed, she would be drawn into it. If she left, perhaps she could escape it.

Fear seized her as a pair of dark eyes flashed before her, a man's dark eyes, framed by winged eyebrows. Love, pleading poured forth from that momentary image and burned itself into her soul.

Lips, sensual and inviting, spoke softly, "Elinor, Elinor, don't leave me. Please, come home."

Emily rose quickly from the chair, banishing the unwelcome thoughts. She walked out of the kitchen door to get a breath of fresh air. She had to make a decision. If she was going to go to New York, it would have to be now.

She walked over to the swing she had used as a child and sat down in it. She wished she could go back and be a little girl again. Grams had always known how to make everything all right. Now, Grams was gone and Emily was alone.

She planted her feet on the ground and, holding the chains on either side, pushed herself back in the swing. Then, lifting her feet up, she went gliding forward. She put her feet down and repeated the process until she was soaring out over the embankment the way she had as a young girl. It always brought her a feeling of omnipotence and helped clear her mind of worrisome thoughts.

She pumped again, going higher and higher as she gazed at the jade ribbon of water sparkling in the sunlight.

"What should I do?" she asked herself aloud.

As if in answer to her questions, a gray, smoky mist rolled over the river. She hadn't seen it coming. It was suddenly just there, like it had been that other day. She put her feet on the ground and stopped the swing. Standing up, she walked over to the middle of the embankment to get a better view. She stared, mesmerized, and could not have turned away had she tried.

A prickling of her scalp accompanied the thinning of the fog. Emily waited, knowing what she was going to see. A new manor house stood in place of the ruins. A man and a woman, clad in old-fashioned clothes, stood by the river. The man had his arm around the woman and they were looking across the water at Emily.

"It's Nicholas and Elinor," Emily whispered, "and I know they see me as I see them."

Nicholas stood rigid and Elinor's skirt flapped in the breeze. Was that the source of the rustling skirts? Somehow Emily didn't think so. The rustling had been threatening and sinister. She didn't feel Elinor meant her any harm.

Emily wasn't frightened by what she saw. Through some bizarre sort of time travel, she had been Elinor. She had made love to Nicholas.

Suddenly, Emily noticed a movement at one of the upstairs windows at Langford manor and her heart froze. She could not see clearly at the distance but she saw enough to know that it was the crow woman. She was clad in a shiny black dress that caught the sunlight. The sheen was like a blackbird's feathers.

Emily knew the woman meant harm to the young lovers who stood innocently by the water, sending out their silent pleas.

"Help us, only you can help us."

Emily heard them though not a word was spoken. What can I do to help? She thought, shaken by the realization. She continued staring at her beloved Nicholas and his wife, Elinor.

The answer came back clearly, though again, no words were spoken.

"Elinor, come home." Nicholas' loving voice imprinted itself on Emily's soul.

Confused, she whispered, "But Elinor is with you, Nicholas. I am Emily."

"Elinor, my Elinor, come home to me." She heard the resonant sounds echoing again.

Could it be, she thought, that I did live a hundred years ago and in that life I was Elinor? But if that were the case, it didn't seem that she should be able to *see* Elinor.

Another disquieting thought struck Emily. If she made another transition into Nicholas' world, would she end up dying in the fire with him?"

Chapter Thirty-two

Emily heard a twig snap behind her and she whirled around. Mattie Devers stood there gazing across the river.

"I see them too, Miss Emily, and I heard what they said to you."

"Oh, Mattie!" Emily rushed to the old woman's side. "How could either of us have heard anything?"

"Them that's from the spirit world know how to speak to us when it's necessary. Yep, I heard it, miss, yes I did." She put her arms around Emily and spoke in soft tones. "Ol' Mattie's here. You don't have to face this alone no more. I can help you."

"Mattie, if only you could." Out of the corner of her eye, Emily saw the fog creeping over the river. She stepped back from the old woman and as she did so, she saw a black shadow emerge from the mist. A crow, a large black bird soared overhead and then turned toward Mattie and Emily.

"That's the bird that attacked Cap the other evening!" Emily shrieked, backing away.

"That's the crow woman," Mattie said. Lifting her arms in the air and calling out in a clear voice she shouted, "Go, you have no power here, old crow. Begone!"

To Emily's astonishment, the menacing black bird turned and disappeared into the mist.

"Mattie! You did it, you made it go away."

The old woman flashed a grin, exposing the gaps where teeth had once been. "Yes, Miss Emily, I still have a few tricks left."

As suddenly as the mist appeared, it thinned, revealing nothing on the other side of the river except the ruins of Langford Manor.

Mattie took Emily by the arm. "Let's go inside, Miss, we have work to do and it ain't gonna be as easy to deal with as that crow was."

"I have a question for you, Mattie," Emily said as they entered the kitchen. She motioned for the old woman to sit down.

Pulling a chair out and sitting down, Emily gazed across the table at the old woman. "I'm really glad you came when you did, Mattie, but what brought you here?"

"I was home, sittin' in my easy chair and I heard the voices. I knew they had somethin' to do with you and so I rushed over here."

"You heard them from your house?"

The old woman pointed a bony finger to her head. "I heard them up here, not in my ears. Just like you, Miss."

Tears welled up in Emily's eyes. "That's not all there is to it, Mattie, there's more."

"Just tell me, child. We'll work it out."

"I've had another time lapse." Emily choked back a sob. "This time it lasted two days. I've been thinking of leaving here and going back to New York. This didn't start happening until I came back here to Benson." Emily searched the old woman's face.

Mattie shook her head. "Won't do no good, Miss Emily. Things have gone too far. You can't run from them now. You have to stay. We'll figure out what to do."

"Nicholas wants something from me. July Fourth will be the hundredth anniversary of his and Elinor's deaths. They died so young. I'm having flashes of memory, Mattie. I feel as though I've been loved by Nicholas Langford. I can't get him out of my mind. And you heard him from across the river, calling me Elinor and telling me to come to him. Could this mean that I lived back then and that I was Elinor?"

"I don't rightly think that's it. The best way to find out is for me to go into a trance."

Fear registered on Emily's face and Mattie reached over and patted her hand to reassure her.

"It's like being hypnotized, miss. I can go back there and find out what this is all about."

"No, Mattie, I can't let you do that! You told me it would be dangerous for me, so it must be risky for you, too."

"Now, now, Miss Emily, ol' Mattie has been in many trances before and I'm still here, kickin'. I reckon I can handle it."

"If that's the case, then why not send me?"

"Because of the crow woman. I know how to deal with the likes of her. She's a witch, a very evil one. I have some magic of my own. I can't send you there unprepared. I have to be the one to go."

"How can you be so sure that returning to New York won't solve my problem?"

"I just know. Somethin' big is brewing. I think you were right when you said it had to do with that hundredth anniversary. Things are comin' to a head fast. We've gotta find out what the young man and woman want from you. We must take care. The evil crow woman will try to stop you from righting any wrongs. That's why I have to go and find out all that I can."

Arising from her chair, Emily paced back and forth across the kitchen floor with her arms folded in front of her. "Mattie, I'm scared for you."

"There ain't nothin' to be scared of, Miss Emily. I know what I'm doing. I'll be fine, providing you follow my directions."

Mattie stood up. "I think the parlor would be the best place to do this."

Emily followed the older woman down the hallway and into the sitting room. She noticed the lace curtains billowing out from the breeze that came through the open window. It reminded her of something, but the memory was illusive and fragmented.

"I'm going to lie down on the sofa, Miss. It'll be like I'm asleep only it will be more than that. You are not to talk to me or touch me no matter what I say. If someone should come here, don't let them in. They must not look upon me. Do you understand?"

Emily nodded.

"Before we get started I want you to lock the door, close the windows and unplug the telephone."

"I really don't expect anybody, Mattie. Both Mitch and Becky are out of town."

"It wasn't them that I was thinkin' of. The old crow woman might send someone or something to try and stop me. You mustn't let them in no matter who or what they are. You sit quietly in the room and watch over me until I come out of it. Remember, don't touch me, and don't talk to me. Promise?"

"Yes, Mattie, I promise. How long do you think it will take?"

"There's no tellin'. Could be minutes, or hours. Just stay put and don't leave this room till it's over." Mattie walked over to the windows and shut them. "Let's close the door and lock it. There's a reason for doing all of this, Miss Emily. Trust me."

"I do trust you, Mattie." Emily gave the old woman a hug. "Please be careful."

Mattie grinned and patted Emily's face. "You're a sweet one to care about what happens to ol' Mattie. Not too many in this town give two hoots whether I live or die."

"I care."

"I know you do, Miss. That's why I'm gonna find some answers for you."

Mattie stepped over to the sofa, sat down and removed

her shoes. Lying back, she closed he eyes and quickly opened them again. "Now don't forget, don't talk to me, don't touch me, no matter what."

"Don't worry, I won't," Emily reassured her, though she was feeling anything but calm.

The older woman folded her hands across her chest and closed her eyes, giving her the appearance of someone laid out in a coffin.

Emily shivered at the comparison as she watched Mattie's breathing become gradually slower. What if she stopped breathing altogether? Mattie hadn't told her what to do in a case like that. Maybe it was normal or it could mean that Mattie was in trouble. Why hadn't Mattie mentioned it?

Continuing to watch her closely, Emily saw that her slow breathing had leveled off and was staying at about the same low rate. She also noticed that Mattie's eyes were moving rapidly back and forth under her closed lids.

REM sleep, rapid eye movement, Emily had heard it called. It meant someone was dreaming. Mattie must be there already, she thought.

A smile crossed Mattie's thin dry lips and she nodded her head. "Yes," she whispered, "yes, I understand."

Then concern creased Mattie's brow and the smile faded.

"Oh no," she moaned, "no, how awful." Mattie began to move her head from side to side. "We will stop her, we will!" Mattie's feet pumped up and down as though she were trying to walk or run.

It was difficult to watch Mattie in such an agitated state and do nothing. Now, Emily understood why Mattie had kept warning her not to intervene. If she hadn't made such an issue of it, Emily would have instinctively rushed to the old woman's side.

Finally, Mattie settled down and resumed her lower respiration as though she were going deeper into the trance.

Emily watched her, almost afraid to breath herself. She clutched the arms of the chair, her muscles tense as though she were in a state of readiness. For what, she did not know.

An hour passed, then two. Mattie had not moved and neither had Emily. The settlings of the house, as it was buffeted by a stiff breeze, had never sounded so loud as it did now in the absolute silence. The striking of the grandfather clock, fainter because it was heard through the closed door, was still loud enough to make Emily jump.

Then Emily heard something else that prickled the skin on her neck and scalp. It was faint but very distinct.

"Caw, caw!"

She listened. There it was again, only this time it seemed closer.

"Caw, caw!"

Emily's heart raced and her mouth went dry. She was inside, protected, yet that awful cawing struck her with panic. That sound came from no ordinary crow. What if it got inside the house? Mattie hadn't prepared her for that.

Suddenly, a loud, shrieking 'caw' sounded again as something large and black hit the window.

Emily screamed and as she did so, Mattie screamed too.

Sitting upright on the sofa, Mattie opened her eyes.

Another thud hit the window again, just above Mattie's head. This time the window cracked.

Emily rushed to Mattie's side and started to reach out for her, but remembering the old woman's instructions, she stopped short.

There was a vacant stare in Mattie's eyes, a blank, dead stare. She was still in the trance.

Emily heard the cawing of the crow and she knew that if it threw itself against the window pane again, it would break through.

She ran to the closet and crawled to the back of it. Thrusting her hand out, she closed her fingers around the butt of Grandpa's shotgun. Pulling it out, she stood upright and pulled out the step stool, hoping to find the box of shells that used to be there.

"Thank God," she whispered as her stiff fingers fumbled to get a handful of them. Though her hands trembled, she loaded the gun the way Jeff had taught her when they used to go skeet shooting. Taking deep, calming breaths, she sat down in her chair, leveled the shotgun at the window pane and waited.

"Caw, caw!" she heard the ear-piercing cry as the huge black bird hit the weakened pane and broke through.

Emily squeezed the trigger and the resounding explosion echoed in her ears. Keeping her eyes open, she was sure she hit the crow. She had seen its body contort and break apart and she had heard and seen the shattering of the glass in the window.

Suddenly the room was quiet. Emily set the shotgun on the floor and stood up. The room was clean and undisturbed, looking exactly as it had when she and Mattie had entered it two hours ago. Where was the broken glass and the crow's remains?

Emily looked at Mattie, wondering how she had survived the commotion. As she did so, the old woman opened her eyes and turned her head to face Emily. She smiled and reached out to the frightened young woman.

"I'm okay, Miss Emily. I made it there and back and I know what it's all about now. I can help you."

Chapter Thirty-three

"Mattie, thank God you're all right!" Emily bent down and hugged the old woman. "Is there anything I can get for you?"

"I'm fine," Mattie grinned, obviously touched by Emily's concern. "I could use a cup of coffee or tea, if it ain't too much trouble. We can talk in the kitchen."

Mattie's gaze traveled to the shotgun lying on the floor and her face paled. "What happened here?"

"You don't know? Oh, Mattie, a large crow flew against the window. The second time it hit it, the pane cracked. When I heard it cawing in the distance I knew it was heading back, so I was ready for it with the shotgun. When it broke through, I shot it. But now there is no trace of the bird and the window isn't broken. I thought you saw it too."

"The crow woman," Mattie whispered, shaking her head. "Yep, it was her and I reckon you done saved ol' Mattie's life, Miss Emily. If she had gotten through to me while I was in a trance, I would have been helpless against her."

Emily's hands shook as she reached out to help Mattie up. "Let's go to the kitchen."

Emily put on a pot of coffee, giving the old woman time to collect her thoughts. She set out a plate of cookies and when the coffee was perked, Emily poured two cups of the dark, steaming brew.

"You said you understand what's going on now and you can help me?" Emily joined Mattie at the table.

"First of all, you and Elinor are two separate people, Miss Emily, but there is a very special bond between you. Do you remember when your parents were killed in the car wreck?"

"Yes, I could never forget that."

"You were hurt real bad. Did your grandmother tell you that your heart stopped beating for three minutes?"

"Yes, I believe she did mention something about that after I was grown." Emily had a sick feeling in the pit of her stomach. What was Mattie getting at?"

"Well, Miss Emily, your ancestor, Miss Elinor's spirit, came forward and fused some of her young strength with your own. If she hadn't, you would have died. Her life was cruelly taken by the evil crow woman. Now, on this hundredth anniversary, you can return the favor. You have the opportunity to re-write history and give Nicholas and Elinor a second chance at life."

"Me?" Emily's mouth went dry. "What can I do?"

"First, I have to tell you that it might be dangerous for you."

Mattie added a spoonful of sugar to her coffee and stirred. "Their spirits have told me that they will understand if you do not want to help. They won't bother you no more."

"I wouldn't know where to begin, Mattie."

"I'll explain, Miss Emily. The fire at Langford Manor was set to cover a murder. The crow woman, Harriet Langford, slipped into Elinor's bedchamber after drugging her. She carried a black widow spider in a little jeweled case in her pocket. She made sure it bit Elinor, before she killed it and put it back into the box to get rid of the evidence."

"Nicholas discovered his mother coming out of his and Elinor's bedroom. He questioned her. Naturally, she covered herself. She told him that Elinor was sick and might not be going to the Fourth of July Ball after all."

"Good Lord," Emily whispered, "what about the fire? I thought that's what killed them."

"There was a fire, all right. Whether or not Nicholas and Elinor escape is in your hands. Harriet Langford's mind totally snapped when her son told her he was leaving Langford Manor that night, no matter what. The crow woman, whose witchcraft had failed, poured lamp oil up and down the hallways of the house and set it on fire."

"How do I fit into all of this?" Emily took a long sip of coffee. "What could I do to stop her?"

"That's where it gets a little tricky, Miss Emily. No one would blame you if you didn't want to do it."

"Do what, Mattie?"

"Go back and provide the antidote to the black widow venom. You must convince Nicholas to allow you to give it to Elinor or she will die."

"Why would I have to convince him, you said that he and Elinor know about me." As Emily was speaking, she visualized Nicholas, the man she loved.

"Their spirits know about you now in eternity, but they did not know you back in 1900. Except for that one time.

"What do you mean? What time?"

Mattie bit into an oatmeal cookie and followed it with a sip of coffee. "They saw you one day in the swing and they saw that this house was different. They didn't know who you were, but they knew something supernatural was going on. They noticed your resemblance to Elinor. It might be enough to convince Nicholas to trust you. It will be up to you to persuade him."

"Trust me?" But I love him, Mattie. I know he has loved me in return. How can I suddenly be a stranger to him?"

"Yes, you have known his love, but it was with Elinor's body. Your spirit became fused with Elinor's during those times, but the two of you are separate people. If you go back now, you will be going as yourself. Nicholas will look upon you different-like. You have to be prepared for that. I must say though, you do look a lot like Miss Elinor."

Emily thought for a moment. Could she stand for her beloved Nicholas to look at her with distrust or anger? A flood of warm feelings for this dark-eyed phantom lover swept over her. Now she understood her fascination for him and why, as a child, she'd dressed up in the old clothes in the attic and pretended to be Elinor. It all made sense now. Emily knew what she had to do.

"You said there would be danger, Mattie, what kind of danger?"

"You might go back there and not be able to return. That's why you have to think about this real careful-like."

"How will I get there in the first place?"

"Now mind you, Miss Emily, I'm not saying you should go." Mattie took a slurp of her coffee and returned her attention to Emily. "In the next two or three days, the mist will come. It is like a portal, a door to the past. When you see it, you will get in your boat and row into the fog. It will get you back to the evening of the Fourth of July, 1900. I know someone who will give me the anti-venom in a hypodermic needle. You will take it with you. You should get there just in time."

"Since it will be happening on the Fourth of July there, won't it be the Fourth of July here, too?" Emily asked.

"Not necessarily. The times are not exact, so you must watch the river. It could happen at almost any time from tomorrow on."

"Why couldn't I go back a little sooner and stop Harriet Langford before she tries to kill Elinor?"

"It doesn't work exactly like that, child. Even evil people still have free will. She must be allowed to follow her own choices, for on that her poor soul will be judged. We can overcome that evil, after it strikes but not before. That is just the way the law of the Universe seems to work in these cases. Mind you, this is a rare situation. It's not often a person has a chance to go back and right a wrong. You have a great privilege but I have to warn you again that it could be dangerous for you. You must also guard yourself against the crow woman. She won't like your interference."

"All right, Mattie, I'll do it."

"One more thing, Miss Emily. You must tell Mr. Nicholas that he is to take Miss Elinor away and they can never look back, return or contact anyone back here. When you change history you must not change people's perceptions. Everyone will think they perished in the fire, but with your help, they can survive. They must allow everyone to believe that. Knowing this, do you want to think it over a bit?"

"No, this is something I have to do. I have to try to save Nicholas' and Elinor's lives. After all, I owe Elinor mine."

Suddenly, Emily thought about Nicholas and his loving gaze. She could be with him. She and Nicholas could leave the manor house before it burned. She could become his Elinor.

"It wouldn't work, Miss Emily. You couldn't live with yourself."

"You knew what I was thinking, Mattie?"

The old woman nodded.

"I'm so ashamed. Elinor saved my life and it is she who Nicholas loves. It was her he looked at with adoration. It was her he made love to. But that part of my spirit that was infused with hers loves and desires him."

"It won't be easy, Miss. Like I told you, no one would blame you if you didn't want to do this."

Emily stood up and went over to the window. As always the tree blocked her view of the ruins. "How long will I be gone and where will you be?"

"I don't know how long it will take. Like I said, the times ain't exact. I don't know when you'll get back but I'll be waitin' here for you. I'll know when you've been called just like I knew today."

"What if Becky or Mitch shows up? What will they think? Emily asked.

"You leave that to me. I'll cover for you."

Mattie stood up and walked over to stand beside Emily. Patting her on the shoulder, she said, "You'll be all right, child. Ol' Mattie will see to it even if she has to come back there and get you herself."

Emily could think of little else the rest of the day. People would think she was crazy to listen to Mattie. Yet, she knew the old woman's words were true. She had witnessed the strange phenomena herself.

That night, in her dreams, Emily remembered it all. The scent of lilacs, the love-making, the mother-in-law who hated Elinor.

When she awoke the next morning, she was more convinced than ever that she must follow through with her plans.

Mattie showed up. "Here's the anti-venom." She handed Emily a hypodermic syringe. I'm going to check on you often. If possible, I want to be here to help when the portal opens. But if I'm not here, don't fetch me. There won't be time. Those time warps can be tricky and can close up real fast."

Emily caught the look in Mattie's eyes. "What if it never opens again, that's what you're thinking, isn't it, Mattie?"

"Now, Miss Emily, I'm supposed to be the mind reader around here. I'll come back later and see how things are goin'."

Becky called right after Mattie left. She'd gotten a summer cold and was going to stay home from school for at least a couple of days to nurse it. She wanted to be in good shape for the Fourth of July festivities.

"Is there anything I can do, Beck?"

"No chicken soup, thank you. You just stay away until I am better. I don't want you catching my cold and spoiling the holiday with Professor Whittaker. Fred's got a cold too. Isn't that sweet?"

"Yes, Beck, that's very sweet. Actually the timing is rather interesting because I need to fly back to New York for a day or two. My agent called and insists on speaking to me face to face." Emily felt a twinge of guilt for lying, but it was the best way to keep Becky from worrying. Cold or not, she knew her friend would be calling constantly unless she thought Emily was going to be away from home.

"Em! You'll be back for the Fourth of July, won't you"

"I should be."

"What do you mean, 'should be'?"

"All right, Beck, I will be. Now relax. Incidentally, Mitch is out of town. If he should call looking for me when he returns, would you explain where I am, please?"

"Sure, Em. When did you say you were leaving?"

Emily told her that her flight was for that evening and that she would call her when she returned.

Mattie dropped by after dinner and, seeing that everything was all right, she said she would check on her the next day.

Emily fixed a cup of herbal tea, hoping it would calm her. She carried it outside to watch the fiery sun set over the mountains. It was a pleasant, balmy evening. The scent of lilacs permeated the air, setting Emily's skin to prickling with anticipation.

She looked at the dark shadowed ruins of the old manor house as the sun dipped behind the mountain, settling a blanket of twilight over the valley. Suddenly a faint wisp of fog appeared over the river. It quickly grew, it's eerie fingers creeping just above the darkening waters until it settled directly in front of the river that fronted Langford Manor.

There was no time to call anyone. Emily's heart slammed in her chest as she grabbed the hypodermic needle Mattie had given her. Her knees were shaky and weak when she began the steep descent to her boat.

Chapter Thirty-four

When Emily reached the boat she looked back and saw Mattie waving from the top of the embankment. Knowing the old woman was there made her task easier. Emily knew this was her last chance to turn back, but she also knew she would not. She pushed the little skiff out into deeper water, getting her skirts wet in the process. Then she climbed in and oared the vessel toward the darkened mist.

Her hair stood on end and gooseflesh rose as she steered into the dank smog. She continued rowing in what she hoped was a straight line.

"I can't believe I'm doing this," she uttered, her voice shaking. Just when she thought the fog would go on forever, it suddenly thinned.

Emily gasped when saw the solid stones of a new Langford Manor waiting for her just ahead. She now remembered the times Nicholas had brought her here as Elinor. Stopping for a moment, she took a few deep breaths and tried to still her trembling hands before heading toward shore. Emily stepped out on wobbly legs and pulled the boat up on the river bank. Then she did a quick check to see if anyone was watching her. The only light in the house came from Nicholas and Elinor's bedroom, and that gave off a very faint glow.

Harriet Langford is in there now, Emily thought. Because of the dreams the previous night, Emily knew the layout of the house. Adrenaline pumping through her veins, she opened a back door and stepped into the deserted kitchen. She thought about the time she and Nicholas had eaten cold chicken after one of their boat rides. *It wasn't me, it was Elinor*, she reminded herself.

Emily stepped into the darkened hallway. This time she was grateful that frugal Harriet Langford had neglected to have the sconces lit. Quickly, she mounted the same stairs she and Nicholas had climbed, and turned down the hallway just in time to see Nicholas.

She gasped and her heart thundered. She was looking at him, her beloved. Standing next to him was Harriet Langford, the crow woman.

Surprise registered on his face as he gazed at his mother, who stood just outside of his and Elinor's bedroom. "Mother, what are you doing here?"

"Nicholas, dear, I was just checking on Elinor to see if she was finished with her nap and was ready for the Ball. She seems indisposed. I told her you would be returning for her soon." Harriet Langford shook her head and put her hand on her abdomen. "I don't feel so well myself. I think we both got some tainted food earlier." Harriet averted her eyes and then glanced back with lowered lids.

"Elinor is ill?" Nicholas frowned and started to push past his mother and enter the bedroom.

Realizing she could not give Harriet a chance to get away, Emily took a deep breath and stepped out of the shadows.

"Nicholas, wait. There's something you must know!" Emily called out as she stepped from the shadows and approached him and Harriet Langford. Her heart lurched when Nicholas glared at her as though she were a stranger. The look of love was now replaced by a brittle questioning and distrust

"Who are you? How did you get in here?" he demanded.

Apparently welcoming the diversion, Harriet leveled a curious gaze at Emily.

Emily ignored her and looked directly at Nicholas. "You know me, Nicholas. You saw me that day on the river bank, you and Elinor."

Nicholas studied her face and then glanced at her short skirt and bare legs. "Yes, and you were dressed strangely then, too. You are so like my Elinor. Where do you come from?"

"How I am dressed and where I am from isn't important. It's your wife's life that matters. I have come to save her."

Nicholas' face paled. "What kind of talk is this? Elinor is in some sort of danger?"

Emily looked at Harriet, whose contorted face was marred with red blotches. "Yes, she is. Your mother has just tried to kill her."

"How dare you say such a horrible thing." Harriet lunged at her, digging her long fingernails into Emily's shoulder before Nicholas could pull her away.

"Miss, I don't know what you are up to, but your little joke is over. I think you had better leave. You can see how you have upset my mother."

Nicholas' look of contempt stabbed Emily's heart but she did not waiver. "Look in her pocket, Nicholas. You will find a small box. Inside, are the remains of a dead black widow spider. After putting it on your wife's pillow and making sure it delivered a deadly bite, your mother killed it. She was successful at doing this because she first drugged Elinor's wine. Oh, Nicholas, don't you know that Elinor is afraid of your mother? That fear is well-founded. Look in your mother's pocket."

Nicholas glared at Emily for a moment, but when his mother tried to break his grip on her wrists, he wouldn't release her.

"Let go of me this instant, Nicholas! I must send for the constable," Harriet hissed her words.

"By all means, send for the constable but look in her pocket first!" Emily demanded.

Nicholas looked directly into Emily's eyes and for a fleeting moment, she thought he recognized her. Then he turned away and looked at his mother.

"I want to see what's in your pocket, Mother."

"Thank you, God," Emily whispered, her knees growing weak. She couldn't allow herself to faint now. There was still a life to be saved.

"Nicholas! I'll not be treated this way." Harriet again tried to jerk free.

"I'll show you," Emily said, stepping to Harriet's side. While Nicholas continued to hold his mother's wrists, Emily reached into Harriet Langford's pocket and pulled out the little jeweled case. She wasted no time opening the lid to reveal the remains of the spider concealed inside.

"So it's true," he said, releasing his mother and dropping his hands to his side.

Harriet pointed her knobby finger at Emily. "She planted it there. She's a witch! Look how she's dressed and she has even changed herself to look like Elinor so you'll be taken in by her. Don't be a fool, son. Ask her again where she's from. She's a witch, I tell you."

"That's not true. It is you who are the witch, Harriet Langford," Emily said. Then she heard that nightmarish rustling of taffeta skirts as Harriet pounced on her. The older woman put her claw-like fingers around Emily's neck and began squeezing.

"Stop it!" Nicholas pulled his mother away and shoved her so hard, she hit against the wall.

"Nicholas, my son." She reached out to him.

Turning away from her, he opened the bedroom door and went inside.

Emily followed closely behind. She could hear the sound of rustling taffeta as Harriet Langford ran off to another part of the house.

Nicholas grabbed Elinor by the shoulders but she did not respond. He looked at Emily. "Can you help her?"

"Yes," Emily said, stepping forward and removing the hypodermic syringe from her pocket. She stole a quick look at Elinor's face, so very like her own. The kinship she had always felt was enhanced a thousand times.

"What are you going to do with that?" Nicholas pointed to the syringe.

"It contains anti-venom. It will save her from the bite of the black widow spider."

"Anti-venom?" Nicholas asked. "What's that?"

"You must trust me. Without it, Elinor will die. At this very moment, your mother is setting fire to the house. I have to give Elinor this medicine now and then we must leave. You and Elinor will go to California and I will go back to where I came from. One more thing, Nicholas. You must promise that you and Elinor will never come back here or contact anyone in any way. Your survival depends on everyone thinking you died in the fire that will destroy this house tonight. Do you promise?"

Nicholas looked into Emily's eyes. "How do you know these things?" Without waiting for a reply, he said, "I trust you, God knows why, but I do. Go ahead—save my Elinor. I will do all that you ask."

Quickly, Emily injected the unconscious woman with the anti-venom. "Now, get her out of here. Put her in a carriage and get away from the house. She will come around in a little while. There's no time to worry about your belongings or your mother. She has created her own fate. You must save yourself and Elinor. Now go, and God Speed."

Suddenly, Nicholas wrapped his arms around Emily and held her close for a moment. "Thank you. We will never forget you." He brushed her forehead lightly with his lips as he released her.

For that brief moment, Emily savored this last embrace as the memories of all those other touches, kisses, love-making washed over her.

Then Nicholas picked up Elinor and Emily followed them into the smoke-filled hallway. Harriet had not wasted time. Now, Emily's destiny was very much intertwined with Nicholas' and Elinor's. Either all three of them would break free of the burning house or they would all perish together. She refused to believe they had come this far only to die in the far.

In spite of the smoke, Nicholas' sense of direction held and though coughing and choking, they were able to make it outside.

Nicholas looked back in time to see his mother standing in one of the attic windows. He placed Elinor on the grass and called to Harriet. "Mother, come down, save yourself!"

In spite of the warmth of the fire, Emily was chilled to the bone when she looked up and saw the crow woman, Harriet Langford, poised in the window. As her taffeta skirts whipped in the wind, orange and yellow flames licked behind her. She looked like the guardian of hell. She opened her mouth and a horrifying shriek came out as her sharp face became even more elongated and her nose lengthened into a beak. The flapping taffeta skirts transformed into beating wings and the shrieking changed into a "Caw, caw!"

Nicholas and Emily watched in disbelief as the giant crow pushed off in flight, like the Phoenix with its wings and tail feathers tinged with fire. It flew upward and its caws, filled with agony, changed to shrieks of pain as the fire quickly spread over its sleek, oiled body. The flapping wings lost power and the terrifying bird suddenly turned around and headed straight down into the flames of the burning Langford Manor.

"My mother," Nicholas said, his voice catching, "she was a witch? How could I not have seen her evil?"

Emily grabbed his arm. "Don't be fooled. She may still be a threat. She vowed you would never leave here. Go now, and remember, to everyone here you are dead. You must never, ever return."

Nicholas picked up Elinor and turned to Emily one last time. "I don't even know your name."

"My name is Emily."

"Emily. It's a beautiful name. Elinor and I will name our first daughter after you." A frown creased his brow. What about you? Where will you go?"

"Don't worry about me, I'll be fine."

She watched as he turned and headed for the stables. A carriage was already waiting in preparation for the evening's celebration. Emily watched them ride away before she headed for the river.

She turned and took one last look at the manor house where red and orange flames licked menacingly out of the windows. Suddenly, a great explosion shook the ground and lit up the sky as the roof caved in.

Looking across the river, Emily pushed the boat into the water. Black mists hovered ahead, blocking the view of the other side. Was the time portal open, or was it smoke from the fire? She said a silent prayer as she seated herself inside the vessel and began rowing toward the dark fog. Tears spilled down her cheeks.

"Nicholas, be happy my darling," she sobbed, remembering the chaste kiss he had placed on her forehead after folding her in his arms. A faint scent of lilacs permeated the smoke and clung to her nostrils.

It only lasted a moment and she again noted the acrid smell of smoke. As she coughed from the burning fumes, she feared anew that she would be trapped forever in the year, 1900.

Just then, the dark fog parted and suddenly she was bathed in glorious sunlight. "I'm home!" she shouted when she saw the yellow Victorian house in the distance.

Four people were standing by the river. Becky was one of them and she was waving frantically. Standing next to her were Fred, Mattie and someone else Emily didn't know.

Or did she?

An odd sensation seized her and she oared faster until she was within ten feet of shore.

"I couldn't believe it when Mattie said you were rowing all the way to Charleston just to get some exercise." Becky's voice rang out, but Emily paid no attention.

She was too busy looking at the tall stranger who waded into the water to grab the side of her boat. His hair was as black as a raven's wing and his arched eyebrows framed eyes that were dark pools of liquid heat.

"Nicholas?" Her voice was barely audible.

He leveled his gaze at her.

She could only stare at him.

A smile flashed across his handsome face. "I'm Travis Whittaker. Rebecca did tell you about me, didn't she?"

Emily nodded, aware of the strong scent of lilacs.

"And you are Emily. Emily was my grandmother's name."

When he turned his head to pull the boat into shore, Emily noticed the small strawberry birthmark just beneath his chin and suddenly everything was clear. Elinor and Nicholas had made it! He'd said they would name a girl child after her. Emily had no doubt that the grandmother Travis Whittaker spoke of was the daughter of Nicholas and Elinor. Emily was looking at Nicholas and Elinor's great-grandson. His name might be Travis, but to her, he was her lost love.

"Nicholas, you have come back to me," she whispered.

Time Lapse
by Jane Ann Tun

In an inadvertent trip twenty years into the past, Jake Anderson and Molly Malone are involved as suspects in a murder—a murder still unsolved when they return to their present time.

ISBN 1-929613-12-1 $5.99 US/$8.50 Can

Your special price: $4.20!

Cappuccino in the Winter
by Valerie Rose

African-American Alayna Alexander will do anything to have a family—including marry a man she doesn't love. All is well until Khavon Brighton comes to help her catch a cyberthief.

ISBN 1-929613-08-3 $6.50 US/$8.50 Can

Your special price: $4.50!

Since All is Passing
by Elizabeth Delisi

When Marie Kenning witnesses the kidnapping of a little girl, she embarks on a dangerous chase to save her.

ISBN 1-929613-24-5 $5.50 US/$7.50 Can

Your special price: $3.85!

To order your books, visit our website at
http://www.avidpress.com
and use code #435 in the special offers section,
or complete the attached order form and mail to us!

Special Offer Order Form

Please send me the following titles at your special price:

When the Lilacs Bloom by Linda Colwell quantity: ___
$4.50 US/$6.30 CAN amount: $_____

Shadows of Love by Sally Painter quantity: ___
$4.50 US/$6.30 CAN amount: $_____

Time Lapse by Jane Ann Tun quantity: ___
$4.20 US/$5.95 CAN amount: $_____

Cappuccino in the Winter by Valerie Rose quantity: ___
$4.50 US/$6.30 CAN amount: $_____

Since All is Passing by Elizabeth Delisi quantity: ___
$3.85 US/$5.25 CAN amount: $_____

TOTAL: $_____
Add sales 6% sales tax in Michigan $_____
Add $2.00 shipping and handling $_____
Add 7% GST (Canadian Residents) $_____
GRAND TOTAL: $_____

___ My check or money order is enclosed for the total amount of $_____

___ Please charge my VISA, MC, or Amex card for the amount above.
Acct. Number: _____ Exp. Date: _____
Signature: _____
My credit card billing address is the same as my shipping address below. ____

Shipping address:

Name_____
Address_____
City _____ State _____ Zip _____
Email _____ Phone: _____

Mail or fax order form to Avid Press:
5470 Red Fox Drive, Brighton MI 48114-9079
fax: (503)210-6765

Special Offer!

30% off when you buy
When the Lilacs Bloom
or *Shadows of Love!*

Buy either *When the Lilacs Bloom* or *Shadows of Love* and receive 30% off any other Avid Press books listed below when you order direct from us!

When the Lilacs Bloom   by Linda Colwell

Emily Langford must travel back in time to save the lives of star-crossed lovers Elinor and Nicholas Langford from the devious plots of Nicholas's mother.

ISBN 1-929613-09-1 $6.50 US/$8.99 Can

Your special price: $4.50!

Shadows of Love   by Sally Painter

Buried alive by white slavers, Celeste Bates escapes into the arms of Captain Brent McGraft, who believes she is his assassin.

ISBN 1-929613-27-X $6.50 US/$8.99 Can

Your special price: $4.50!